I0769082

The Hearts We've Broken

The Hearts We've Broken

H.K. GREEN

Editing by Andrea Halland, Editing by Andrea

Cover Design and Formatting by H.K. Green

Paperback ISBN: 979-8-9909156-5-7

For anyone who has only ever wanted to be seen, chosen, and loved.

And for the readers who met Mikey and knew there was a deeper layer to him. I hope you still love him, even if he's not always the funny guy.

playlist

Blame It On My Broken Heart | Avery Anna	3:14
Never Met Anyone Like You | Ella Langley	2:48
Playboys | Midland	3:41
Use Me | Zach Top	3:56
Better Than Revenge | Taylor Swift	3:36
Looking at Me | Sabrina Carpenter	3:01
Casual | Chappell Roan	3:52
Wanna Be Loved | The Red Clay Strays	3:37
False God | Taylor Swift	3:20
Put Me In My Place | Muscadine Bloodline	3:08
we're not alike | Tate McRae	2:59
Silver Springs | Fleetwood Mac	4:48
Nobody Gets Me | SZA	3:00
hookup scene | Kacey Musgraves	3:21
Bury Me | Noah Kahan	3:14
Wish You Well | Avery Anna	3:04

Thank you for picking up *The Hearts We've Broken*. This is book three in The Road and The Rodeo series and can be read as a standalone. However, for the best reading experience, I recommend starting with *The Pieces We've Lost* and *The Chances We Take*.

Additionally, please note that The Road and The Rodeo is a five-book interconnected series. While the main couple gets their HEA/HFN at the end of this book, there may be side stories and plot points that are not immediately resolved and will run through the series.

The Road and The Rodeo is a cowboy romance series, but it's also a sports romance series, so just like the previous books, rodeo plays a major role. Bull riding is the main focus of several chapters, but other events, including team roping, steer wrestling, tie-down roping, barrel racing, and wild horse racing, are discussed.

In rodeo, the animals are extremely well cared for, and that is reflected in my story. Rodeo is not meant to be an act of animal cruelty, and thus no animals are injured during the events of this story (although it can happen).

Content/Trigger Warnings:

This book is intended for adult readers and includes mature themes, on-page explicit sexual content, and explicit language. If needed, please refer to the back of the book for closed-door modifications.

Additional content warnings include:

- Alcohol Consumption
- Bodily Injury
- Cheating (not between main characters)
- Discussion of Deceased Parent
- Emotional Abuse/Online Harassment
- Consensual Restraint
- Physical Violence
- Rodeo Events (Bull Riding, Team Roping, Tie-Down Roping); No animals are injured.

Readers who may be sensitive to these subjects, please take note. It is my sincere hope that I handled these topics with the care they deserve.

rodeo 101

Alleyway: In barrel racing, the entrance to the arena where the horse and their rider begin their timed run.

Bells: A weighted metallic object, often a cowbell, that is attached to the bull rope and hangs under the bull, which helps the rope fall off the bull once the rider dismounts.

Box: In a timed event, the box is the area where the horse and rider back into before they make a roping or steer wrestling run.

Bucking Chute: A specialized pen in a rodeo arena that holds bucking bulls and horses in place before a rodeo event, allowing the rider to prepare and mount the animal securely before the gate opens to start the ride.

Bulldogger: A steer wrestler.

Bullfighter: A specialized athlete who protects a bull rider, after they dismount or are bucked off by the bull, by distracting the bull and ensuring the rider can safely escape the arena.

Bull Rope: A flat, braided rope that a bull rider wraps around the bull's chest, just behind the front legs, then secures to their own hand.

Mark Out: In saddle bronc and bareback riding, an athlete must place their heels above the point of the horse's shoulders and keep them there until the horse's front feet hit the ground on its first jump from the chute. Failure to do so results in disqualification and no score.

NFR: National Finals Rodeo. The premier rodeo event by the PRCA which showcases the talents of the PRCA's top fifteen money winners in each event as they compete for the world title.

Nodding: A signal that a cowboy gives when they are ready for the gate or chute to be opened.

No Score: Failure to make a qualified ride (8 seconds) in roughstock events.

No Time: Failure to make a qualified run (illegal catch, no catch) in timed events.

PRCA: Professional Rodeo Cowboys Association. The oldest and largest professional rodeo-sanctioning body in the world.

Re-Ride: A second chance for a roughstock rider. Allows the rider to give up their first score in exchange for another attempt if the initial ride was unsatisfactory due to the animal's sub-par performance or an equipment failure.

Rosin: A sticky substance that riders apply to their bull rope and glove to increase grip and prevent the rope from slipping during a ride.

Roughstock: Bareback riding, saddle bronc riding, and bull riding. Other events are called timed events.

Short Go: The final, championship round at a rodeo.

Spotter: A person in the bucking chutes who assists the rider in maintaining balance and safety by being positioned to intercept the bull's movements, such as kicks, with their arm or body.

Standings: In professional rodeo, a cowboy's success is

measured in earnings. There are several sets of standings where cowboys can keep track of where they rank.

WRCA: Working Ranch Cowboys Association. A professional association that produces the World Championship Ranch Rodeo, an event that showcases the skills of the working ranch cowboy.

series recap

From *The Pieces We've Lost*—**Ellison** and **Colter** have been happily married for almost a year and are living on the Carson family ranch in Silver Creek. Colter is still team roping with Reid and managing the ranch, and Ellison works as a vet tech in Miles City. She also teaches kids in the community how to ride horses and travels to rodeos with Colter and the guys often.

From *The Chances We Take*—**Isabelle** (Ellison's best friend) and **Reid** are in a long-distance relationship but are very much in love. Reid lives in Silver Creek and still competes with Colter at rodeos, and Isa lives in Houston and works with bookstores managing their social media marketing. They visit each other in Montana and Texas as often as they can.

Jake and **Hayden** are both single and competing in rodeo. Jake is a tie-down roper, and Hayden is a team roper. They both live in Silver Creek and travel with their buddies—Colter, Reid, and Mikey—to rodeos.

I should have realized something was off when neither my boyfriend nor my best friend answered their phones. I'd tried calling both of them at least three times while I was at the store getting supplies for our New Year's Eve party, but the calls went to voicemail.

Every. Single. Time.

Whatever, if they complained about the type of champagne I got, or told me I bought the wrong snacks, it was on them for not answering.

"Hey, babe! Can you—" I pushed the front door open with my hip, arms full of grocery bags, expecting to see my boyfriend in his usual spot playing video games or watching sports on the couch. "Brady?"

I froze when I heard noises coming from our bedroom.

"Fuck," a male voice rasped what sounded an awful lot like a moan.

What the fuck? I set down the bags and pounded on the bedroom door three times. Whoever was in there didn't stop as the slapping of skin and the creaks of our bed started to increase in speed.

"Oh, God, Brady, don't stop!" The muffled voice through the thin wall was enough for me to throw the door open, revealing my boyfriend balls deep in my best friend.

"What the hell?" I screamed, white-hot rage coursing through my veins.

If you're going to cheat on your girlfriend, at least lock the fucking door.

Both of them scrambled out of the positions they were in, Ava covering herself with the sheets—*my sheets*—and Brady rushing over to me butt-ass naked, not even bothering to cover his junk that was just inside my *best friend*.

"Baby, baby, baby, I can explain," he stammered as I walked further into the room to pick up his jeans and fling them at him.

"Explain what, exactly? How you were fucking my best friend?" I snapped as I shielded my eyes and held my temple at the same time. This whole interaction was giving me a migraine.

I'd have to wash my eyes—and frankly, my brain—out with bleach later, because I'd never be getting the horrifying image of them out of my head.

They both rushed to put their clothes on, but I was already storming toward the front door. I wasn't sure where I was going to go, but I sure as hell wasn't going to stay here.

Brady raced after me, presumably to keep apologizing and beg me to stay, but I slammed the door in his face before he could say anything.

The rear door of my car was still open with grocery bags in the trunk. I debated throwing the grocery bags out and leaving them on the curb but decided against it. My money, my groceries. I closed the hatchback then yanked the driver's side door open, sliding in as fast as humanly possible before shutting and locking it.

My phone buzzed in my hand.

BRADY

Baby, I'm sorry, please let me explain.

> Do not start. We were done the moment you started seeing Ava

A separate text from Ava came through after I hit send.

AVA

June, please

I blocked both of their numbers and tossed my phone into the passenger seat before resting my forehead on my steering wheel, fighting the urge to slam my head against it repeatedly.

What a clusterfuck.

I had nowhere to go, but I would've rather lived in my car or a cardboard box on the side of the highway than continue to live in that house after everything I had just witnessed.

How was it that a few weeks ago, I was newly graduated from college, and now I was homeless? To top it all off, my shit was still in the house, so I'd have to go back at some point. I tried to think of friends I could stay with until I found my footing, but I could—pathetically—count them on one hand now that Ava and Brady were completely out of the picture.

What I *needed* was to get out of this town. The plan was always to leave anyway after Brady graduated, but I assumed I had at least five more months. Five months to work in a research lab in Goldfinch to gain experience then find a good job in a place we both wanted to live. Five months to figure my life out.

I shook my head, cursing myself. My entire future was planned around him. A goddamn boy.

What a foolish thing to do.

I scrolled my contacts, trying to think of who I could call in a favor from.

No, she's all the way in Florida now.

Still in Goldfinch.

My finger landed on a friend who I hadn't talked to in a while but still had a good relationship with. She lived in a small, middle-of-nowhere town. I couldn't even remember the name of it, Miles something? Maybe that was exactly the type of place I needed.

What do you have to lose? I thought as I hit the call button.

A month and a half had passed since I caught my ex-boyfriend and ex-best friend together. Within a week, I had completely moved out of our—his—house. Up until that point, I'd been couch surfing, staying with the few friends I did have in town.

A couple of them had offered to let me move in, but I'd turned them down. Goldfinch wasn't large enough for me to stay. I didn't think I could stomach seeing Ava and Brady together around town, so I packed my bags and drove east toward Miles City.

Natalie was one of my friends from freshman year. We had several classes together and quickly became friends.

She'd graduated last spring, so we weren't as close as we used to be, having fallen out of touch once she left, but our friendship was still recent enough that I was comfortable asking her for a favor. Once I told her the situation—she'd met Brady several times since we'd started dating freshman year—she had immediately agreed to let me stay with her for as long as I needed. She wasn't a huge fan of Brady while we were together; now I could see why, but at the time, my judgment was so clouded by what I thought was love that I didn't care.

"I need to find a job," I groaned from my position on the couch. "I feel like a freeloader."

"I mean, it's not like you haven't been looking, right?" Natalie replied from the kitchen, the wall that separated us muffling her voice a bit.

If scrolling aimlessly on job search engines counted as looking, then sure. But all those jobs required a relocation, and I was picky.

"Why don't you look downtown? I'm sure someone would be grateful for the extra help, even if it's only occasional. That way you can work, make some money, and stop feeling so bad about not paying rent. Even though I told you it was fine."

I nodded, though I knew she couldn't see me. "You're right. Don't worry, I'll be out of here before you know it."

"June, it's okay. Seriously. I just want you to be happy." She walked over to the couch and extended a hand to help me up.

I took it, grateful to have a friend who literally and metaphorically picked me up. "Thanks, Nat. I'll be back later. Wish me luck." I grimaced as I let out a pathetic laugh on the way to the front door.

I couldn't believe this was the situation I was in. I knew

a lot of people fresh out of college were still figuring things out, but I assumed I would be looking into places to raise our future kids, not wondering why my boyfriend decided to stick his dick in my best friend. Or why she even *let* him do that in the first place.

For a while, I imagined it was all a bad dream. A really, really bad dream. I'd wake up any moment, and Brady and I would have a nice laugh about it. Unfortunately, it wasn't a dream, but my actual life.

Did I miss something? Was I oblivious to the signs? Surely they weren't *that* good at hiding it.

Mid-February in Montana could be one of two things: negative temperatures with snowstorms every weekend, or a balmy forty degrees without a single speck of snow on the ground. This year happened to be the latter.

Despite the unseasonably warm temperatures, I still huddled in my jacket as I went from business to business asking about employment opportunities. I'd take anything at this point, short-term or on-call, hell, I'd even be happy with one shift a week if it meant I could pull a little bit of my weight with Natalie.

Most people, understandably, didn't know who I was and weren't willing to hire a stranger on the spot or add a new employee to their roster when it wasn't needed. I couldn't blame them for that.

I was about to throw in the towel and go back home when I reached the end of the street and saw the old-timey western sign of Rudy's bar.

What the hell, why not? I thought to myself as I pushed open the double doors. The bar was fairly quiet, with it only being early afternoon. Fluorescent bulbs lit up the space, and the local country western station played over the speakers at a respectable volume. High-top tables occupied the open area to the right of the bar, and the back corner housed a pool table. A few old men sat at the bar, watching a rodeo on the television mounted in the corner.

Brady was a big sports fan—football, baseball, rodeo, you name it. I, on the other hand, would have rather done anything else than sit in a dusty arena that smelled like horse shit. Now that I thought about it, the horse shit was quite fitting for him.

"Hello there, young lady." A booming, yet friendly, voice broke me out of my thoughts. A large man with white hair and kind eyes stood on the other side of the bar. "What brings you in today?"

"Hi." I smiled. "My name's Juniper, and I'm…well, you see, I'm new in town and—" I hung my head a little at how awkward I was being.

"You're looking for a job?" He finished my sentence for me.

"Yes, sir." My chin was still dipped down, but my eyes flicked up toward his. "I understand if you don't need help or don't want to hire a stranger."

"Do you have bartending experience?"

I nodded. I'd done some bartending when I was in school at Sapphire Gulch University. The college bars tended to be packed, so I knew my way around a bar. I could hold my own practically anywhere.

He paused for a beat, tilting his head to the side as he stroked his short beard. "When can you start?"

I blinked a few times. My mouth opened and closed, but nothing came out at first. "A-as soon as possible."

"Why don't you come by tomorrow night, Juniper, and we'll get you started? My name's John, but everyone 'round here calls me Rudy." He reached out his hand, and I took it. "Welcome to Miles City."

CHAPTER TWO

I'll see you around? Maybe we can do this again sometime?" the busty brunette I'd just hooked up with asked as I tried to usher her out of my trailer as quickly as possible.

Doubtful.

"Yeah, see you around."

She looked over her shoulder to shoot me a grin and a flirty little wave. I returned a fake smile and closed the door, my shoulders immediately slumping as I let out a sigh.

Reminder to self: double-check girls with the hot-crazy scale *before* taking them home.

Don't get me wrong, she was cute, but she was also a stage-five clinger. Most girls understood that I was here for a good time, not a long time, and they were okay with that. But some got to the point of being borderline stalkerish. It only took a few of those for me to stop giving out my phone number.

Luckily, most of the crazy ones were only passing

through; I didn't mess with locals. Well, sometimes I messed with locals, but only when they were in it for the same thing as me. One night. Or on very, very rare occasions, a week max.

The guys gave me a lot of shit for it. They'd joke, *Man, you're thirty. Have you ever had a girlfriend?* Or they'd twist it around to say hell would freeze over before I'd ever be in a stable relationship.

They failed to consider that Jake was twenty-eight and still single. I mean, shit, Reid didn't actually start dating his girlfriend, Isabelle, until he was twenty-seven, and I'd never even seen Hayden so much as *look* at a girl. Colter was the only one out of our group who was on a semi-traditional path, meeting his wife, Ellison, when he was twenty-six. I also had to cut him some slack since the first girl he was engaged to at twenty-four didn't work out.

I just considered myself a late bloomer. Besides, I was already married to the thrill of bull riding. And I wasn't a cheater.

In a couple weeks, we'd be heading down to Texas for the Houston Livestock Show and Rodeo, and man, was I ready. For the bull riding *and* the women. Mostly the bull riding, though. I was entering this season with a vengeance.

At the age of thirty, I was supposedly on the downhill slope of my bull riding career. At least, according to the media, I was. They assumed because I wasn't ready to settle down, I was distracted, and as a result would continue to have a mediocre career—never quite making it to a gold buckle—until it eventually fizzled out. They claimed I'd be better off retiring now while I still had a shred of dignity.

Everything they said was bullshit, though. Yes, thirty may have been the average age most bull riders retired, but, in my opinion, I hadn't sustained severe enough injuries to retire. I was determined I'd make it to a world championship one of these days and prove them all wrong. With or without a ball and chain.

Besides, last year I'd made it to the NFR, so that was already proving them wrong. You don't get to the top fifteen in the world with a *mediocre career*.

After throwing on a pair of jeans and a T-shirt, I hopped in my pickup to drive over to Reid's place. There was a slight chill in the air when I escorted that girl out of my trailer, so I reached into the backseat to grab a hoodie to put on when I arrived.

The guys were all gathering to get some practice in before we hit the road. I technically didn't have to be there since my training was a bit different from theirs, but I liked the company. And they liked having someone to open the chute.

Gravel crunched under my tires as I pulled into Reid's driveway. Hayden and Colter's pickups were already here, but Jake's wasn't, so at least I wasn't the last to arrive. I shrugged on my sweatshirt and shut the door to my vehicle, not bothering to lock it. The last time I actually happened to lock the doors, my keys were inside. I liked to think I learned from my drunken mistakes…at least sometimes.

As I approached the arena, the sound of hooves against the dirt and some whoops and hollers from the boys greeted me.

"Nice of you to show up!" Jake called out to me in a teasing manner.

Well, shit. He must have gotten a ride with Hayden.

I threw my hand up in a wave, not bothering to walk any faster. "What can I say? I was preoccupied." My lips quirked up in a grin.

"No surprise there." Hayden chuckled.

Colter and Reid were on horseback, and Hayden leaned against the fence by Jake. When I got closer, they rode their mounts by the edge of the arena to say hi.

"The day that Mikey gets a girlfriend will be the day that hell freezes over," Reid joked.

"Man, I'd pay good money to see that," Colter added. "It'd be a waste of money, because I doubt it would last more than two weeks, but it'd still be interesting to see."

"Hey! If I *wanted* a girlfriend, I'm sure I'd have no issues getting one." I thought back to this morning and the girl who was practically drooling over the idea of seeing me again.

Jake walked over to me. "Wanna bet on it?" He pulled out his wallet and started rifling through the bills. "Fifty bucks says you can't keep a girl for longer than two weeks."

"That's a pretty big wager, you sure he's gonna take that?" Hayden cocked an eyebrow, seemingly staying out of the betting.

I shot him a glare then threw out a counteroffer. "One hundred."

"Sure confident there, buddy." Colter laughed. Both he and Reid had dismounted at this point and joined our circle.

Jake thought about it for a moment then said, "How about this? You keep a girl for two weeks and you get fifty. Keep a girl for more than a month and I'll double it for you."

Colter and Reid exchanged a glance then nodded to each other before Colter spoke up. "We'll even join in at that point. Fifty from each of us for an extra hundred. Hell, if you can convince a girl to date you until Houston is over, I'll give you an acre of land. You can finally build yourself a house and put down some roots. I'm sure your future girlfriend will appreciate it."

"And if I can't?"

"Then you owe Jake fifty bucks. I think this one's a gamble we're willing to take." Reid shrugged.

"You boys have got yourself a deal, then. A month will be nothing." I scoffed and rolled my eyes.

They all looked at each other as though they didn't believe me. I couldn't say I blamed them with my…history. But for a bit of cash and land, I could suck it up. It wouldn't be a real relationship anyway. I wasn't going to catch feelings for a girl.

Not with a gold buckle in December calling my name.

Whoever the lucky lady was would get a damn good fuck buddy for a month, and then I could collect my winnings and get back to my regularly scheduled programming. It was a win-win.

Now I just had to find a woman worthy of my time.

"All right, then." Jake extended a hand to shake on it, and I accepted it firmly. "Let's get back to it, shall we, boys?"

"Mikey, you want to man the chute?" Reid asked, although I knew it wasn't a question.

I gave him a mock salute and headed back behind the roping boxes.

After about thirty minutes and approximately fifteen runs later—we tended to shoot the shit between turns—

Ellison arrived at the arena. She and Reid had made a deal that she could use the arena to give local kids riding lessons as long as it didn't interfere with any of our schedules.

"Ellie, you're here early!" Reid called out to her. "Thought you didn't have a lesson until two this afternoon?"

She shrugged before leaning up against the fence by me and Colter. "Figured I'd come hang out. Maybe get in some runs myself to put you all in your place." She winked after the last part. Ellison was good, but she didn't compete professionally. She'd started putting her name in for breakaway at a few of the smaller rodeos and jackpots, but she seemed pretty content at her job in Miles City as well as teaching young kids.

"Hi, baby." Colter leaned in to peck her on the cheek. Ellison jokingly made a show to wipe it off, but then gave him a kiss of her own.

"You slacking off over here, Michael?" she teased, reaching out to punch my arm. "Sure you don't want to get up on a horse today?"

I huffed out an amused breath. Ellison asked me this question every single time they roped in the practice arena. "Nah, I'm good. I don't feel like risking my health to ride a horse." I wouldn't be caught dead on the back of one unless I was blackout drunk—like last year's Bucking Horse Sale—or lost a bet. Those things were terrifying. Not that I'd *ever* admit that out loud.

"You ride bulls for a living, dumbass!" Jake snorted, throwing his head back in a laugh.

"Yeah, and? I don't see your point here."

"Aw, come on. You can ride Lucille. I'll even lead you around the arena like I do with my five-year-olds." Ellison chuckled, which caused a chain reaction of laughs around the group. I answered them with a middle finger, but it was all in good nature.

"Have you talked to my girl lately?" Reid asked.

He and Isabelle finally got together last year after Colter and Ellison's wedding. Everyone knew they had the hots for each other—from the moment they met, really—but they kept beating around the bush and denying their feelings. She still lived in Houston, so they were in a long-distance relationship, but she came up to visit pretty often.

"Yeah, she's good. Excited to see us all in a couple weeks."

Colter interjected then, nudging Ellison with his elbow. "Speaking of girlfriends, you'll never believe the bet that Jake and Mikey just made."

She eyed me curiously. "Oh? What was it this time? Please don't tell me you bet him to try to ride a bison again."

"Hell no! I wouldn't have taken that bet anyway!" *I probably would have.*

"I bet him fifty bucks he wouldn't be able to keep a girl for more than two weeks," Jake answered. "And then I said if he could make it longer than a month he could have a hundred."

Ellison raised an eyebrow, like she was waiting for him to continue.

"And I might have said that if he could keep a girlfriend longer than the Houston Rodeo I'd give him fifty more and an acre of land." Colter dragged out the *might.*

Her mouth gaped open, and she lightly smacked him on the arm. "You did not!"

"If it makes you feel better, I only bet fifty if he could make it past Houston and Hayden didn't bet at all," Reid added.

"It doesn't, but then again, I'm not sure Mikey's ready for that kind of commitment." Her eyes glimmered with mischief, and a cheeky smile spread across her face.

I shook my head, crossing my arms and grumbling. "I'll show you guys. You'll be eating your words soon enough."

juniper

A few days had passed since Rudy offered me the bartending job. Bartending was pretty universal, so it was easy enough to learn the ropes and pick everything up. On my first day, I shadowed another one of the bartenders, Nico, but by my third shift, I was basically on my own.

Rudy's was a small bar, so it never got too busy. Not much exciting happened in town in general, but I was told when May rolled around, Miles City would get crazy for something called The Bucking Horse Sale.

I was wiping down the bar when my coworkers, Nico and Liv, walked up next to me. Both of them were students here at the local community college, but they weren't that much younger than me.

"Sup, Junie." Nico threw his arm around my shoulders, and I resisted the urge to brush him off.

I gave him a side-eyed glance. "Don't call me that."

"Sorry, sorry." He put his hands up in mock surrender, but his eyes shone with a playfulness that screamed trouble.

Liv cleared her throat. "How have your first few days on the job been? Enjoying it so far?"

I nodded. "Yeah, I like it. The people here in town are nice. Pretty easygoing."

"This is your first time here in Miles City, yeah?" she asked.

"Yep. Just moved here a few weeks ago."

"Have you done much exploring?" Nico leaned against the bar casually, like he was trying to seem nonchalant and not like he was prying for information.

"Not really. I'm living with one of my old friends from college, and I've gone to the grocery store with her a couple times, but I've mostly stayed home." I gave him a noncommittal shrug. "I was mainly focused on finding a job, to be honest."

"Well," he drew out the word, "a bunch of us are having a bonfire this weekend, if you want to come by? Bring your friend, too."

"Oh, I don't—"

"It'll be super fun!" Liv chimed in, a pleading look in her eyes. "We'll introduce you to everyone and you'll make loads of new friends. It'll be great."

That was what I was worried about. I wasn't planning on staying here long-term. While I was grateful for Natalie and Rudy, Miles City wasn't going to be my final destination. I'd give myself a few months tops to get my footing, then I'd be out of Montana for good. Maybe I'd go back home to Michigan, or maybe I'd travel. At some point in the last few weeks, I'd decided that small town life ultimately wasn't for me. I wanted to be able to date and not have to see them at the grocery store if we happened to break up.

"I'll think about it." I finally decided to give them a

sort of nonanswer, and it seemed to get the two of them off my back for now.

"Well, if you change your mind, you know where to find us, Junie." Nico flashed me a crooked grin as he walked back to the end of the bar.

I let out an amused sigh then went back to wiping down the bar.

Tonight wasn't slow, but it wasn't packed, either. There weren't a ton of bars in town, but Rudy's was more popular with the older folk. Rudy had tasked us with coming up with theme nights to get more of the college students to come in, and we planned to announce our first soon.

Apparently, though, there was a group of men—cowboys—in their mid- to late-twenties who frequently came into the bar. They didn't live in town, but they lived close, in a little community called Silver Creek.

Liv told me about them on my second day of work.

"They're pretty cute. I know two of them aren't single anymore, but I haven't seen the others with girls before. Well, except for one of them. But he's a notorious playboy, so I wouldn't even dream of going there." She wrinkled up her nose.

"Don't you think they're a little bit old for you, Livvy?" Nico teased her with a laugh.

She immediately blushed and sputtered out, "I'm twenty-one! There's only a five-year age difference between me and the youngest one!"

We both laughed at her outburst, but she crossed her arms and mocked a pouting face.

"What about you, Junie?" Nico asked.

"What about me, what?"

He wiggled his eyebrows suggestively. "Are you on the market for a man?"

"Ew, Nico, never say it like that ever again," Liv groaned, to which he rolled his eyes and said, "I'm just teasing."

I just shook my head, still deciding if I was going to answer his question. "No. I'm definitely not interested in dating."

Before he could respond, Liv spoke up. "Wait, but what about you and—"

Nico made a face of what seemed to be slight contempt in the middle of her question. Liv gasped, and then they both walked to the back, leaving me amused and by myself at the bar for about an hour.

The bells on the front door jingled, pulling me from the memory, and I lifted my head to see who it was.

Rudy flashed me a bright smile as he sauntered up to the counter. "Juniper, how's everything been for you so far? Feeling at home here?"

"So far, it's been going really well. I'm used to the bars I've worked in being, er…" I paused for a moment, not wanting to offend him.

The corners of his eyes crinkled. "Busier?"

Heat rushed to my cheeks. "Uh, yeah." I let out a nervous laugh. "I didn't mean it in a bad way, I just worked in Goldfinch and you know how those college bars are."

"Don't you worry, I know very well what you mean. I had my fair share of rowdy nights as a youngster." His eyes seemed to glass over, but the expression was gone just as quickly as it appeared. "I'm sure Nicolas and Olivia have filled you in, but we get good business during The Bucking Horse Sale, so it'll be nice to have you on staff so I don't have to drag my old ass in here." He let out a deep, belly laugh, and I couldn't help but crack a smile.

"I'm happy to help."

"Well"—he patted the counter a couple times—"I just wanted to check in." Then he disappeared around the corner, presumably to go to the back office.

The next few hours were slow. Only a few people trickled in and out of the bar, giving Nico and Liv plenty of time to pester me about the bonfire. I gave them the same kind of answer as before, but I had a feeling I'd be hearing about this gathering—and plenty more in the future—if their facial expressions were any indication.

Around nine o'clock, I was in the middle of pouring a whiskey and Coke for one of the regulars when the front doors opened and a group walked in, led by an average-height man with dark-brown hair that curled under the baseball cap that he wore backward and tattoo sleeves covering both his arms. He had a thick mustache, but the rest of his face was fairly clean shaven, with a bit of stubble on his jawline.

"First round's on me, boys!" his slightly deep, masculine voice rumbled.

I couldn't pinpoint where I recognized the voice from, but I was sure it would come to me later. Probably didn't matter in the long-run, but it made me curious all the same.

I slid the drink I had been making to Jim—the regular —and he thanked me, handing me a five-dollar bill. The group of cowboys had already gathered in front of Liv, and she was working on pouring them shots of Pendleton.

"How's your evening going, Livvy?" the tattooed cowboy who offered to buy the drinks when they walked in asked her.

The blond one standing beside him elbowed him in the ribs. "She's already told you she's not interested, Michael, leave the girl alone."

"I'm just being nice, Flynn!" He elbowed him right back.

"Don't mind him, Liv, he's just being his usual self."

The youngest looking cowboy—who was shorter than the other three but taller than the tattooed one—apologized for his friend.

Liv's face immediately flushed to beet red. "Can I get you guys anything else?" She stumbled over her words a little but recovered quickly.

"Nah, thanks, Olivia." One of the final two who hadn't yet spoken thanked her. "Let's get a move on, shall we, boys? Jake and Hayden against me and Reid?"

They all nodded and grabbed their shots, making their way to the pool table in the back. Now that I was thinking about it, they looked vaguely familiar. Especially the short one.

"Who were they?" I whispered to Liv.

"Those were the Silver Creek cowboys. Colter Carson, Reid Lawson, Jake Flynn, Hayden Watkins, and Michael Tucker. But everyone calls him Mikey."

Mikey Tucker? No fuckin' way.

"Cover for me, will you, Liv?" I asked, earning a puzzled look from her. "I'm about to do something reckless tonight."

CHAPTER FOUR

I huffed out a breath as I set down the barbell and checked my watch. It was a little after six thirty, which meant I needed to wrap up my workout soon. Luckily deadlifts were near the end of my leg day routine anyway, so I wouldn't have to skip anything.

I trained in the gym several times a week, focusing heavily on balance and core strength, and bolstered strength training with actual practice bulls up at the community college. Sometimes the guys would train with me, but most of the time they were off doing their own thing. It was nice, though, being able to focus on bull riding and really hone in on bettering myself.

We had plans to go out to Rudy's tonight, so the goal was to run home, take a quick shower, and maybe eat something before heading over to the Carson Ranch.

I finished my last set then gathered my belongings. On my way out of the gym, I stopped at the counter to grab a protein shake.

"Good to see you, man," the guy working at the desk greeted me.

"Hey, thanks." I, admittedly, couldn't remember his name, and he didn't have a nametag on. I didn't want him to feel bad, so I played it off. The TV behind the counter had an old rodeo playing, and he looked up at it.

"Looks like there's going to be some tough competition again this year."

I let out a grunt. "Mm-hmm." I didn't like talking much about my rodeo career. People always had something to say.

"Well, here's your shake, brother. Hope you have a good one. Good luck out there."

I took the drink, thanking him. I wanted to get out of here and be home as soon as possible. I was ready for a night of fun.

The minute we stepped through the doors of Rudy's bar, I headed to the counter where our favorite bartender, Liv, was working. A new girl—another blonde—was working, too, but she was helping one of the regulars. I swore I'd seen her before but couldn't place where. Then again, faces kind of blurred together for me between fans, the press, and women.

"How's your evening going, Livvy?" I jokingly laid it on thick.

Jake elbowed me in the ribs, and I elbowed him right back as Hayden apologized for me, something he didn't need to do. Liv knew I was just messing with her. Besides, not only was she a local, she went to school at the community college here.

I got involved with a college student over in Goldfinch

once—granted she was twenty-one and in her last year—and liked to think I learned my lesson from that one. She was a bit too clingy for me, so I broke it off fast.

I didn't miss the way Liv's cheeks flushed when Hayden talked to her. I gave him a subtle grin, which he immediately brushed off.

"Can I get you guys anything else?"

"Nah, thanks, Olivia." Colter scooped up his shot glass, nodding toward the pool table in the back. "Let's get a move on, shall we, boys? Jake and Hayden against me and Reid?"

The guys nodded and started walking away from the bar. The new girl scooted over to Liv, but I didn't get a chance to speak to her before I realized the guys were going to leave me out of the game.

"Hey! What about me?" I protested as I took a few large strides to catch up to the boys.

Jake wrinkled his nose. "No offense, man, but you kinda suck at pool."

I huffed. "I do not."

"Remember that time you immediately hit in the eight ball?" Reid just *had* to remind me of *the one time* I hit the eight ball in and lost the game on default.

"He has a point." Hayden shrugged. He had filled in for Colter right before Eight-Ball-Gate.

"It was *one time*," I groaned. "But fine. I'll sit this one out."

They all looked satisfied, and I leaned against the wall as Jake racked the balls. "Good Time" by Alan Jackson blared from the speakers overhead, and I scanned the room in hopes of finding someone good enough to play my fake girlfriend for a few weeks. Looks were always a factor, but this time I knew I had to find someone with a good personality. Someone who could keep up with me and not only take jokes but dish them out, too. A firecracker like Ellison, although maybe not as ruthless…to me at least.

A group in the corner caught my eye for a brief moment, but I recognized one of them, so that was an immediate no. A redheaded woman sitting at the bar had a nice smile, and I'd never seen her before. However, was a tourist passing through the right option for this? The question was enough for me to hesitate. Good thing, because shortly after, a big burly man sat next to her, placing his hand on the back of her stool.

Finally, a brunette in bootcut jeans and a flannel walked through the front doors. I'd seen her around town a couple times, but I didn't think she was enrolled at the community college. May have been a vet tech or something. I was pretty sure I'd seen her helping out behind the chutes at the Bucking Horse Sale. Fine enough for me.

I rolled my shoulders back a couple times before I started toward the woman—whom I'd made eye contact with now.

But before I could reach her, a flash of blonde hair and piercing blue eyes stopped me in my tracks.

The new girl. The bartender.

"You're Mikey Tucker, right?" she asked. She wasn't much shorter than me, and I was able to look her straight in the face, meeting her eyes.

I nodded, my eyebrow quirking up.

"Perfect," she muttered before smashing her lips against mine.

My eyes widened before I leaned into the kiss, closing my eyes and placing my hands on her jaw. She wrapped her arms around me, running one hand through my hair and resting the other on my back.

When she opened her mouth, I slid my tongue past her lips, swiping it against hers. She tasted like peaches, a delicate sweetness with a hint of something tart.

"Let's get out of here," she murmured against my mouth as she ran one hand down the front of my chest.

I pulled away, eyes snapping open. "Wait, but aren't you the new bartender? Don't you have to work?" I glanced toward the bar where Liv and the other bartender, Nico, were standing behind the counter watching us.

"They've got it covered. Come on, Casanova, you really gonna turn me down?" Her lips curved up in a sinful smirk, and blood rushed to my crotch.

I raked my eyes up and down her body, surveying her. Her hair fell just below the swell of her breasts. Her figure, although slim, sported generous curves—hips I wanted to squeeze while pounding into her from behind.

Fuck.

I was supposed to be finding a girl to *date*, not a one-night stand. But she practically threw herself into my arms. Maybe she'd be up for it. I was willing to find out.

"Come on." I took her hand, pulling her out of the bar to my pickup. The guys would figure it out soon enough when they noticed I wasn't there. They wouldn't need to come looking for me.

The chill of the night air did nothing to cool me down as I pressed the girl against the passenger door of my pickup and our tongues tangled together. My dick swelled in my pants, and I ground my hips against her front, craving the friction. Someone whistled as they passed, and I flipped them the bird.

"Maybe we should…" She turned her head toward the people passing.

As I lightly grasped her chin, pulling it back toward me, my voice rumbled in my throat. "Ignore them."

Her pupils dilated at the sound of my voice, and she pulled her bottom lip between her teeth. Before I could move my lips toward hers again, she reached down, cupping the front of my jeans over the visible outline of my hard-on. A sharp breath escaped her lips, and she flicked her eyes down then back up to me.

"Like what you see, Peach?" I teased, flashing her a cocky grin.

"Still deciding," she fired back.

"Well, then, let's not waste any more time. I'd hate to disappoint." I grinned as I pulled her away from the door, opening it for her. She climbed in, and I shut it, jogging around the front to the driver's side.

I broke about all of the traffic laws in the book on the way home, blowing through stop signs and going ten over the speed limit. You could say I was a bit eager. I didn't know what it was about blondie, but she didn't seem like the other girls I'd hooked up with. She may have approached me, but I had a feeling she wasn't going to try to hang around.

I peeled into the trailer court, parking in my "driveway," and cut the engine, mentally kicking myself for not tidying up the place a little bit. Whatever, she probably wouldn't care. It was obvious to me she just wanted to get fucked, and that was fine. I could do that. It was the conversation after that I was worried about.

She stepped out of the pickup, and I fumbled with the door handle, finally getting it open. Before she could say anything about the state of my trailer, I kissed her, grabbing her waist and backing her into the bedroom. Once the backs of her thighs hit the bed, I lifted her up, gently tossing her onto the comforter. I pulled my shirt over my head, tossing it to the side then crawling over top of her.

My lips made their way from her mouth to her jaw to her neck. When I kissed up her neck to the spot just below her ear, she drew in a quick breath, the air quivering as she exhaled. I nipped at her earlobe, and a moan escaped her lips.

One of my hands grasped her wrists, holding her arms over her head on the pillows as the other trailed down her body to the waistline of her jeans.

"Are you sure you want to do this?" I asked, wanting to have her full consent before going any further. I may have enjoyed having sex with different partners, but I wasn't an asshole.

"Yes. I want this," she panted, her voice laced with lust.

"If you want to stop at any point, just say the word and we'll stop, okay, Peach?"

She nodded, but when I raised my eyebrows, she verbalized an *okay*. I undid the button and zipper of her jeans with my free hand, sliding my fingers inside until they reached the apex of her thighs. Her silk panties were slick with her arousal, and I groaned at the feel of them.

"What do you want me to do to you?" I began rubbing circles on the fabric over her center. Her hips bucked, and her chest rose and fell in a steady rhythm. "Tell me what you want…" I hesitated. I didn't even know her name, yet I was about to fuck her with my fingers. *Good lord, Mikey.*

"Juniper." As if she read my mind, she said her name. "I want your fingers. I want you to make me come with your fingers."

Juniper.

Before I could disappear into my head wondering where I'd heard that name before, I snapped back to the moment. Releasing her wrists from my grip and sitting up, I used both hands to pull her jeans and underwear down, tossing them to the floor in a heap. Nudging her thighs apart with my knees, I dragged a knuckle down her center, letting her wetness coat my finger before slowly pushing it inside her.

"More. I need more," Juniper whined, lowering her hand down to her clit.

"Uh-uh." I smirked, removing the one finger I had inside her. Once again, I took her hands in mine, pressing them above her head. "I'll make you come, Juniper, but I'm going to take my time. Watch you squirm and beg for it."

Most women protested when I took my time, slowly building them up to an orgasm before taking it away only to start again. But they always came back for more. I was *good* at sex. I knew how to please a woman, and tonight was going to be no different. There was a chance this would only be one night, so I was going to make the most of it.

Juniper didn't say a word. She didn't complain or beg. "Go on, then. Just know that I plan to do the same to you."

My cock twitched at that. I liked the sound of her doing to me exactly what I was about to do to her. Unbuttoning my jeans, I let my cock spring free from my boxers. Juniper's eyes flicked down, but her expression stayed the same.

I plunged two fingers inside her, pumping them in and out. Her back arched off the bed, and her head lolled back. My thumb circled her clit, and her pussy clenched around my fingers. Removing my fingers again, I brought them to my cock, stroking my length to coat it with her arousal. I moaned as I imagined her pussy wrapping around me. When I looked at Juniper, her pupils were blown out and she was biting her lip, clearly enjoying watching.

I let her hands drop to the pillow and stripped my pants off my legs, leaving nothing to the imagination. "Take off the rest of your clothes."

She obeyed, pulling her shirt over her head at an achingly slow pace like a strip tease, leaving her in a black bra. I would have been shocked if I didn't look like a drooling dog, watching her undress for me. Her breasts spilled out as she unclasped her bra, and she brought a hand up to pinch her nipple.

Bark, fucking bark.

A low, throaty moan slipped from my mouth at the sight, and she pinched her lips together in a smile.

"Two can play this game, Michael Tucker." She slid her hand down the front of her body until it reached the space below her navel. Her fingers pressed against her clit before disappearing inside her. My mouth gaped as I watched her touch herself until her eyes rolled back and her breathing became rapid.

"Fuck, Juniper." I was about to come like a teenager, just by watching her. "I need you."

"What was that?" She tilted her head toward me, still fucking herself with her fingers. "I don't think I heard you."

"Please let me fuck you." The plea—filled with desperation—left my lips before I could process what was happening.

With a satisfied grin on her face, Juniper pulled her fingers out of her pussy, bringing them up to my lips. I sucked her fingers clean like she wanted then stood, reaching into the nightstand for a condom.

"I was going to take my time, but it seems you had other plans, Peach. I don't want to wait another second to be inside you." Sliding on the condom, I stood at the edge of the bed. "Now, turn around and let me fuck you like I've wanted to all night."

CHAPTER FIVE

juniper

I was not expecting Mikey Tucker to beg me to have sex with him. Making him watch was just a bluff, but for some reason, it worked.

What I was *really* not expecting was for him to stop me at the door to his trailer after. I assumed he'd want to skip all the awkward post-hookup talk. He didn't seem like the kind to want to cuddle, either. Based on what I'd heard from Liv, he was a one-night-stand-only guy. No strings attached, never see you again, type of thing.

"Wait, you're telling me you want me to be your *girlfriend?*" I cocked my head to the side, raising an eyebrow.

He ran his fingers through his hair. "Fake girlfriend, but yes."

Why the hell does he need a fake girlfriend?

I wasn't sure I wanted to know.

I thought about it for a second, though, and something dawned on me. Yes, being able to say I hooked up with the bull rider Ava had so desperately wanted a chance with was great, but *showing up on his arm?* That was even better revenge. Even though we would know it was fake, no one else would, so she'd think he chose me and not her.

It was brilliant.

I wasn't just going to agree to this arrangement, though.

"What's in it for me?" I crossed my arms, knowing full well what I was going to be getting out of this but not willing to show all my cards.

"Whatever you want." He shrugged at first then backtracked. "Within reason. Don't go asking me to write a check with more than two zeros. I may be a bull rider, but I'm not loaded."

"Make an appearance with me at an event this summer in Goldfinch." It would have to be summertime for it to be an event that both Ava and Brady would be at, but if I was doing this for Mikey now, I felt like it was reasonable for him to return the favor later.

He nodded without hesitation. "Deal. I just need you to do this for a couple weeks. A month or two tops. Nothing serious."

"Before we shake on this, we need to set some ground rules," I pointed out. "Do you have a pen and paper anywhere?" I looked around the trailer and pursed my lips, finally noticing the disarray. It looked like a tornado of frat boys had rolled through. I fought the urge to gag, instead focusing my eyes on the ceiling.

"Here." Mikey handed me a piece of notebook paper with a stain I hoped was coffee and a pen.

"Okay. First rule: both of us, obviously, have to stay single. No bringing other girls home. No going out with anyone else. If this is going to work, we have to be exclusive. Agreed?"

He nodded, and I wrote it down.

"What's next?"

"Make it believable, but nothing extra. No offense, but I don't want to be spending money on fancy jewelry or shit like that."

I rolled my eyes but wrote down the second rule. "I don't want your money, Casanova. But I agree. This isn't real, so there's no need to be flashy with it. Third rule: no kissing in private. There's no reason for us to do that."

"What about sex?" he asked, because *of course he did*.

"I don't think that's a good idea. However, if we're going to be kissing and pretending to be intimate, I do think you should get tested. You know, in case something does happen again, which it won't, but in case." In hindsight, I probably should have brought up his sexual health *before* we hooked up, but I wasn't exactly thinking logically in the heat of the moment. I wouldn't be making that mistake again. "I'll get tested, too, and share the results if it makes you feel better." I'd gotten a test shortly after I caught Brady and Ava, because if he was so quick to cheat on me with her, then I had to assume he was cheating on me with others. I knew I was in the clear then, but the last thing I wanted was to catch something— especially now—so even if Mikey insisted I didn't need to, I'd be going. Offering to get tested and share the outcome made my request feel more fair, too.

I expected him to complain, to protest and say he was fine, but he simply replied, "Whatever you want, Peach."

I raised a brow at the name he'd called me four times now before scribbling *NO SEX* next to *No kissing*. Normally, I'd find something like that annoying, but coming from him, it was almost sweet. Endearing in an odd way, if you could even describe strangers who'd just hooked up as that. It'd work just fine to make our relationship look believable, so I didn't want to tell him to stop.

"Final rule, but arguably the most important." I looked up at him from the paper to make sure he was paying close attention. "Absolutely no—under *any* circumstances—falling in love with each other." I finished writing, underlining the bullet point a few times for emphasis, and slapped down the pen. "Sound good?"

"That shouldn't be an issue. No feelings and no one gets hurt. Sounds perfect to me."

"Great." I picked up the pen that I so dramatically threw down a few seconds earlier and signed my name under the rules. I handed him the pen, and he scribbled his signature next to mine. "Do you want me to keep it or do you want to?"

His eyes made a quick sweep over his trailer. "Uh, you keep it."

"I figured." I folded up the agreement and put it in my pocket. "Oh, I didn't think about this until now, but what happens if your friends expect me to stay at your place?"

"You can park your car here, and I'll drive you back to yours. Then pick you up to get your car the next day or something," he offered.

"What about your neighbors?" I'd noticed a couple other trailers in the horseshoe court when we pulled in. Word tended to get around fast, and while I didn't know if the people in Silver Creek liked to gossip, I usually assumed residents of a small town would.

"There are like three other people who live in this park. We're spaced out, so the odds of them noticing are slim. Besides, they're all older and they mind their own business. We'll figure it out. It'll be fine."

"Right. We'll figure it out. It's not that long anyway, it'll be no big deal," I agreed, unsure if I was trying to convince him or myself more that this arrangement wouldn't go south.

"Can I have your phone?" he asked, catching me off guard. When I didn't respond, he explained. "My fake girlfriend should probably have my phone number."

I blinked a few times. "Right, right. Sure. Here." I unlocked it, handing it to him.

Mikey went straight to the contacts, not taking any time to snoop or invade my privacy. After typing a few things then sending himself a text, he gave the phone back to me.

"B.D.E.?" I frowned. "What's that supposed to mean? Big Dick Energy?" That would be getting changed later.

"Or Best Dick Ever. Whatever you want it to mean."

"How about Biggest Disappointment Ever?"

He shrugged, a goofy smile on his face. "It was worth a shot."

"Don't give yourself too much credit." I smacked him lightly on the chest.

My comment only made him smirk even more. "I mean, you seemed to be enjoying yourself, so I think I'm crediting myself appropriately."

Images of him fucking me from behind, face contorted into pleasure and breathy moans falling from his lips, flashed through my mind, and I was sure my face had turned red as a tomato.

"I-I should probably get back. I don't want my roommate to think I got murdered by a serial killer or something," I mumbled. I reached for the door handle, but he beat me to it, following me out of the trailer. "What are you—" I started to ask before I remembered that he drove me here and my car was still at Rudy's.

"Come on, Peach." He laughed as he opened the passenger side door and guided me up into his truck.

The house was dark when I pulled into the driveway. Careful not to wake Natalie, I crept through the front door, expecting to disappear into my room like any normal night. Instead, an amused voice greeted me from the couch.

"Fun night?"

I spun around, attempting to make my expression as neutral as possible, knowing damn well I got caught like a teenager sneaking in after curfew. "Yeah, you could say that." I wasn't even going to try lying to her.

"Liv told me you left the bar early." Natalie chuckled. "Do I want to know who the guy was?"

"Probably not," I admitted with a scoff.

"Just be careful, okay, June? I know you're smart, but make sure you take time to heal. I know you want to make it seem like the breakup was no big deal, but I don't want you to do anything you might regret later."

"Thanks, Nat." I started walking toward my bedroom, but then stopped. "Hey, my coworker invited us out to a bonfire this weekend. I wasn't going to go, but maybe it would be fun?"

As much as I wanted to lie low and keep to myself, it would have been a mistake not to make *some* friends. Especially since I didn't know how long I would be living here. And Nico and Liv were cool.

"I think that would be great! I know you don't plan to

be here for a long time, but it wouldn't hurt to have some fun."

"Great. Well, I'm going to head to bed then. Night." I gave her a half-hearted wave then disappeared into my room, shutting the door and immediately tossing my phone onto the bed so I could get changed.

My phone buzzed next to me, the screen lighting up with a text message notification.

B.D.E.

Sweet dreams Peach

I huffed out a soft laugh, opening my messages. Before responding, I changed the name in my contacts to Tucker. Mikey would have been too obvious if anyone got ahold of my phone, and despite our fake-dating arrangement, I wasn't in a rush to have to explain to Natalie why I was in Mikey Tucker's bed. She knew his reputation better than I did and would almost certainly consider hooking up with him a regrettable decision.

After brushing my teeth and pulling my hair up into a messy bun, I typed out a quick text to Mikey, so he wouldn't think I was ignoring him.

Good night

My phone buzzed again, but I didn't check it as I put it on the nightstand and crawled under the covers, succumbing to slumber almost immediately.

Rudy's Angels

NICOOL

Sup Junie

Don't call me that

Why are you in my phone as "NiCool"?

LIV

Because he's dumb lol

NICOOL

Took you long enough to notice

Are you coming to the bonfire?

LIV

Omg please Juniper?

Hmm

NICOOL

She's totally going to say yes

Well now I don't want to

LIV

Ignore him

It wouldn't be the same without you

Pleeeeeaaaaseeee?

Okay

NICOOL

I can give you three reasons why you
should come

Wait

OKAY?

SHE SAID YES

LIV

You act like she just accepted your
marriage proposal lol

Can my friend Natalie come?

LIV

Wait that's the friend you're living with? Of
course! I love Natalie.

NICOOL

The more the merrier Junie

I'll send you the address

Don't call me that

But thanks. I'll see you guys

LIV

See you!!

NICOOL

Where did you go off to the other night, Mikey?" Jake asked as we helped Colter prep the barn for calving.

"Ah, you know. Home." I shrugged as I shoveled old bedding into a wheelbarrow.

"Oh?" He raised an eyebrow. "And what did you do at home?"

"Why are you suddenly so interested in my personal life, Flynn?" Normally, the guys would complain if I talked about my sex life. "Thought you didn't care to hear about my sexcapades?" Their wording, not mine.

"We don't!" Ellison yelled from the side-by-side parked outside the barn.

"Nosy woman." I snorted, shaking my head.

"Yeah, but what we do wanna know is if this girl is a keeper or not." Jake waggled his eyebrows. "You gonna be able to keep this one for a whole month?"

"I'll have you know, I'm fully capable of keeping a girl. I just choose not to, because most of them are nuttier than a fruitcake. I'm surprised none of them have tried to trap me with a fake baby or something."

Reid chuckled. "I'm kind of shocked none of them have come to you with a real baby."

"Be nice to him, he's just now learning about commitment, you guys." Colter patted me on the shoulder as he passed.

"When do we get to meet the lucky—or maybe unlucky—lady?" Jake poked at me.

"You'll meet her eventually. I don't want you guys to scare her away."

Colter tapped his lips. "Hm, I don't know, Mikey. I'm not sure I'm convinced this girl even exists. I'll believe it when I see it."

It was a joke about me giving him shit about Ellison when they first met, but I just shrugged. "Fine by me, Carson. Make fun of me all you want, but that money's going to be mine at the end of this." *And no one will even have to get hurt in the end.*

They quieted down after that, giving me a break from being the butt of all their jokes. I loved the guys, I really did, but sometimes it weighed on me. I knew I wasn't stupid or a complete dumbass, but sometimes it was easier to be the funny guy. That didn't mean I wanted to be a punchline, though. At least not all the time.

A few hours later, we'd finished helping Colter with the work that needed to be done on the ranch and had gathered on the back porch with a case of cold beer.

"Only a couple weeks until Houston, boys." Jake plopped down into an Adirondack chair as he popped the tab on his beer can. "You all ready for another year of this?"

"Yessir." Colter held up his can in acknowledgment.

It'd been three years now since he'd met Ellison at the Houston Rodeo. Since then, he and Reid had brought home plenty of gold buckles.

This was my year to bring one back from Houston. I could feel it in my bones. I was also ready to prove everyone wrong at the NFR, too. Although I'd made it last year—an accomplishment in itself—it didn't seem to be enough for the media or the "fans." It was always the same thing.

If Tucker had been more focused on riding those bulls than riding women, he'd be the number one bull rider in the world.

That guy is off his game.

Maybe it's time for him to hang up his chaps and give it a rest.

The comments I'd seen on social media flashed before my eyes, and I squeezed them shut to make it all go away.

"Everything all right?" Reid broke me out of my trance.

"Yep. All good." I nodded, fighting to think of something to change the subject. "Bet you're excited to see your girlfriend again. Houston seems to be the lucky gold mine for finding women. Maybe it's time we got Hayden a girl." I wiggled my eyebrows to add to the joke.

While Reid technically hadn't met Isabelle in Houston, that seemed to be the place where the fire between them ignited. At least until they friend-zoned each other... probably because of me. Oops.

Hayden's cheeks flushed as he shook his head.

"Ah, why not, man? I've never seen you with a girl before, there's gotta be one out there for ya."

He grumbled something under his breath that I couldn't quite make out, but I swore I heard, "Doesn't matter, because none of them will ever be her."

"Hey, maybe instead of focusing on our love lives, you can focus on bull riding, eh?" Colter raised his brows.

I tried not to dwell on what he said, but the words hit me like a sucker punch to the gut. I knew Colter didn't mean to hurt me, and his intentions weren't malicious, because he—and everyone else—had no idea the pressure I was under. I wanted to be better. Hell, I should have been winning by now. It was already difficult not to accept what the people on the Internet were saying as truth—that I was past my prime and there was no way I'd ever be able to claw my way to the top.

Instead, I plastered on a fake smile and fired back, "I like what I like, Carson." Kicking my feet out and leaning back into my chair, I added, "I'm only after three things. Danger, buckles, and buckle bunnies."

"Well, you've got at least two of the three down." Ellison snorted.

I sighed, letting my shoulders droop. *They don't mean it.* "Yeah, yeah. I'm working on it. This is my year."

"That's the spirit." Jake raised his beer.

I started riding bulls when I was nineteen. It started as another stupid bet, but then I realized I was actually good at it. I spent a few years riding in smaller rodeos in the WRCA before getting my permit card for the PRCA when I was twenty-four. It'd been six years since I joined the PRCA and almost twelve since I'd sat on my first bull.

It was damn time for me to start winning bigger prize pots.

There were several elements to bull riding. While it was absolutely about skill and your level of training, luck of the draw played a role in it, too—literally. There was a chance you'd draw a good bull that matched your style of riding, but there was also a chance you'd draw a bull that bucked differently and you'd have to adapt.

Then came the element of mental toughness. I was sure every bull rider experienced some level of fear sitting atop the bucking chutes, but it was all about how you grabbed hold of the reins and controlled that fear. To focus on the end goal of eight seconds. To have that courage to do the hard thing. Like the old saying went, being scared to death yet choosing to saddle up anyway.

At the end of the day, the adrenaline rush of bull riding overtook the fear for me. After my fair share of vicious bulls, I was convinced anything was possible if you had the mental fortitude to hang on for eight seconds, to push through the pain and fear of the uncertain and come out on top.

Sometimes those eight seconds felt like a lifetime, but the minute you heard that buzzer go off, it was like a weight being lifted off your shoulders. Getting out of the arena safely was another story, but that was what the bullfighters were there for. They were trained professionals who put their lives at risk every ride. Combine it all and bull riding was an art.

One I wasn't quite ready to give up on yet.

CHAPTER SEVEN

Conversational chatter and the thump of bass music got louder as Natalie and I approached the address Nico sent. If we weren't sure this was the place from the noise, the flames billowing behind the dark silhouettes of people definitely gave it away.

"Is it weird that we're coming here since we're out of school?" A bit of hesitancy came out in my voice, but she shook her head.

"No, not weird. It's not just a college bonfire. People who are a few years older than us come to these things, too."

Her comment didn't do much to reassure me. This kind of felt like the equivalent of going out to the college bars every single night even though you were five years graduated and well past your prime.

Now I just sounded pretentious. Especially since I worked at a bar.

I had *just* finished my degree, though, and it was perfectly normal for a twenty-two-year-old to go to the bars and still party. A small part of me was still slightly uncomfortable with the idea of drinking around a fire with freshmen. Then again, it wasn't like it was any different at the house parties Ava and I went to in Goldfinch.

The deeper rooted issue was that I was supposed to have my life together by now. Or at least be on my way to having it together.

I let out a small sigh, but it was enough to catch Natalie's attention.

"Are you okay? Do you still want to go? I can turn around." Concern flashed in her eyes.

I shook my head, shaking away all my thoughts about college and post-grad. "Yeah, I'm fine. Just having an existential crisis, apparently."

"Nothing a little alcohol can't fix," she joked as she pulled into a makeshift parking lot in the middle of the field.

The moment my feet hit the ground, Liv was yanking me toward the bonfire.

"There's someone you need to meet!" she practically screamed in my ear.

"Hello to you, too." I chuckled. I tilted my head away from her face, if only to prevent further eardrum damage. I caught a glimpse of Natalie following us out of the corner of my eye, so I let Liv continue to drag me along.

"You're gonna love—"

"You came!" Nico threw his arm around my shoulder when we got to him. He staggered a bit on his feet, and his grip on my arm tightened.

I rested my hand on his back to hold him up while flashing him an amused grin. "How much have you had to drink tonight, Ni*Cool*?" I teased.

The heat from the fire warmed my face, and he looked at me with a sly smile.

"Are you flirting with me, Junie?" His words slurred together, and he wiggled his finger in my face. "Don't go doing that. I can't have my heart broken twice in the same week."

I raised my brows at Liv, hoping for some kind of answer, but she just shrugged. Looking back to Nico, I replied, "Nope, not flirting with you. You didn't answer my question."

"I don't even remember your question. But if it was about the person who streaked down Main Street last weekend, then no, I definitely do not know who did that."

Liv looked him up and down. "He's had a few beers?"

"I've had *more* than a *few* beers, Livvybug," Nico cut in. It was pretty evident he'd had a bit to drink tonight by the way he was still swaying.

I grabbed his arm. "Let's get you away from the fire. The last thing we need is you taking a tumble into it."

"I'm going to grab a drink. Do you want something?" Natalie asked when she caught up to us.

"No, I'm okay, I need to drive," Liv replied.

I shook my head. "I'll go grab something in a minute. You might want to get Nico—"

"BEER!" Nico hollered.

Water, I mouthed to Natalie as I subtly pointed to him.

She nodded, an amused grin on her face. "Be right back."

We moved a couple paces back from the fire, and the night air instantly provided cool relief.

"What would I do without you two?" Nico's arm was still around my shoulders, but he wrapped his other one around Liv, pulling her close.

Liv giggled. "Well, for one, you'd probably be passed out somewhere."

"You'd come save me, though, wouldn't you, Livvybug?" He didn't wait for an answer before he took his arm off me, using his finger to boop her nose. "You would. I know you would. You're always saving me."

I didn't know what that meant, but I also didn't know how reliable Nico's storytelling was at the moment.

Liv rolled her eyes, but her cheeks flared pink as she whispered, "Probably."

Natalie came back shortly after with two drinks.

"What's this?" Nico tilted his head at the solo cup Natalie offered him.

"It's something new. You'll like it. Go on," Natalie urged.

He took the cup from her and downed it in a couple gulps, letting out a loud burp at the end. Nodding vigorously, he smiled lazily. "You're right, that was good!"

Liv yanked on the arm of a guy who looked to be a taller, male version of her. They had matching green eyes and the same blond hair. "Juniper, this is Tommy. He's my older brother."

"Hi." I raised my hand in a polite wave, pursing my lips in a soft smile.

"June just moved here from Goldfinch! She graduated from SGU in the winter," Liv explained, her hands moving in wild gestures. "Tommy graduated a couple years ago, so I thought you two would get along. You should go talk!" She pushed her brother toward me.

Tommy let out an awkward laugh at Liv's attempt at matchmaking. "Sorry for my sister's inability to be subtle. Do you want a drink?"

"Yeah, now that Nat's back, I think she and Liv can handle Nico." I laughed. "We'll be back, guys."

Liv and Natalie nodded and Nico sort of waved as we

stepped away from the bonfire. We walked side by side toward a few coolers, and Tommy handed me a seltzer that I pointed out.

"So, do you live here?" I asked him.

"No, I'm just visiting for the weekend. I don't know how much Liv has told you about herself"—he laughed—"but we grew up in a tiny town here in Montana. You've probably never heard of it. Reverie?"

I shook my head. "Nope, can't say I've heard of that one."

"You'll have to come visit with Liv. In the fall they put on this big festival and the town population basically doubles. It's like the Bucking Horse Sale level popularity, but with cozier vibes."

"I've heard a lot about this Bucking Horse Sale thing."

He laughed. "It's a big deal around here. It's one of those 'the ones who get it, get it' type of things."

"I guess I'll take your word for it then."

We lost track of time and talked a while longer—or rather, Tommy talked—then walked back to the bonfire to find Liv and Nico. He was interesting, but a nagging feeling in my chest kept me from getting too involved in the conversation. I'd made a deal—didn't matter that it was a deal with the devil himself—and I was going to stick to it for the sake of my own agenda.

"I'd love to get to know you better. Maybe in a setting that's not so crowded with college kids." Tommy chuckled.

Before I could turn him down, a hand dropped onto my shoulder.

"There you are. I was wondering where you'd gone off to."

Speak of the devil.

I spun around, coming face to face with Mikey. He

looked good, in a baseball cap and a Henley with the top button undone. His facial hair had grown to a five o'clock shadow since the night we met in the bar, and his mustache was neatly combed.

"Oh, I—" Tommy stuttered. "I didn't know you had a boyfriend, Juniper. I'm sorry. Liv didn't mention…" His voice trailed off as he realized who I was with.

"No worries." Mikey brushed him off.

Tommy pointed over his shoulder awkwardly. "I'm gonna…go." He walked away, and I could practically feel the embarrassment radiating off him.

I pulled Mikey aside, away from the other people. "What the fuck are you doing? Aren't you a little old to be here?" He had to have been the oldest person at the bonfire.

"Damn, Peach. Good to see you, too." He snickered.

I crossed my arms, huffing out a breath. "Are you keeping tabs on me?"

Mikey raised his eyebrows, a playful glint in his eyes. "No, but maybe I should, girlfriend. Have you forgotten rule number one?"

"*Fake* girlfriend, and no, I didn't forget. Good to know you're taking that seriously, though." I patted his arm as I tried to walk past him.

He took hold of my arm as our shoulders brushed, pulling me back. "Come on, Peach. At least act like you like me. It's a little too early in our *fake* relationship to be fighting already, don't you think?" Although his tone was teasing, there was a silent plea in his expression. For whatever reason, he needed me as much as I needed him.

"I'm sorry. I've never been in a fake relationship before, so this is all new to me."

He mumbled something under his breath that sounded

a lot like, "I've never been in a *real* one before, so this is also new," but I chose to ignore it.

"You didn't answer my question, though. Why are you here?"

Mikey shrugged. "Heard through the grapevine that you'd be here and thought it'd be a good opportunity to pilot this relationship. Thought if it went well and we could make it believable enough, I'd introduce you to the rest of the guys."

Oh. I hadn't thought much about the rest of the cowboys in his friend group.

I sighed and gave him a reluctant nod.

"They don't believe that you're real. They thought I made you up to get them off my back, so, you know."

"I see. So, we've gotta make it believable."

"Believable but not flashy, right?" He winked. "It'll be a piece of cake."

Right…

"All right. Let's put on a good show, then." I gave in, taking Mikey's hand in mine and dragging him back to the crowd of people congregating around the fire.

"June! Where did you…" Natalie called out to me, but her voice faltered as she took in the man next to me. "Uh, hi?"

"Hey, I'm Mikey." My fake boyfriend extended a handshake to Natalie, and she took it hesitantly, the look on her face akin to one someone would have if they were picking up a dead animal.

"I know who you are." She whipped her head toward me and raised her brows with the silent accusation of, *This is the guy you went home with?*

"This is my friend, Natalie. We both went to school at SGU, and I'm living with her here in Miles City." I introduced her, shooting her a glare and mouthing, *Be nice.*

"I'm sure I've seen you around town, but it's nice to formally meet you." Mikey nodded at her, flashing her a wide smile.

"Mm-hmm," Natalie hummed, dropping his handshake and not bothering to hide her look of disgust as she glanced down at her hand and rubbed her fingers together like they were covered in dirt.

"Don't mind her," I cut in, trying to save this conversation. She and I would be having an in-depth talk about this later, but for now, I was just trying to make us look believable. I looped my arm through his, resting my hand on his bicep. "Where did Liv go?"

"She and her brother just left. They took Nico with them." She flicked her eyes toward Mikey. "I'll probably head out soon, too. Unless you want me to stay to give you a ride home?" She asked the question like she was giving me an out. As though this was a hostage situation and not something of my own volition.

"That's all right. I can give her a ride home, right, Peach?" Mikey answered for me.

Annoyance prickled at my skin, but I nodded, not wanting to give the impression that I was in distress, because I wasn't. If Natalie picked up on anything that seemed like hesitancy or trouble, she would have said something and the whole act would have been ruined.

"Yeah, Mikey can drive me. Thanks for the offer, though. I'll see you at home." I nodded enthusiastically, even though my brain was screaming at me that this was all fake and my acting sucked.

She nodded, although suspicion was still written all over her face. "Call me if you need anything, okay?"

"I will. Promise."

"Goodnight, then. Bye, June. Mikey…" She side-eyed him as she brushed past us to head to the car.

My eyes tracked her until she got in the vehicle and drove away, tires kicking up dust and headlights disappearing into the night.

"Your friend doesn't like me, does she." Mikey's words came out more as a statement than a question.

"It doesn't matter." I pursed my lips. "She just worries about me. It's fine. I'm sure she'll warm up once she gets to know you."

Ironic, considering I hardly knew him. I knew his reputation, though, so it didn't come as a shock that Natalie was wary of him. I expected nothing less.

"Seems like we've got our work cut out for us, then. Add her to the list of people to convince, I guess." He took off his backward ballcap, running his fingers through his hair before placing it back on his head. "Are you ready to head home?"

We hadn't been there for very long, but I didn't know anyone else here since my friends had all left. Considering I agreed to come to the bonfire for Nico and Liv, I didn't see any reason to stay longer. "Yeah, let's go."

"How do you feel about meeting the guys later this week?"

"I guess it's now or never." *Why the fuck not?* "Let's do it."

mikey

All right, so we've got the team ropers: Colter, Reid, and Hayden. Colter and Reid are roping partners, and Hayden is the youngest of the group. He's also pretty quiet, so don't let it surprise you. Jake is a tie-down roper and bulldogger—which is just another name for a steer wrestler." I ran through the guys' names once more as we drove down the gravel road toward Colter and Ellison's house. "Ellison is Colter's wife. Honestly, you'll probably get along with her. You're both firecrackers."

Juniper tapped her fingers against the back of her other hand and hollowed out her cheeks. On instinct, I reached over and took her hand in mine. She gave me a puzzled look, but I didn't pull back.

"What are you doing?" Her eyes narrowed. "We aren't in public, you don't need to hold my hand."

"You're nervous." I pointed out the obvious.

"Yes, and? I stand by the fact that we aren't in public. We don't need to pretend right now. Rule number two, remember?" She pulled her hand out of my grasp.

Juniper fell silent for a few moments, but then spoke up, her voice barely a whisper. "What if they don't like me?"

I turned my head toward her and blinked a couple times, trying to process her question. "Don't like you?"

"Yeah. What if they don't think I'm good enough for you?"

I couldn't help but scoff. "Not good enough for me? June, they're probably going to say the opposite. That you're *too good* for me."

Her expression fell blank, and the urge to reach out and find the reason pulled at my chest, but I didn't pry. We were still getting to know each other, still strangers. I didn't expect her to pour her heart out to me, but when she was ready, I'd be there to listen.

"I think I'm just nervous. It's been a minute since I've had to impress anyone," she admitted softly.

"I've got your back, Peach." I gave her leg a reassuring squeeze then turned my attention back to the winding road and the endlessly sprawling Montana landscape.

When we arrived at Colter and Ellison's house, I killed the ignition and raced around the pickup to open Juniper's door for her. She threw me a suspicious glance, and I winked in response. Just because there weren't people around to judge our fake relationship didn't mean I couldn't show her basic decency.

Was this a bit out of character for me? Yes.

But something about Juniper made me want to turn over a new leaf. At least for the duration of our arrangement.

"Ready?" I asked her.

"No, but I don't have a choice." She swallowed and took a deep breath. "Let's do this."

I nodded and took her hand in mine, if not for show,

then for the small ounce of reassurance it gave me heading into this gathering.

"We're here!" I announced as we walked through the front door.

If I had a camera on me, I would have immediately captured the looks on everyone's faces.

Shock. Pure shock.

Too many seconds of awkward silence passed before Ellison finally got up, seemingly the only one to have a bit of sense not to make Juniper more uncomfortable than I was sure she felt.

"Come on in." She waved us along before walking up to Juniper. "Dinner's not quite ready yet, but it should be soon. I'm Ellison."

"Juniper."

The rest of the guys followed Ellison's lead and stood from their spots at the dining table.

"I'm Colter. Better known as Ellison's husband." Colter shook her hand, and I thought his joke lightened the mood a bit, because Juniper let out a small laugh. I gave him a look of gratitude before following behind Juniper as she went down the line of cowboys.

"It's nice to meet you, Juniper. I'm Reid." His eyes— reflecting with what looked like uncertainty—flicked to me and back to her, but I didn't think she noticed.

Jake introduced himself, giving her a handshake and a nod, and Hayden smiled at her while offering his name.

Once formalities were all exchanged, we sat at the table, Juniper on the end across from Hayden, Jake, and Reid. Colter was at the head while Ellison sat on my right.

It'd been a long time since we'd had one of these formal dinners. But Colter and Ellison had insisted, saying they wanted Juniper to feel comfortable instead of throwing her into the arena. Truthfully, I thought they didn't want any distractions so I could be interrogated. I just hoped they went easy on her.

"So, how did you two meet?" Jake wasted no time getting to the point, the sole purpose of this meal. I stared at him with wide eyes and pursed lips, as though to send him a message of, *Really?* He responded with a nonchalant shrug like I should have expected this.

"I'm a bartender at Rudy's," Juniper answered. "We met there."

Jake tilted his head, raising his brows in recognition. "Ah, so that's what you were doing when you left us the other night, huh?" He couldn't elbow me in the ribs like he normally did when he was teasing, so he just plastered on a stupid smirk.

Before I could speak, Juniper retorted, "I saw what I wanted, and I went for it. How did you all meet?"

I held back my smile as I looked down at the table. She was just like Ellison. Fiery and not afraid to dish it out. I liked it, and not just because it was nice not to be the one who that energy was being directed toward for once.

"Colter, Jake, and I all competed in college rodeo together in Goldfinch. Hayden, too, but Colter and Jake had graduated before he started school. We also met Mikey at a bar," Reid answered.

"Ah, I just graduated from SGU with a degree in Molecular Biology."

Heat flared in my cheeks.

Well, that's a new development.

I hadn't paid enough attention in the bar, or even after the fact. Juniper didn't act like she was in college, though. She had a mature air about her that I didn't even think to ask her how old she was. And she was clearly smart, I didn't need to know what she studied in college to figure that out.

The boys all exchanged subtle glances.

"Damn, I didn't even know SGU had a degree like that." Reid looked impressed.

"They added it my sophomore year of college, so I changed my major." She shrugged. "Originally, I was going into chemical engineering, but I'm interested in biotechnology so the switch made sense."

For a minute, the room fell silent, but then Colter was the one brave enough to cautiously ask, "How old are you?"

"Twenty-two."

One of the guys coughed like they were choking down laughs, and I sighed. Did that really matter?

"What brought you here? Especially with that degree, I'm surprised you decided to come to a small town in Montana." Ellison changed the subject, seemingly sensing the uncertainty in the room. "Not that you can't do that kind of stuff here, but a bigger city with greater resources makes more sense."

Juniper shuffled her feet under the table, her jaw hardening for a quick moment. "I needed a change in scenery. One of my friends offered to let me stay with her for the time being, and I took her up on her offer to get out of Goldfinch."

"Do you plan to stay, or?" Ellison continued.

Juniper's face paled. I didn't think it was anyone's business what Juniper chose to do with her life. This agreement didn't span more than a couple months, and while we were playing the part, there was no reason to put the idea in their heads that this was more serious than it was, especially since we'd just met. Besides, their questions were more a reflection of me and my behavior than of Juniper.

"I think that's enough questions," I cut in before things could get out of hand. "We didn't come here for an interrogation," I added with a stern look.

A few apologies were muttered from around the table. I reached down to find Juniper's hand, giving it a light squeeze to let her know I had her back. That I acknowledged the awkwardness of the conversation and was sorry.

A timer conveniently went off, and Ellison scrambled out of her seat to go to the kitchen.

"Need some help, Blaze?" Colter called after her. Before she could answer, he was already up from his chair, following her.

Jake cleared his throat. "I'm gonna go grab some drinks that I brought over."

Reid got up next, holding his phone to his ear. "Honeybee, what's up?"

I guessed no one wanted to sit in the uncomfortable silence that they'd caused.

"I'm sorry for everyone's questions," Hayden murmured before softly chuckling. "We're not exactly used to Mikey bringing someone around. Doesn't excuse it, but I hope we haven't scared you off or made you feel bad." He gave her a tight-lipped smile before patting the table and getting up himself.

Juniper pulled her lips to the side and mumbled, "Well, that could have gone better."

I lowered my voice so Colter and Ellison couldn't hear. "Don't worry about them, Peach. Their reactions are more a reflection of me than of you. Like Hayden said, they're not used to me bringing girls around, much less *having a girlfriend*, so I'm sure it was a shock. I'll have a talk with them later."

God, what had I dragged her into? She'd made the move on me first that night, but part of me thought I should have just let her go when she tried to leave. I had to remind myself it was only until the end of Houston and then whatever she wanted me to do this summer. A bit of discomfort would make it worth it for both of us by the end.

Anything was possible if you just hung on for eight seconds.

"What if this just isn't worth it?" she whispered, voicing my exact fear.

"Nothing's binding, Juniper. If you want out, just say the word and we can end things." It would cost me money and my dignity, but I wasn't going to force her into an arrangement she didn't want.

She paused, as though a billion thoughts were rolling through her brain. "No. I don't want out. I can do this."

I couldn't tell if she was trying to convince me or herself. Whatever her motivation for this was, it was strong enough to keep her here.

"The offer still stands. If at any point you decide you can't do this anymore, we'll end it. Add it to the list of rules."

The front door creaked open and Reid and Jake appeared, carrying a couple cases of beer, cutting our conversation short. There wasn't much left to say anyway. But I was secretly hoping Juniper wouldn't give up on me.

Hayden came back next with a plate of rolls from the kitchen, and Colter and Ellison followed suit, each carrying a plate.

"Here, let me take that from you," Reid offered to take one of the plates—pork roast—from Ellison's hands.

"Anything else that I can grab?" I asked her.

"Yeah, do you want to grab the empty plates and silverware from the counter?"

I nodded, heading into the kitchen before hearing Juniper ask if she could do anything.

"No, you're our guest. And I apologize for prying earlier. We really do want you to feel at home here. Our group can be a bit chaotic at times, especially with Mikey." Ellison laughed. "I should have afforded you the same respect the guys all gave me when Colter first introduced me."

"To be fair, I thought you were going to clock Mikey in the face the first time you met him," Jake pointed out.

I started walking back just as Ellison shrugged, and a small smile tugged at my lips. "I'm sure I would have deserved it."

"I kicked your ass in pool, so that was enough for me," she teased.

The rest of the evening was much lighter as we all shared jokes. They didn't drill Juniper with any more questions, and it made me think this whole fake-dating masquerade might actually work.

"Wait, so how did you and Colter meet?" Juniper asked.

A few awkward laughs filled the room.

"She quite literally ran into me in a bar, and I accidentally said something about her eyes. She didn't want anything to do with me, but I wasn't willing to give up on her. It took a bit of time, but I finally got her to soften up." Colter planted a kiss on Ellison's head.

"If it were any other cowboy, I don't think it would

have worked on me. But Colter was different. Special. I'm grateful it worked out the way it did," Ellison added.

Juniper smiled. "That's sweet."

Juniper excused herself to go to the bathroom, leaving me alone with my friends.

"Is it just me or does she look familiar?" Jake asked. "I feel like I've seen her before."

I'd also felt the same way, but I couldn't place where I'd recognized her from.

Hayden and Reid exchanged a look, but neither of them said anything.

"She doesn't look familiar to me. Maybe you just recognize her from Rudy's. After all, she said she started working there." Ellison shrugged, providing a reasonable explanation.

The rest of the guys, except Reid, seemed to accept her answer. I raised a brow at Reid, hoping he'd speak up, but he didn't. Probably a good thing, because Juniper was coming back.

"Thank you for having me over. I had a fun time."

"You're always welcome back. Next time the guys rope, you'll have to come with Mikey. Really see them all in action." Ellison grinned.

Juniper nodded.

"I'll take you home?" It was getting late, and I was slightly worried something would come up to scare Juniper away. I offered her my hand, and she took it. "I'll see you all later. Thanks for dinner, Ellison."

We waved and headed out the front door.

Juniper let go of my hand the second we were out of the house and the door was shut behind us.

Once we got in the pickup and started back down the road, I said, "I think that went well."

"I think so, too. We were definitely believable. Now we just have to keep the act up for a few more weeks, right?"

"Yep." I couldn't pinpoint why, but my heart dropped a little. It definitely wasn't because of the reminder that all of this was fake, though. It couldn't have been. It was my idea, and I didn't have time for a real relationship.

My phone buzzed in the cup holder after I'd dropped Juniper off at her house.

LAWSY

You sure you don't remember that girl from somewhere?

Nah. Do you?

LAWSY

I have my theory, but if you don't remember her, then I'm probably wrong

It's not important. Anyway, I think this will be good for you. Settling down, that is

Maybe

juniper

After meeting Mikey's friends, I felt good about our fake-dating arrangement. If it was believable enough to them, even if they were skeptical at first, then it would be believable enough for Ava and Brady this summer. I could just imagine the looks on their faces, especially Ava's, when they realized who I was with—the one-night stand who tossed my ex-best friend to the curb and who also happened to be my ex-boyfriend's favorite bull rider.

Maybe it would all blow up in my face and they'd think I was just another hookup, but the idea that I could get the same man Ava had once wanted was enough to propel me forward with my plans.

Over the course of the last few days, Mikey and his friends would pop into Rudy's bar when I was working, and even though I was on shift, our act never fell through the cracks. The old man himself even cracked a smile at the sight of the two of us.

"You look happy." Liv sidled up next to me at the bar.

I quirked an eyebrow. "What do you mean?"

She gestured to me as a whole. "I don't know, you just have this glow about you. Compared to when you started working here, you just look more content."

Heat rose to my cheeks at the idea of Mikey actually making me happy in a romantic kind of way.

"See! This is what I mean. You're literally blushing," Liv pointed out.

I made a show of patting my face, if only to stop my lips from curving into a smile, and tried to come up with some excuse for my changed demeanor. "I—"

"It's okay to be happy, June. I don't know why you moved here or your reasoning for anything, but if I'm being honest, you looked kind of sad when you first started working here."

I opened my mouth to protest, but quickly shut it because Liv kept going.

"I don't know if it's Mikey that's making you this happy, but if he is, I won't judge. I'm surprised, but good on him if he's the reason. As long as he doesn't hurt you in the end, I'll support whatever it is you two have going on. Even if it's not my brother." She chuckled.

"For what it's worth, Tommy seems like a great guy," I offered.

"He's all right for a big brother." She winked as a customer called her over for drinks.

A group of college girls came up to the bar wanting white tea shots, so I started pouring them. Out of the corner of my eye, I caught a flash of Natalie's dark-brown hair as she walked in the door. I gave her a nod of acknowledgment, and she waited behind the group I was serving.

I wondered why she was in the bar, but then I got a better look at the expression on her face.

"Five white tea shots. Open or closed tab?" I asked the girls as they thanked me for the shots.

"We'll leave it open, please!" A pretty girl with dirty blonde hair and doe-like eyes handed me her card.

"You got it." I kept her card, and they walked off with their drinks. When I came back to the bar, Natalie was leaning against it. "What are you doing here? Is something wrong?"

"You tell me, Juniper. You've been avoiding me for the past week. Since the bonfire." She crossed her arms.

"I'm sorry, I've been busy." I shrugged.

She cocked her head to the side, lifting an eyebrow. "What the hell are you doing with Mikey Tucker?"

I guessed we were getting straight to the point. I let out a sigh. "We're dating."

"Mikey Tucker doesn't date."

"I'd beg to differ. He's dating me." I put one hand on my hip.

Her mouth gaped. "You've known each other for a week and a half!" Her facial features pinched, and she shook her head. Forcing out a breath, she put her hands on the bar. "I'm sorry, I just worry about you."

"I understand that. But I'm fine."

"It's just…your boyfriend cheated on you, June. You should be eating ice cream in the bathtub *Aquamarine* style, not jumping into a new relationship, much less one with *him*."

"*Ex-boyfriend*, Nat," I corrected.

"I know they say the best way to get over someone is to get under someone else, but you couldn't have picked literally anyone else?" She kept babbling on. "I mean, *my God*, Juniper, he's got one of the biggest reputations in Montana, and not in a good way."

"Nat—"

"You should probably go to the doctor, because God forbid—"

"Natalie!" I cut her off then leaned in. "Listen to me. You *cannot* speak a word of this to anyone, but it's not real, okay?"

"Huh?"

"The relationship. It's fake. I want revenge."

She blinked a few times, as though she was processing the information I just gave her. "Well, that's healthy," she muttered, and a twinge of regret for telling her the truth rose in my chest. "I suppose it's better than you actually being in a relationship with Silver Creek's notorious playboy but, again, you couldn't have chosen anyone else?"

I huffed out a breath. "Come on." I gestured for her to follow as I walked behind Liv to the end of the bar and disappeared around the corner to the back office. Rudy wasn't in tonight, so it was the best place to have a private conversation with her. "I needed it to be Mikey because of Ava. I can't just have *any* fake boyfriend," I explained.

"I'm not sure I'm following."

"Ava and Mikey had a one-night stand last year. I recognized him when he came into the bar, so I made a move. Was it the most mature thing to do? No, and I acknowledge that, but neither was fucking my boyfriend—sorry, *ex*—behind my back."

Natalie blew a raspberry. "Wow, okay, that's…a lot. I can tell you've already made up your mind, but just be careful. I know I've said that before, but I mean it. He's got a reputation bigger than his entire career. I'd hate for your heart to get broken twice in a year."

I winced a little. "The whole purpose of this fake-dating arrangement is so neither one of us gets hurt. We have a whole set of rules written out. The system is in place so no one catches feelings." Sure, rules could be broken, but they existed so we could check one another when things started to get out of hand. Besides, I had no intention of breaking our rules.

My goal was to help Mikey with whatever it was he needed, and then get my end of the bargain. I'd be using him just as much as he'd be using me.

"All right. I believe you." She raised her hands in surrender before laughing softly. "You're something else, Juniper. Remind me not to get on your bad side."

I smiled in response. "Come on, let's get out of here before Liv comes looking for me."

TUCKER

So I have a request

> I didn't know requests were in our agreement

TUCKER

This one's kind of important...

> What is it?

TUCKER

The Houston Rodeo is coming up

I was hoping you'd come with me

J uniper never answered my text about the rodeo, and I was starting to get anxious. We'd be heading out on the road soon, and a key component to getting the most out of the bet was being able to prove I had a girl until the end of Houston. I didn't think it'd be too believable for the guys if my girlfriend didn't come support me at one of the biggest rodeos of the year.

The guys had been bothering me about it all week, too.

The Silver Creek Cowboys (And Ellison)

ELLISON'S HUSBAND

Your girl coming to Houston with us?

Dunno yet

FLYNN

She break up with you already? Damn. That was quick

LAWSY

We probably scared her off at the dinner

ELLISON'S HUSBAND

Oops.

ELLISON

I thought my questions were valid

HAYDIE

You guys are kinda scary when you get into interrogation mode

Thanks Haydie. Glad you've got my back

HAYDIE

I was more talking about Juniper, but sure

I sent back the emoji that had lines for the eyes and mouth then opened my text thread with Juniper.

I needed to convince her to come on the road with us. It was a big ask, but since it was crucial to the believability portion of our agreement, I was certain it fell under the rules.

Peach I really need this favor

PEACH

I don't know if I can. I have a job.

Let me handle that

Please. We can end things after Houston. Promise

PEACH

But you'll still do my thing this summer, right?

Of course. I'm not gonna bail on you Peachy

Can I take you to work? We can go talk to Rudy together

PEACH

Sure

I rehearsed a speech in my head the entire drive to Juniper's house, brainstorming ideas of how I was going to convince old man Rudy to let her take a month or two off work to come be a roadie.

Yeah, the more I thought about it, the less I was convinced he'd let her take that much time off. But it didn't hurt to ask.

Juniper was waiting for me on the front steps when I made it up the driveway and quickly hopped in the truck.

"Hi," she huffed.

"What's on your mind, Peachy?"

She buckled her seatbelt and slumped in the seat. "This Houston thing. Natalie thinks it's a bad idea, and honestly, I have to agree with her."

"Why's that?" Her hesitation both intrigued and frightened me.

"For one, it's not like I can just leave my job for a month. Not only because it'd make me a shitty employee, but I need to make money."

"I've got you covered. You're my girlfriend—" I started.

"Fake girlfriend," she cut in.

"Yes, like you love to keep reminding me. You're my *fake* girlfriend, so it wouldn't make sense for me to not pay for your food in Houston, and you'd be staying with me, so that's also free. Getting a hotel room would be suspicious, don't you think? I'll handle Rudy."

Juniper wrinkled her nose but didn't say anything.

"What?"

"Staying with you is a bit much, don't you think?"

I sighed. Sure, we agreed not to do sleepovers here at home, but Houston would be different. "Not if we want to make this thing believable."

"See, that's what I mean. This all sounds like more hassle than what it's worth," she protested.

Fuck. I needed her to come with me if I was going to get that patch of land.

"What else do you want? What's going to convince you to do this?" I asked, hoping my question didn't come off as desperate as it sounded.

She gave me a puzzled look then tapped her lips in thought. "I mean, I have something, but I don't think you'd be down for it."

After she explained her idea, my stomach dropped. "I don't think that's a good idea, Juniper. We'd have to stay together for much longer if we did that."

"I mean, we wouldn't *have* to. Think about how many celebrities are only in a month-long relationship for PR. We do one appearance together and that's it."

Yeah, but they don't have the media hounding them for being "distracted."

"I can't."

"Then I guess I can't go to Houston with you." She faked a yawn and kicked her feet up on the dash.

I ticked my jaw. "Surely there's a way we can compromise here?"

She shrugged. "Possibly."

Brat.

"Why do you want media attention so badly?"

Her face blanched, and she planted her feet back on the floorboards. "Just forget it."

We pulled up to Rudy's, but as she reached for the door handle, I locked the pickup.

"What are you doing? I need to get to work."

"Answer my question." Sure, most girls wanted their fifteen minutes of fame by getting a picture with me to post on their social media or whatever, but Juniper didn't seem like that type of girl.

"I just need to prove a point, okay?" she grumbled.

"Listen, Peach. I can give you as many pictures as you want, hell, I'll even give you a video, but media attention is where I have to draw the line."

She scoffed, unlocking her door and hopping out of the truck, setting off the alarm.

I followed as she stalked off to the bar. "Dammit, Juniper, wait." I reached out to grab her arm.

Her eyes darted to mine, icy blues piercing my soul, chilling my bones.

"You do realize that if I agree to this, it's going to extend our agreement, right?"

She nodded. "I don't see the issue. Even if we 'break up' now, we're just going to have to 'get back together' this summer."

She had a point. Conflicting feelings settled in my stomach as I thought about it. Maybe if the fans and reporters saw me with a girl, they'd stop hounding me about being distracted. I could attempt to repair my playboy image *and* win the bet.

I closed my eyes, letting my lungs fill with air before slowly exhaling through pursed lips. "Fine. The likelihood of the media finding us anyway is pretty high. I guess avoiding each other at the event while our friends believe we're dating would have been off the table anyway."

"Exactly. Now you just have to convince the boss man to let me go." She strutted away, her hips swaying with each step.

I followed her into the bar. It was pretty slow with it being mid-afternoon. There wouldn't be a rush for another couple hours. Rudy stood behind the bar, wiping down the counter.

"Hey, Rudy, can I talk to you for a minute?" Juniper's voice was barely above a whisper.

"Sure thing, what can I do for you, Miss Juniper?"

"I was wondering if I could take a few weeks off work." She pulled her lip between her teeth, obviously not having high expectations for the request.

"You wanna do what now?" Rudy's booming voice filled the bar. But his tone wasn't mean or accusing, just curious.

"I want her to come with me to the Houston Rodeo. To support me as my girlfriend," I explained, thinking it might come better from me. Not that Juniper couldn't fight her own battles or advocate for herself, but Rudy knew who I was and how big of a deal this would be.

Juniper shifted on her feet. "I know it's a big ask, and I absolutely don't expect you to say—"

"Well, now, yes, that's fine! You should have led with that! It's about time this mustang here got roped in. I thought I'd be dead before he ever settled down." Rudy let out a deep belly laugh.

"You...what?" Her face contorted in confusion.

"Go on, have fun. I'm sure Olivia and Nicolas can handle things here. We won't be terribly busy until May anyway, and I assume you lot will be back for the Bucking Horse Sale, yeah?"

I nodded. "Wouldn't miss it, you know that, Rudy. We'll be back in mid-April since we're driving and hitting some rodeos on the way back."

"Then I don't see what the problem is. Your job will be

ready for you when you come back, Juniper. Make sure you keep this one in line. It's nice to see him behaving for once," Rudy teased, slapping me on the shoulder as he headed to the back office, his soft chuckles audible even after he turned the corner.

"Well, there you have it. Guess you're coming with me on the road. You ever been to Texas before? They say everything's bigger there. Definitely true when I roll into town." I winked at the innuendo, and she rolled her eyes.

"Whatever helps you sleep at night. Now, let me get to work, Casanova."

"Yes, ma'am." Leaning in to kiss her cheek, I whispered, "Thank you for this. You're doing me a huge favor."

juniper

I'd never been to Houston before, and my jaw dropped at the sight of the city skyline before us. The drive down had been long—just under twenty-four hours—but we'd survived without ending our fake relationship early.

The long road trip was actually helpful to get to know each other better. Luckily, since the relationship was new, we had an excuse for not knowing every single minute detail about each other. But eventually, we'd be expected to know simple facts about one another.

"Where are you from originally?" I'd asked on a long, boring stretch through Wyoming.

"Colorado," he replied. "The southern part. Where are you from?"

"I'm from Michigan."

"What made you move to Montana, then?" He looked over at me with curiosity in his eyes.

"It truly was for a change of scenery. Admittedly, I'd seen photos of the wide open spaces and big blue skies and was immediately drawn in. SGU had the program that I wanted to go into, and even

though it was more expensive than an in-state school, I was ready to get out. How about you?"

"It was a similar whim. I'd been traveling from place to place for a while, never really finding anywhere to settle. Colorado is where I grew up, but I wouldn't necessarily call it home anymore. When I met Colter and Reid, it felt right to come up to Montana. I honestly didn't plan to stay, but somewhere along the line it became home. I don't have a house or land, so I can always leave if the urge to roam comes up again, but I do consider the guys family," he confessed, the words seeming to pour out of him. "I think Montana may be the place I finally settle."

I didn't mean for it to slip out, but I still confessed, "Sometimes I'm not sure what to do with myself. I had this whole future planned out and then…"

"Then what?"

"Things changed. I changed, I guess." I didn't want to divulge what had happened for fear that I'd be found out, but it wasn't necessarily a lie either. Brady cheating on me was humiliating enough as it was; I didn't feel the need to open that can of worms.

"Was it at least a good change?"

"Yeah. It was, I think."

Once we'd gotten settled and everyone had unhooked the trailers, we started to make a plan for the evening.

"I think Colter and I are going to take a trip out to the ranch, but we can meet you all later?" Ellison explained.

I'd learned from Mikey that she was born and raised in Houston. Her father was once a famous cowboy, but a rodeo accident had taken his life when Ellison was a child. By a stroke of fate, she'd run into Colter at a bar then saw him again on the one day out of the entire year she went to a rodeo. The rest was history, a love story for the ages.

"Isa should be coming around soon," Reid said.

"We could wait for her then grab some food or something. Meet you two at the bar later?" Jake suggested.

A few murmurs of agreement rose within the group.

"Juniper's never been to Houston before, so I say we give her the full experience." Mikey winked at me.

Heat flushed into my cheeks. I hadn't told anyone else that I'd never been. I wasn't sure why it was embarrassing to me, but for whatever reason, it made me feel almost inadequate. I'd never been involved with the rodeo, or particularly well-traveled, so I didn't feel part of this circle. Brady had tried to get me to go to the Goldfinch rodeo before, but I always made up some excuse. I couldn't help but wonder if he'd flirted with other girls at the events. Ava never protested going to a rodeo and, now that I thought of it, they'd gone without me a few times.

"Oh, this is going to be so fun." Jake rubbed his palms together.

"Don't do anything I wouldn't do. Please." Ellison spun around on her heel, pointing at the guys as she and Colter started walking away.

"Didn't you almost punch a guy in the mouth the night you and Colter met?" Hayden asked.

"Yes, but I'm a changed woman, Hayden. Don't do anything I wouldn't do *now*. We aren't going to talk about my past," she joked.

Colter and Ellison jumped in the truck and headed out, leaving the rest of us to wait for this Isa they'd all been talking about. From what I understood, Isabelle was Ellison's best friend and Reid's long-distance girlfriend.

I admired them for being able to maintain a relationship thousands of miles away. I don't think Brady and I would have ever survived long-distance. We didn't even survive close proximity. You can't get much closer than living together. He was practically under my nose and still cheated on me.

Damn, I needed to think about something else, otherwise my mood was going to get depressing really fast.

Before I could let my mind wander any longer, Mikey pulled a cooler out of the bed of the pickup truck and dropped it on the ground. The sound was enough to distract my restless mind.

"Anyone want a beer while we wait?" Mikey asked the group.

"Toss me one, yeah." Jake nodded.

Hayden and Reid declined.

"Peach?" Mikey raised his brows at me.

"No, I'm okay. Thanks." I gave him a soft smile. I wasn't much of a beer girl.

"So, how was the last leg of your drive?" Reid turned to me, pulling out some lawn chairs for everyone to sit. He set mine up, not letting me lift a finger.

I sat, crossing my legs. "Thanks. And it was good."

"Mikey hasn't driven you insane yet? You're not about to run for the Texas hills are you?" Jake teased, nudging Mikey with his elbow.

I puffed out a small breath of air, shaking my head. "No, it was fun. Learned a lot about you all, in fact."

"Uh-oh. Not sure I want to know what he told you about us. Probably can't be anything good." Jake laughed.

"Nothing good about you, at least," Mikey jabbed back, a wide grin on his face.

"Figures."

Before anyone else could poke fun at Mikey, a gray Honda Civic pulled up to the trailers.

"That's Isa." Reid practically jumped from his chair.

I turned my head toward the vehicle just as Isabelle

stepped out. The guys weren't lying when they said she was short. But she was like a real-life version of Barbie, with perfectly curled blonde hair, long eyelashes, and pouty lips. Even her clothes looked perfect. A twinge of envy rose in my chest as I took her in.

"Oh my goodness, hi! I missed you all!" she squealed, walking right past Reid to hug the other guys.

Reid just laughed, his eyes sparkling at the sight of her. Like he wasn't even bothered that she didn't go to him first. Reid looked at Isabelle like she was the only girl in the world. As if she hung the moon and every single star in the sky.

"You must be Juniper! I'm Isa. I've heard so much about you!" She came up to me next, immediately pulling me in for a hug, too.

I blinked a few times, never having been one for physical affection. "I've heard a lot about you, too."

"Hopefully nothing bad." She smiled.

"Only good things," I replied, pulling back. "I hope you haven't heard anything bad about me."

"What? No, never. Anyone who can keep Mikey in line is a good one." She shot him a teasing look. "I like her already. I'm sure we'll have lots to talk about." Isa laughed. "You probably have tons of stories already just from a couple weeks with him."

I knew Mikey had a reputation for being a playboy, but I didn't realize how often he seemed to be the butt of everyone's jokes. Don't get me wrong, he had a decent sense of humor and was a good sport, but he was almost always the target.

"Have you eaten anything yet?" Reid asked, pulling her away from me. "Also, it's nice to see you again, Short Stack."

"I just talked to you on the phone, you're fine." She stuck out her tongue. "I haven't eaten yet. Is that what you're planning to do? I'm guessing Colter and Ells went out to her mom's?"

Reid nodded. "Yeah. They said they'd meet us later tonight at the bar."

"For someone who claims to hate the bars, she sure goes to them a lot." Isa snorted. "I guess it's different now that she's married."

"Well, let's head out then?" Hayden stood, stretching his arms out. "Who's riding with who?"

Isa glanced at me then directed her attention to Mikey. "Hey, you should go with Hayden and Jake, and Juniper can come with me and Reid! I want to get to know your girl."

My eyes widened. That wasn't part of the plan. Not that I only wanted to hang out with Mikey, but I wasn't exactly prepared to spend alone time with his friends.

"You'll be okay?" he asked, and I reluctantly nodded because what else was I supposed to do? "I can go with you, if you want. It's up to you."

I shook my head. Eventually I'd have to hang out with Isabelle—and Ellison—alone. Once the guys started competing, Mikey wouldn't be attached to my hip. Might as well start to get to know her now.

"Perfect! Finish your beer, Jake, let's go!" Isa put her hands on her hips, ordering him around like a tiny drill sergeant.

Jake shrugged then chugged his practically full beer, tossing the can in a trash bin close to the trailers.

"Man, I didn't even get to open mine." Mikey sighed when Isa shook her head at him.

That evening, we strode through the doors of the Ace in the Hole Bar. Apparently, it was sentimental to the group. I couldn't tell if the bar had a nostalgic vibe to it or not because of how crowded it was. I imagined when it wasn't overflowing with people, it had an old-timey western feel. The music definitely gave that impression. Most of the songs being played were from the eighties and nineties instead of the top twenty radio hits.

"Do you know how to dance?" Isa yelled into my ear over the music.

"No."

"You're going to learn!"

"Wait, what?" My stomach dropped as she yanked me out on the dance floor, pulling Ellison with her other hand.

"You'll get used to it." Ellison chuckled. "Dancing is also a bit of a requirement to be friends with Isa."

The corners of my lips drooped as I gave her a downturned smile. "Noted." Out of the corner of my eye, I noticed Mikey leaning against the bar with a beer in hand, an amused look on his face.

More people joined us on the dance floor, lining up in rows.

"What's going on?" I admittedly hadn't been to a lot of country bars, surprising considering I went to school in a town where cowboying was popular.

"A line dance." Ellison sighed. "Don't be afraid to bail out if you have to. She won't expect you to stay on the floor the whole time."

My chest thrummed with nerves as the song started.

Isabelle stood on my right and Ellison on my left. Immediately, I knew I wasn't going to last very long. Everyone else made it look easy, but I felt like my left foot was on my right side and my right foot was on my left. Eventually, I stumbled backward into someone, embarrassment flaming red-hot into my cheeks.

"Sorry," I muttered. She gave me a sympathetic smile, and I decided that was enough. I maneuvered my way out of the formation of people, finding the guys sitting at a table near the dance floor.

"What happened out there, Peach?" Mikey teased, and I shot him a glare.

"I don't want to talk about it."

"Don't worry, here comes Ellison." Colter grinned as Ellison approached the table, sweat slicked across her forehead.

"I tell her every single time that she's going to end up out there by herself, but does she ever listen?" Her words came out shaky as she caught her breath.

"No, never." Reid laughed softly, although his eyes still sparkled with adoration.

The song ended, and Isa came strutting back to the table. "You guys left me out there all by myself!" She pouted in mock disappointment.

"It's on you at this point, Is." Ellison shrugged.

"Come on, Short Stack, let's go dance." Reid grabbed her hand and tugged her back onto the dance floor as a slower song came on.

"Want to?" Mikey offered his hand.

"I clearly don't know how to dance, so as long as that doesn't bother you." I snorted.

"We can struggle together." He winked as he led me out, placing his hand on my waist and positioning my free hand on his shoulder. My skin tingled at the contact, and butterflies attacked my stomach when he murmured, "That's it, slow and steady."

"How did you learn how to dance?" I asked as we swayed to "She's Everything" by Brad Paisley.

"Started going to street dances and bars after rodeos. There's always people looking to dance, so it wasn't hard to pick up on it. Besides, it's good to have rhythm. Helps with riding bulls, you know?"

"Makes sense. I never would have pegged you as a dancer."

"No?" The corners of his eyes wrinkled as he cracked a small smile, his lips curling up slightly underneath his mustache.

I shook my head, but then light flashed on our left side. I turned my head just in time to see someone holding up their phone then quickly putting it back in their pocket.

"What was that?"

Mikey looked over to where my eyes were, but the person was already gone. "Huh?"

"I thought someone took a photo." Maybe they weren't taking a photo of us. It probably didn't matter anyway, as I was sure plenty of people took pictures of Mikey without him knowing.

"If they did, it's probably not a big deal. Don't worry about it. Hey, you're getting the hang of this." He changed the subject. Probably spoke a bit too soon, though, because a moment later I stepped on his toes.

"Sorry." I laughed quietly. "So, what's the plan for tomorrow?"

He spun me quickly, my hair flying into my eyes as we turned to face one another again. "We'll probably watch some of the competition tomorrow night. It's the last night of the first series, and then I'll be competing the next day."

"You don't compete every day?"

"No, definitely not. There are five different groups that compete on a set of days and then the semifinals and championship if you make it that far. That's why we didn't need to be here right away," he explained.

"Got it. So, like a bracket, kind of?"

"Yeah, exactly. It'll be fun, and I think you'll really enjoy all this. I mean, as long as you enjoy watching me win the whole thing, we'll be golden." He flashed a bright smile, and I couldn't help but grin back.

CHAPTER TWELVE

A mix of earth, leather, and hot dogs filled my nostrils as we walked into the stadium where the rodeo was being held. Crowds of people passed us in waves, shuffling in lines toward the arena. I'd never seen anything like this before. Sure, football games were busy at SGU, but this was on an entirely new level.

"How are you feeling?" Mikey squeezed my hand as we followed Colter, Ellison, Reid, and Isabelle to find our seats. Jake and Hayden were behind us, forming a whole convoy of cowboys.

"I don't know what I was expecting, but it wasn't this. It's huge."

He smirked as though I'd said an inappropriate joke.

When I picked up on what he was probably thinking, I rolled my eyes. "Get your head out of the gutter. You know that's not what I meant."

"You're the one who said it, not me, Peach." His smirk widened into a grin, the corners of his eyes creasing. "But, no, this is the biggest rodeo in the world."

"You did say everything's bigger in Texas, so I suppose I should have believed you."

"Now you're getting it. Just wait until we get to our seats. You're going to love it all."

We entered the arena, and my jaw dropped. This was where professional football games were also held, so I knew it would be huge, but the space was completely transformed for the rodeo. The floor was entirely covered in dirt with fences lining the edges in front of the stadium seats, and the bucking chutes were set up at one end of the oval with an open space at the other end.

"Incredible, isn't it?" Isabelle looked at me with an amused expression.

"Where are we sitting?" I asked, looking around at the thousands of seats.

"Down there." Ellison pointed to the section right in the front.

My eyes felt like they were bulging out of their sockets, and the girls must have noticed, because they started laughing.

"Best seats in the house, baby." Mikey threw his arm around my shoulder. "Right up close and personal with all the action."

When we walked down the steps to our section, murmurs rose from around us.

"Is that Colter Carson and Reid Lawson?"

"Wait, that's Mikey Tucker! The bull rider!"

"Who the fuck is that girl with him?"

"I didn't know he had a girlfriend!"

"I swear a month ago he was seen with a different girl?"

"He definitely wasn't with her at the NFR last year."

Self-consciousness prickled at my skin at the comments directed toward me. As if he sensed my discomfort, Mikey pulled me closer, rubbing circles on my arm. Then, to my own shock, he planted a kiss on my temple.

"I thought you didn't want extra attention?" I whispered teasingly in his ear.

"Not when the comments they're making are being directed at my girl."

Even though I was sure he was only saying that to keep up the act, warmth burst in my chest at his comment. I pulled my bottom lip between my teeth, looking down at my feet as a flush crept into my cheeks. "Thanks."

"I'm going to protect you, Juniper. Just because you're my"—he coughed—"girlfriend, doesn't mean my reputation gets attached to you. It's not going to follow you around."

We reached our seats, and although the comments hadn't ceased, I felt better knowing Mikey would stand up for me.

About twenty minutes later, the lights in the arena went low and spotlights danced across the floor. Pyrotechnics shot up fireworks on the arena floor and in the sky. The national anthem was played, but when it concluded, the lights stayed down low instead of coming back up.

"Good evening, ladies and gentlemen, and welcome to another night of rodeo! We've got an action-packed night planned!" The rodeo announcer's voice echoed around the arena. "But first, please direct your attention to the screens."

A video of horses and rodeo athletes played as the announcer explained the significance and impact of bucking horses. My eyes were so focused on the jumbotron that I didn't notice the spotlight fixed on the arena right by the chutes where a beautiful white bucking horse ran out.

The announcer explained that the horse was a great-

great grandmother and had fourteen babies who were all born to be bucking horses. Then one of those fourteen came out, the announcer continuing to say that she had five more babies. Soon, more and more horses of all ages and sizes ran out onto the arena floor, showing several generations of this family of bucking horses.

Tears pricked at my eyes as I watched them run. I realized the significance of rodeo and these animals, and a wave of pride washed over me to be part of the special moment, even if I was only watching.

When the lights finally came back up, I wiped a stray tear. Looking around me, I noticed that several other spectators were also emotional. At least I wasn't alone in that.

Cheers rose from the crowd as the announcer yelled, "Who's ready for some rodeo? We're kicking it off with bareback bronc riding!"

The first cowboy climbed onto the back of the horse in the bucking chute as rock music played in the background. In a split second, the gate was opened and the horse whipped out of the chute like a flash of lightning, kicking its hind legs, trying its hardest to throw the rider off.

My heart pounded in my chest until a buzzer signified eight seconds. A couple other men on horses rode next to the bucking horse as it galloped around the arena until the cowboy was able to grab one of the men's arms and hop off the back of the bucking horse.

"Let's give him eighty-two points, shall we?" the announcer called out.

"Is that good?" I asked Mikey.

"It's not a bad score by any means. It's out of one hundred, so the higher the better, but it's not bad for the first round."

I nodded in slight understanding. After watching a couple more, I thought I had grasped the idea of it. But then one of the athletes made it to eight seconds and still didn't get a score.

"What happened there? He made it to eight seconds."

"Didn't mark out," Jake answered from my left. When I raised my eyebrows at him, he explained. "When the horse initially jumps out of the bucking chute, your spurs have to be held above its shoulders until the front hooves hit the ground. If you don't do that, you fail to mark out and don't get a score."

I was still confused, and he must have picked up on it.

"Essentially, you hold your feet out in front of you until the horse's front hooves hit the ground for the first time, then you can kick them back."

"Ah, okay."

The events went by fairly quickly. My favorite was probably the bronc riding or the team roping, much to Mikey's dismay. He'd told me, "Just wait until the bull riding. That's the real action."

I was told the event right before bull riding was barrel racing, which was one of the few things I actually knew a little bit about.

"Ladies and gents, up next we've got a cowgirl hailing from the great state of Montana. She's running on Ace's Lucky Charm. Let's hear it for Sierra Bayley!" The camera focused on a dark-haired girl whose horse turned in a few circles in the back of the alleyway before exploding into the arena at a run, hooves pounding against the dirt. Her hair, tied back in a braid under her beige cowboy hat, flew behind her.

I looked over at the others. "Do you guys know her? Since she's from Montana?"

Isabelle and Ellison shook their heads.

Colter gave a noncommittal shrug. "Heard the name a couple times, but I don't know her, no."

Reid followed with a similar sentiment, but Hayden's face had turned white as a sheet. He looked like he was on the verge of throwing up and quickly excused himself.

"What's his deal?" Mikey turned his head toward Hayden's retreating figure. No one knew, so we all turned back to the arena as she rounded the last barrel and her horse sprinted home.

"Fourteen-point-six-seven seconds!" the announcer cried out as the camera focused on her once again, a small smile creeping into her cheeks at the recorded time.

"Do you need anything from concessions?" Mikey patted my knee as he stood.

"No, I'm okay, thanks." I shook my head.

When he left, Isabelle moved over into his seat. "So, how are you liking it so far? Pretty fun, isn't it?"

"I'm enjoying it much more than I thought I would," I admitted. On the rare occasion I'd go to a rodeo with Ava and Brady, I usually spent the time on my phone, not caring to watch the events. I'd count down the minutes until we could go home and get away from the dust and crowds of people.

"I can relate to that. I hadn't gone to many rodeos before Ellison met Colter and before I met Reid. But now I can confidently say I'm hooked."

"You could say she got *roped in* to all of it." Jake nudged me playfully as he wiggled his eyebrows, a goofy grin on his face.

"Ha ha, you're *so* funny," Ellison deadpanned.

"I mean, they thought it was funny." Jake gestured to Colter and Reid, who were chuckling quietly.

"They would." Isa scoffed. "They're team *ropers*, of course they think it's funny."

"I'm a roper, too," Jake pointed out.

"I don't know if that helps your case," I muttered.

Isa smiled. "See, she's on our side."

"Does she really get a say, though? I mean, she's dating Mikey." Colter laughed.

I narrowed my eyes. "I don't see how that has anything to do with this. Why do you guys give him so much shit anyway? He's not that bad." I tried to keep my tone neutral, but the way they always made fun of him kind of annoyed me.

"To be fair, he wasn't like this a couple weeks ago," Ellison suggested. "Maybe he's changing." She looked at the others, giving them a bit of a pointed look, and they quieted down. "It's a good thing. He needs someone to rein him in a little bit."

Too bad I wasn't going to be the one to do that, at least not long-term. I still wasn't exactly sure what Mikey's motive in all of this was, but I didn't really care. I had my own agenda, too, and I knew he and his friends would see me differently if they found out.

Rule number four: no feelings.

Mikey came back just before the last barrel racer started her run, holding a hot dog and a large soda. "You guys were nice while I was gone?"

"Your girl actually told us off," Reid told him, and Colter nodded beside him, affirming what happened.

"What do you mean?" Confusion shone in his eyes.

I shrugged. "I just said I didn't understand why they give you so much shit, because you're not that bad."

Something like gratitude flashed across his features, but

then cocky arrogance overtook them. "Well, she's right. I'm the best. You guys would be lost without me."

Why does he do that?

Before I could say anything, the lights in the stadium went low again, and the announcer introduced the bullfighters and the rodeo clown who would be protecting the bull riders.

Mikey leaned forward in his seat, eyes trained on the arena as the lights came up again and the first bull rider matchup was read out. He had a fire in his eyes. A passion that I wasn't sure could be extinguished any time soon.

The bull thrashed in the chute, knocking against the gate. On the big screen, the cowboy set himself on the back of the bull and adjusted his grip on the rope. Once he was ready, he nodded and they opened the gate. The bull spun and kicked right off the bat, but the cowboy held on as cheers from the crowd drowned out all the other noise in the arena.

Clouds of dust rose up on the floor as the bull switched directions, kicking its legs out behind it, doing whatever it could to throw the man off its back.

Eight seconds felt like an eternity before the buzzer finally went off. He jumped off the bull and scrambled out of the arena as the bullfighters distracted the bull and guided it out of the arena.

"You do *that* for a living?" I hadn't realized I'd said it out loud until the words were already out of my mouth.

"Sure do, Peach. And I'm damn good at it, too."

After the rodeo concluded, the goal was to get out of the stadium as quickly as possible, avoiding the media and any rabid fans who saw us walk in.

Things hardly ever went according to plan, though, and right as we stepped out of the arena, a reporter stopped us.

"Mikey! Who do you have with you tonight? Is this your girlfriend?" she asked as she shoved a microphone in his face, a cameraman standing next to her. "Or is she just another one of your flings?"

I wasn't sure if he meant to or not, but Mikey flinched beside me. Annoyance flared in my chest, traveling up my throat. I didn't think. I just defended him. "I'm not just a fling. I'm his girlfriend, and my name's Juniper, thanks for asking." With that, I pulled Mikey, still frozen in shock, away from the reporter as she called after me, drawing attention from everyone around us.

"Mikey! How long have you two been together?" someone else yelled from our right.

"Where's she from?"

"Are you going to drop her after Houston like you do every other girl?"

Fuck. That was cold.

Soon enough, everyone in close proximity to us had their phones out and were snapping pictures.

"I'm sorry," I whispered in a panic. "I just wanted to help."

He sighed as we continued walking. "It's all right, Juniper. I appreciate you standing up for me. We've got a new problem on our hands now, though."

"What's that?" I asked.

"People are expecting us to break up after Houston

now, so we're going to have to play this out longer than planned."

Even though we'd planned for this—accounted for the media inevitably talking about us—it still came as a shock. I hadn't expected everyone to think we'd immediately break up or that I was just a fling to him. Perhaps that was naive on my part.

"Oh…well, that's fine, right?" I didn't sound too convincing. I wasn't sure if I could have convinced myself with that tone.

He responded with a small hand squeeze. "We'll make it work."

@therealbucklebunny: Did you see the girl Mikey Tucker was with tonight at RODEOHOUSTON?

@roughyforlifee356: Don't expect this one to last that long

@ropingandriding.podcast: We plan on getting the full scoop on this. Stay tuned, rodeo fans.

mikey

TRAVIS

Call me later. We need to talk about those photos going around.

You got it.

TRAVIS

Good luck tonight.

My phone was blowing up with notifications—text messages from my agent, Travis, and tags on social media. Photos of me and Juniper from last night were all over the Internet, and fans speculated in the comments about how long our relationship would last, or if it would last at all.

I could handle the comments about me; I'd been dealing with them for most of my career, but I couldn't stand the harsh things people were saying about Juniper.

Luckily, no one knew her social media handles, so they

couldn't tag her. Unfortunately, it was likely only a matter of time before someone found her.

"Stay off social media. Please," I pleaded with her. "I can handle this."

"Do they always say such horrible things about you?" she asked as she scrolled through the comment section of a western influencer's video about us.

"It comes with the territory. I just try to ignore it." I shrugged. "But you shouldn't have to deal with it, so please, Peach."

"This one called me a buckle bunny whore." Her face fell for a second then contorted into something that looked a lot like anger. "That person doesn't even know me! I don't even know what the fuck that means!"

I took the phone out of her hands, turning it off and setting it on the counter. "Exactly, and that's why you shouldn't be reading the things people are saying online. I'll handle this. Just stick with Ellison and Isa today, okay? And stay off social media, damn it." With that, I exited the trailer, stepping into the morning sunlight.

"How's she doing?" Reid walked up and patted me on the shoulder.

"She's fine. Just frustrated, I think. But she won't get out of the damn comments."

"I can have Isa talk to her, if you'd like," he offered. "You've got to focus on riding today, man. The best way to get them to eat their words is to prove them wrong."

I looked down at the ground and nodded. Reid was right. This wasn't unlike anything I'd dealt with before, except this time it didn't just affect me. "Yeah, have her talk to Juniper. At least to distract her. I'll talk to Colter, too, see if Ellison can do anything since she's been in the public eye before. It's not something I thought to prepare her for, and that's on me. But I also didn't think people would come after her like this."

"We've got your back, Mike." He gave me a solemn look then headed back to the trailer he and Colter shared.

Tonight was the first night of the second Super Series —the one I was competing in. Colter and Reid were competing in the fourth, and Hayden and Jake were competing in the fifth. The rest of the guys weren't required to be here until the days they competed, but we had a habit of all traveling together.

Truthfully, it meant a lot to me. It'd been a long time since I'd traveled solo, and sometimes it would get lonely. I didn't like being alone. Early on, meaningless hookups helped fill the void. After a while, it just became a habit. Then a punchline.

But I also knew I was good at jokes and people liked me for them. Sometimes I worried if I wasn't the funny guy or the person to take the heaviness out of a situation, the guys wouldn't like me anymore.

I wasn't sure who I was—who I could be—without my friends.

Jake and Hayden were sitting in chairs outside their trailer.

I walked over to them, kicking a small rock as I went. "Morning, fellas."

"You haven't been looking at the media, have you?" Jake asked.

I shook my head. "No, and I told Juniper to stay away from social media, too."

"Sorry, man. That sucks. Not the type of thing you need going into tonight."

"It's all right. I'll just perform well and they'll have

something else to talk about." I brushed it off. It was all I could do not to overwhelm myself.

Hayden gave me an encouraging glance. "That's the spirit."

"I've gotta get to the arena," I muttered. Unfortunately, I was scheduled for an appearance this morning. The timing couldn't have been better, at least for the media.

A few of the other bull riders were already at the spot where fans could meet us. Kids were getting pictures taken with them, and it looked like it was pretty calm. I wasn't too worried about reporters hounding me here, not with so many fans and the other athletes around. My concern was after the appearance.

I stood in line next to a rider I didn't recognize.

"Hi, I'm Cody." He shook my hand.

"Mikey."

"Oh, damn, you're that guy all over social media right now."

I blinked a few times, trying not to let my annoyance show. I clearly didn't do a good job at it, because the kid quickly threw out an apology.

Both of us were saved from the awkward interaction when a young boy in a pearl snap shirt, jeans tucked into his cowboy boots, and a hat too big for his head came up to me.

"You're my favorite bull rider. I want to be *just like you* when I grow up." He looked up at me with awe in his eyes.

"Is that so?" I chuckled. "What's your name?"

"Devon."

"Well, it's nice to meet you, Devon. Do you want a picture?"

He nodded vigorously, a huge smile forming on his

face. I squatted down to his level, putting my arm around him as the camera flashed.

"Thanks, buddy. Keep up the good work." I signed his cowboy hat then sent him along. The kid bounced on his feet the entire time he walked away with his parents.

Kids like that both made my heart feel full and like someone had driven a knife through it. On one hand, I was honored to be considered a role model in their eyes, but on the other hand, what right did I have to *be* a role model for them? If I was a parent, I wasn't sure if I'd want my kid to look up to me. Especially not with the media and fans' perception.

Another kid walked up, and I tossed away all my negative thoughts and feelings. For an hour, I wasn't Mikey Tucker the playboy bull rider. For an hour, I could be Mikey Tucker the role model.

After the appearance and the phone call with my agent, I stood behind the bucking chutes taking deep breaths to ease my racing nerves. Spectators hadn't arrived at the arena yet, so there was a type of tranquility in the air. Soon enough, the uproar of fans would fill the space, drowning everything out like a symphony.

I'd drawn Iron Tornado for my matchup earlier and stood face to face with him now, the back pen's fence separating us. He huffed, warm air blowing in my face. These bulls were bred to buck, were made for this, but I wondered if he knew what was coming. If he was as determined to throw me as I was to hold on.

"Mikey." A gruff voice behind me caught my attention, and I spun around.

"Maverick." I nodded.

Maverick Oakes was one of the best bull riders in the league. He'd won the World last year and was projected to have another good season. He was younger than me, but he had a maturity about him, a confidence that radiated off him in waves. It was difficult not to admire him at least a little bit.

"Been seeing a lot of you on social media lately."

I snorted. "You know a lot of it's bullshit."

"Yeah, I know. I'm looking forward to seeing you ride out there tonight, Tuck." He patted me on the back as he passed, walking toward the tunnel to exit the arena.

"Thanks. Yeah, you, too." I started to say goodbye then stopped myself. "Hey, Maverick."

He paused in his tracks.

"How do you deal with it all? The media, pressure from fans, staying at the top of your game?" I regretted the words as soon as they came out, not wanting to show any kind of weakness, especially not to my biggest competitor, but he turned around, his face reflecting understanding instead of judgment or pity.

"You just keep ridin'. Remember why you're here and do your damn best, putting in one hundred and fifty percent every day. The majority of those people would never attempt to get on a bull, so they don't know what it's like," he said simply. "Keep your head up." With that, he disappeared through the tunnel, leaving me with the beast I'd take on later tonight and the thoughts I battled daily.

"Folks, our next rider comes from Silver Creek, Montana. He's a three-time RodeoHouston athlete and last year competed in the NFR. Tonight, he's up against the bull they call Iron Tornado." The announcer rattled off information about me, but it was purely background noise to the pounding in my ears.

Everything around me faded away as my breaths started to shallow. I hopped back and forth on my feet, the tassels on my chaps swinging with the movement. Wringing my hands together, I waited for the right moment to wipe my sweaty palms on my jeans, then I climbed onto the chute gate from the platform behind it.

The guitar riff of a rock song played, and the cheers from the crowd magnified. Adrenaline pumped through my veins as I looked up, seeing my face on the big screen until it panned out to the arena and the crowd.

I handed the rope to the man on the platform who would pull it to tighten it and sat myself on the top of the chute before putting a foot on the bull's back and grabbing both sides of the pen. Lowering myself down, I sat on the bull, warmed up the rosin on the bull rope and my handle, then shook down my bells before adjusting the rope on his back.

To a normal person, it would seem like there were a lot of steps, but this was second nature to me. I went through the same routine every single time I rode, no matter what bull I was on.

Iron Tornado rocked back and forth in the bucking chute, hitting the sides and kicking the gate.

"Pull," I ordered. The rope was tightened, and I wrapped it around my hand. Once I adjusted my seat on the back of the bull, leaning slightly so I wouldn't be immediately thrown, I nodded, pushing my hips toward the rope as the gate swung open and the bull launched out of the chute, unleashing his anger.

As he twisted and kicked, I flowed with the bull's movements like we were partners in a choreographed dance, adjusting my body and adapting to his rhythm with each chaotic spin. Even though my muscles ached from the strain and each lunge jarred my bones, the thrill of riding —of proving to everyone I was tough enough— outweighed it all.

Sweat dripped down my brow as I pushed on, willing myself to just make it to eight seconds. In the background, music blared and yells of encouragement rose from the crowd. The bull kicked up dust as it went, cutting through the hazy clouds as hooves pounded against the dirt.

The buzzer went off, penetrating through all of the other sounds in the stadium, and I blew out a breath of relief. I released my grip from the rope then leaned back, dismounting toward the bull's hips. My feet met the earth, and I scrambled out of the way to safety as the bullfighters guided the beast out of the arena. Taking off my helmet, I stared up at the big screen, awaiting my score.

"Ladies and gentlemen, let's give our judges a moment to tally the score." The announcer kept the spectators— and me—on their toes. "How 'bout an eighty-seven for the first round!"

I pumped my fist in the air, satisfied with the score and the ride. Could only go up from here.

Once the rodeo concluded, I hung back by the bucking chutes. Maverick had scored an eighty-nine on his ride, leaving me in second place, but I'd take it. Every night was a brand new rodeo and a fresh opportunity to get a better score.

"Good ride out there tonight, Tuck." Maverick patted me on the shoulder.

"Thanks, man. You, too." I dipped my chin in acknowledgment.

"That was amazing! You were incredible out there!" Juniper exclaimed when I found the group.

"Thanks, Peach." I made a show of planting a kiss on her cheek.

"What's the plan for tonight, boys?" Jake asked, throwing his arms around Reid and Colter.

They both shrugged, and Hayden and the girls didn't say anything either, looking to me. They probably expected me to say we should go celebrate my ride, but the truth was I was exhausted.

"I actually think I'm going to go back to the trailer for an early night."

Shock painted their faces at my announcement.

"Are you sick, Michael?" Ellison teased, bringing the back of her hand to my forehead before wrinkling her nose and wiping it on her jeans. "Sweaty, that's for sure."

"Go on, it's okay. I'm sure you'll all manage without me," I joked.

"Do you want me to go back with you?" Juniper asked, raising a brow.

I waved her off. "Nah, go have fun. I probably won't be too much fun anyway." I planned to take a hot shower, crawl into bed, and pass the fuck out.

"Oh, okay." She gave me a small smile. "Good job tonight. I'm proud of you." She whispered the last part, and I tried to ignore the way my heart doubled in size.

CHAPTER FOURTEEN

The energy in the arena seemed to crackle around us as we watched night two of Mikey's Super Series. I hadn't seen him since the morning because of his busy schedule, and nerves swirled through my body in anticipation of his ride.

I didn't realize I was bouncing my leg until Isa looked at me and rested her hand on my knee to stop it.

"Sorry," I mumbled an apology as the steer wrestling began. "I'm just nervous?"

"That's understandable," she reassured me. "I'm just here to let you know everything will be okay. Things can happen, but he's a professional."

"How do you get past it? The fear of something terrible happening?" I asked, biting my lip. Hypothetically, my question would just be part of the act, but I was genuinely concerned.

Ellison chimed in. "Honestly, you don't get past it, you just get used to it. They know the risks when they sign up for this. You just have to trust them and the animals."

On the trip down to Houston, I had made a comment

about being surprised that she was still involved with rodeo after her dad died but was promptly corrected and told that she avoided them until she met Colter.

"Doesn't all of this hurt the animals?" The question slipped out, but none of them seemed to be phased by it.

"Some people do think that rodeo is animal abuse, but they're truly so well taken care of," Ellison explained without judgment. "This is what they're born for, and animal care is at the forefront when it comes to rodeos. A lot of these events are actual practices used by ranchers. Once you consider the events in a working, practical context rather than for entertainment, you see it in a different light. Of course, there are some people who will never understand, but these athletes and the ranchers and cowboys who do this for a living take great pride and care in these animals. They're just as much athletes as the humans."

I nodded in understanding, although I still rolled my lips.

"Ellison could go on and on about this topic, June, so just understand that accidents can happen, but for the great majority, these animals are treated like royalty." Isa chuckled, giving the SparksNotes version of Ellison's lecture.

"Hey, I'm just trying to provide a different perspective. Education on the topic leads to understanding." Ellison shrugged. "Seriously, though, if you have questions, any of us who grew up around the sport and the culture would be more than happy to answer."

The guys nodded and grunted in agreement, not having anything to add to Ellison's statements.

"She's also a vet tech and has been on call for some of

the smaller rodeos back at home to help. She knows her stuff," Reid pointed out.

I clasped my hands in my lap. "I definitely wasn't trying to discredit the sport or lifestyle. It's just very different from what I'm used to," I admitted. "I'm grateful to be learning, though. Spending time with you all has opened my eyes a lot to this life."

Jake, who was sitting behind us, clapped me on the back. "We'll make a cowgirl out of you before you know it. We can be quite convincing. Just ask Isa." He gave her a playful wink, and Isa just rolled her eyes with a grin.

"Noted." I snorted.

The rest of the events went off without a hitch, and bull riding was up next. After the lights went low and the bullfighters were introduced, the first bull rider exploded out of the gate on a nasty bull named Diablo. Although he did his best, he didn't stay on for eight seconds.

"Folks, you all saw his eighty-seven-point ride last night. Tonight, the bull he's drawn is Payback. Michael 'Mikey' Tucker. Let's go!" The announcer drew out Mikey's name, and shortly after, the chute gate was pulled. The bull flew out, kicking its legs back and spinning wildly in a circle.

My eyes widened, and I clenched my fists, digging my nails into my palm. It wasn't a long time, but the seconds seemed to drag as Mikey continued to hang on, his free arm flailing in the air.

"Come on now, Mikey! Get it!" the announcer yelled out.

The bull whipped around, thrashing its head from side to side, dust flying up all around it.

The eight-second buzzer went off, and a wave of relief washed over me as I released a breath.

"How're you doing over there, June?" Jake chuckled, probably noticing my anxious demeanor.

I waved him off as the announcer called out Mikey's score. "Eighty-five for the Montanan!"

After Mikey's recent performances, the comments on social media seemed to calm down a bit. The fans were starting to realize that he was serious about bull riding and didn't come to Houston to play around. There were the occasional comments about his relationship status, but they were few and far between at this point. I knew he told me to avoid them, but I couldn't help it.

Reid, Isa, Ellison, and Colter slid into a half-moon booth in the back corner of the bar, leaving just enough space for Jake, Hayden, and Mikey to squeeze in. I stood at the end of the table, awkwardly shifting my feet.

"Should I just go get a chair or something?" There wasn't enough room for all of us to fit. There was hardly enough room for the seven of them as it was.

"Oh, Juniper, here, you can have my spot." Jake started to slide out of the booth on the opposite side of the table, but Mikey waved him off, grabbing my hand and pulling me onto his lap.

"She's good right here, aren't you, Peachy?" He flashed a cocky grin as his hand settled on my denim-glad waist, fingers splaying out.

Before I could answer, a server walked up to our table. If our seating arrangement phased her, she didn't show it. "Can I get y'all some drinks?"

The guys ordered themselves a round of Pendleton

shots and some beers, while Ellison ordered a tequila soda, and Isa ordered a Malibu lemonade. You could tell a lot about a person by their drink order, something I'd learned from a few years of bartending. I'd decided all of their drinks were fitting based on what I'd seen from their personalities.

I ordered a Cosmo with Tito's and Cointreau instead of Triple Sec, and specifically requested that the bartender go light on the cranberry, asking for a lime wedge instead of concentrate. The server raised a brow at me, but I was particular and knew what I liked.

"I'll be right back with those." Our server spun around on her heels, walking toward the bar, and I couldn't help myself from stealing a glance at Mikey to see if he was watching her leave.

But he was only looking at me, something like admiration in his gaze. Butterflies stirred in my stomach, and I did my best to hide my smile.

Mikey brushed a stray hair out of my eyes, planting a gentle kiss on my cheek.

My phone buzzed with a text message notification.

Rudy's Angels

LIV

Juniper!!!!

You do realize you're famous right?

NICOOL

Dude you're all over social media right now

Trust me, I know

LIV

How's it feel?

Besides the comments telling me I'm a buckle bunny whore who will get dropped in a week? Fine, I guess lol

NICOOL

Damn Junie that sucks

I was about to type out *don't call me that* for the millionth time, but I stopped myself, a stupid grin pulling at my cheeks.

LIV

Don't listen to the haters. You're a badass, June.

AND YOUR BOYFRIEND IS A FAMOUS BULL RIDER

Thanks guys

Giggling to myself, I turned off my phone, sliding it into my back pocket.

"Who was that?" Mikey put his hand on my shoulder.

"Liv and Nico." I playfully rolled my eyes at their antics. "They wanted to let me know I'm famous."

He chuckled. "Sounds about right."

"I mean, people seem to be letting up on you guys, that's a good thing!" Isa said, never looking up from her phone. "Hopefully it means they've accepted that you guys are a legit couple."

Mikey and I exchanged a look, but it was so fast the others wouldn't have noticed.

I'd spent the morning with Isa and Ellison, because Mikey had media appearances. The topic of Mikey and my relationship came up briefly, but I thought I'd handled it well enough.

"How are you doing with everything?" Ellison asked as she sipped on her iced white chocolate mocha.

We'd ended up at The Corral, a coffee shop not too far from the stadium. Ellison and Isa had said it was one of their favorite places to go.

I picked at the label on my drink. "I'm fine. I think it's Mikey you should be checking on. This has more to do with him than it does me."

Ellison hummed in acknowledgment, and Isa cocked her head.

"Wait, so you're actually dating Mikey?"

I narrowed my eyes at her. "Yes?"

She leaned back in her seat, straightening her posture and raising her hands a little. "I'm not judging. I'm just…surprised? You seem so normal."

"Thanks?"

"Mikey just isn't the type for commitment," Ellison interjected. "It's been a bit of an adjustment for all of us."

"Interesting." I looked at my drink, still pulling at the corner of the label, the condensation from the drink dampening it.

"I hope you know we're happy for you guys." Isa recovered, like she thought she might have offended me.

Heat rose to my cheeks, and I looked up. "Thanks. Deep down, I think he's a good guy, he just has a weird way of showing it."

I'd wondered early on why exactly he needed a fake girlfriend, but I didn't really question it. At the time, I wasn't sure I wanted to know the answer. Now, the further we leaned into the act, I wondered if there was something deeper behind it.

"What, you think the media suspects it's a fake relationship?" Ellison nearly choked on her drink, bringing me back to the conversation.

"I mean, plenty of celebrities get into relationships for

the sake of PR." Isa shrugged. "I'm not saying that's what this is." She gave us a quick once-over. "I mean, look at them. Mikey can hardly keep his hands off her, and he's never brought a girl around us as much as he does Juniper. There are too many factors for it to not be real."

"I'd say this is your hopeless romanticism coming out, but you have a point." Ellison seemed to accept what Isa was saying, and the rest of the guys nodded like they couldn't see any flaws in her reasoning.

I pulled my bottom lip between my teeth. We were clearly faking it well if the people closest to Mikey weren't suspicious. I mean, that was what he was obviously doing. Faking it. Making it believable.

None of this was real.

"We're right here, guys," Mikey cut in.

A guilty expression flashed across Isa's features. "Yeah, sorry. Don't mean to be speculating about your relationship in front of you." She laughed without humor.

"We're happy for you, man," Colter added. "I think this is good for you. I like seeing you focused on the rodeo. It's also nice not having to meet someone new every week. We might have been wrong about you."

I didn't think anyone else noticed, but Mikey's smile faltered, all emotion draining out of his eyes. I didn't want to see the other guys as bad people—I didn't think they were. But I also didn't think they understood the effect their little jabs and comments had on their friend.

No one deserved that, no matter how many bad decisions they'd made in the past.

CHAPTER FIFTEEN

I scored an eighty-eight-point-five in my SuperSeries championship, securing my spot in the semifinals alongside Maverick and two other bull riders out of California and Arizona respectively. I had just over a week before I'd compete again, but the other guys were competing in the upcoming rodeos, so I'd still be in the arena as a spectator.

Until then, though, we had a few days where none of us were competing, and I had big plans for me and Juniper. I wanted to get the most out of the trip and make sure she experienced things in Houston outside of the rodeo.

"Where are we going?" she asked as we drove down the streets of Houston.

I grinned at her curiosity—and her persistence, as this was about the fifth time she'd asked on the fifteen-minute drive. "I told you, it's a surprise."

She huffed from her seat next to me in protest but didn't ask again as we neared the building.

"Mini golf?" Suspicion laced in her tone as I pulled into the parking lot.

"Come on, it'll be fun." I got out of the pickup and walked around the front to get to her door. I grabbed the door handle right as she swung it open, only barely avoiding getting hit in the face. I held it open for her as she stepped out, the sun shining through her golden hair.

"If this is your idea of fun, I think I've had you wrong this whole time," Juniper muttered as we made our way across the parking lot.

I shrugged. "There's a lot you don't know about me. Good opportunity to get to know me better since we're here, don't you think?"

She mumbled something I couldn't quite make out, but once we walked through the front doors, her eyes widened.

The entire space was cloaked in neon, with spotlights dancing along the walls and green turf floor. Bright LED signs hung on the walls among paintings in frames, murals, and greenery. Near the front desk, gumball machines filled with vibrant-colored golf balls lined the wall across from a row of putters in all lengths and colors.

"I can confidently say I was not expecting this." She laughed awkwardly as we stepped up to the counter.

"How can I help you?" The teenager who was working looked, and sounded, bored out of his mind.

"We'll do eighteen holes," I said. "There's two of us."

"That'll be forty dollars."

Juniper raised her brows and her eyes flicked to me at the employee's tone, but I just pulled out my wallet and handed him my card.

"Grab a putter and a ball over there. There's three different courses you can choose from. You'll do two of them for eighteen holes. Have fun."

I had to suppress a laugh, because how could any normal person expect to have fun when the person working sounded like Roz from *Monsters Inc.*? I, however, was just happy to have time alone with Juniper without cameras, or fans, or even my friends around to make fun of me.

We headed over to the gumball machines holding the golf balls.

"What's your favorite color, Peach?" I asked.

"Blue," she replied.

"What? Not peach?" I teased, moving over to the machine with the blue balls and trading the quarter to dispense one. It fell into the chute with a clunk, and I lifted the flap, grabbed it, and handed it to Juniper before grabbing my own red golf ball. We both grabbed a putter then walked past the bar to the hallway to get to the courses.

Immediately, it was clear that this wasn't your typical mini golf course. Each hole wasn't very long, and they were all themed in some way with an untraditional spin. The first one was set up to look like a graveyard, and another hole was an arcade-looking game. Each hole had a placard with instructions next to it.

A fit of laughter from Juniper erupted from beside me. "This is the weirdest thing I've ever seen."

"I told you we'd have fun." I winked as I stepped up to the first hole, dropping my golf ball behind the line. I—admittedly—hit the ball a bit too hard, completely missing the hole and causing Juniper to snort next to me. "What? Don't laugh at me until you hit."

She shrugged, stepping up to the line and hitting her ball with the perfect amount of force and power, sending it ricocheting off the corner and stopping right before the hole. Juniper raised her brows at me as if to say, *What was that you were saying?*

I rolled my eyes playfully and took my second shot, getting it much closer this time. Juniper hit the ball in on her next turn, and I made it on my third stroke.

"I was just warming up," I teased.

"Sure, Casanova. Whatever makes you feel better about yourself." She laughed, gently elbowing me in the ribs.

The next hole took us into one of those money chambers, where the air blew cash in the air and you had to grab as much as possible. The air blew Juniper's ball through the hole—a stroke of good luck—while mine didn't make it out of the booth.

"Damn, we're gonna have to go play a game I know I can win. Maybe a mechanical bull." I sighed as she beat me once again.

"I hardly think that's fair."

"What? Afraid to lose?"

She shot me a mischievous look. "What, like how you're losing now? I don't think you can taunt me with losing when I'm the one winning and you're complaining about it."

I waved her off. "Pfft, it's only the second hole. We've got sixteen to go, I can make a comeback."

Making a comeback was wishful thinking. By the tenth hole, Juniper was leading by at least six strokes. It was possible that I was throwing some of them because I liked the way she shot me a smug grin every time she beat me, but I'd never reveal my secret.

"This was much more fun than I expected," Juniper admitted at the fourteenth hole. "I've never played mini golf this way, but it's a cool twist on the game."

"I'm glad you're having fun." The statement was sincere. It was nice to see her playful side, even if she was kicking my ass. "I didn't expect you to beat me so easily, though."

She rolled her eyes, lips quirking up in a grin. "I'm competitive."

"Did you play any sports?"

Juniper shook her head as she took her next shot, the ball rolling around the corner of the art gallery themed hole. "No, but I still don't like losing. Hate it even."

I chuckled. "Fair enough. I like that, though. Maybe not the hating losing part, but the determination. I think it's a good quality to have."

"What, you like losing?"

"I mean, I don't think anyone likes losing, but it's a part of life. Sometimes you have to fall off the bull to get better. If you never fail, then I don't think you can learn."

The expression on her face shifted into something curious. "That may have been the smartest thing you've said all day, Mikey Tucker."

"I'm not a complete idiot," I mumbled.

"I know you're not." Her voice was soft, gentle, and her eyes burned into me.

I suddenly felt self-conscious.

"Hey, what's that?" I pointed toward another hole, and she turned her head, giving me just enough time to slide in front of her and rest my hands on her waist. By the time she looked back at me, my lips were on hers. She kissed me back, but the moment was cut short when she pulled away.

"What was that for? Rule three, remember?" She slid out of my grasp, walking over to her golf ball to take her next shot.

I knew the rule, but I didn't regret the kiss, even if I did it to get the subject off me. The moment felt a bit too vulnerable for comfort. Did the trick, though, and the game was back on.

We finished all eighteen holes, and Juniper ended up beating me by an embarrassing length. As we left the course, her stomach growled, so I pulled her to the bar for drinks and snacks. We didn't have anywhere to be today, so it may as well have been five o'clock.

"So…" Juniper stirred her drink.

"So?" I lifted a brow.

"You said I don't know much about you. Tell me something about you."

I placed a finger on my lip, tapping it as I thought up something interesting enough about me. "The first time I got on a bull, I got thrown off so hard, I couldn't get out of bed the next day. But I kept coming back and got better at it to the point that hitting the ground hurt a little less."

Her eyes widened. "If it hurts, why do you do it?"

"The thrill is unlike anything I've ever experienced in my life. Yeah, it's dangerous, but not many people can say they've ridden hundreds, hell even thousands, of bulls in their lifetime and lived to tell the tale."

"Couldn't you get the same thrill out of a roller coaster, or I don't know, skydiving?"

I huffed out a laugh. "Pretty sure skydiving and roller coasters both have risks associated with them."

She threw her arms in the air. "Mechanical bulls, then."

"You worried about me, Peach?"

Her gaze held mine, frozen in time. But then she whispered, "Yes," and my heart fluttered in my chest.

"It's what I love most in the world. It may be dangerous, but I've gotta say, it wouldn't be the worst way to go. I'd at least know I went out doing something I was passionate about."

She rolled her lips, changing the subject. "What are your tattoos?"

I looked down at the ink on my arms. I had full sleeves and a hand tattoo. I was surprised she hadn't noticed the one on my hand and said something about it sooner. It usually got a laugh out of people.

I pointed to each of them, describing what they were. "I got this skeleton in Colorado when I was twenty-three and the hand of cards when I was twenty-six. It's an ace-high royal flush, the luckiest hand in poker. I thought it wouldn't hurt to have some extra luck on my side."

"And your hand tattoo? What does that say? Say… when?" She tilted her head, a frown appearing on her face.

"*Tombstone* reference." I gave her finger guns, showing off the tattoo fully.

She gave me a blank stare.

"I'm your huckleberry?" I continued, but was met with nothing. "Doc Holliday? Don't tell me you don't know…" My voice trailed off when her expression changed into subtle guilt. "*Peach*," I whined, drawing out the word.

She shrugged. "Sorry, I don't watch movies."

"You're breaking my heart."

"Better that it gets broken now rather than later, right?" she teased.

I hummed. "I'd rather no hearts get broken."

She tapped my arm. "That's why we have rules in place. No feelings and no one gets hurt."

Even though I was the one who'd initially brought up that statement, I was having a hard time believing there'd never be any feelings involved. At least not for me. Not with how the trip was already going. But I'd humor her for now. "Right. No feelings, no heartbreak."

juniper

Over the last few days, Mikey, the rest of the group, and I explored Houston. During the day, we perused shops downtown, and in the evening, we watched the rodeos. Surprisingly enough, the fans left us alone, and the press was too focused on the other athletes actually competing to go after Mikey, although the buzz on social media hadn't stopped.

Today marked the beginning of the fourth SuperSeries, so Colter and Reid were busy practicing and doing appearances, leaving me, Mikey, Hayden, Jake, Ellison, and Isa to find things to do without them.

"Tonight after the rodeo, I say let's hit the bars." Mikey, sitting in a lawn chair next to mine, threw an arm around me, squeezing my shoulder.

"Ugh, we just went out." Ellison groaned. "Haven't you had enough? You have a girlfriend, how is that shit still fun for you?"

I eyed Mikey, curious to see what his response would be. It was obvious that he mostly met girls at the bars before we made our arrangement, but now I was in the picture. Or at least that's what everyone thought.

"Not everyone's a grandma like you," Isa piped up before Mikey could defend himself. "You never thought the bars were fun *before* you started dating Colter, so I don't think you're the most representative of the group. *I*, for one, think going out would be fun!"

"What do you think about all this, Juniper?" Jake asked.

I shrugged. "As long as he's not hitting on other girls, I don't see the issue in it. I mean, I work at a bar, so I don't think I have any right to tell him what he can or can't do."

The silence around our circle was deafening, as though they'd never heard someone say that about Mikey before.

"Erin texted me." Isa broke through the awkwardness. "She's on her way into town."

"Who's Erin?" I asked, wanting to be caught up in the friend group.

"She's one of our friends that lives here," Ellison explained. "She was one of my bridesmaids."

Jake laughed. "Erin's a fun girl. Thought for sure Mikey would have tried to go after her."

Mikey just shook his head. "Nah, man, she's so tall."

I twisted my facial features, turning my head to look at him. "She can't help it. Maybe you shouldn't be so short," I teased. "Then again, all you bull riders are so short. I don't get it."

He shrugged. "We can't all be J.B. Mauney."

"Erin's got a boyfriend now, anyway." Isa rolled her eyes, sass lacing her tone. "Not to sound like Mikey, but maybe you should focus on finding yourself a girlfriend, Jakey."

"Fair enough, Izzy Bee," Jake teased.

I'd never heard that nickname for Isa—granted I'd only known her for a short time—but judging by the expression that flashed across her face, she hadn't either.

"Yeah, I don't think that one's gonna stick." She cringed, her smile looking more out of pity than amusement. "Anyway." She drew out the word. "She's probably going to stick around for a bit until the rodeo."

"Is there anything you guys want to do until then?" Ellison asked.

Jake kicked his legs out, leaning back in his chair. "Honestly, I just want to chill. We've been go, go, go all week."

Mikey nodded next to me. "I agree. Guys, I just want a day to not have to deal with the media and fans. Why don't you girls go meet Erin? Have fun, and we'll meet you at the rodeo tonight."

"Are you sure?" The question slipped out. Not because I didn't want to spend more time with the girls, but I didn't want Mikey to feel alone or left out.

"Yeah, I'm sure. Go. Have fun," he reassured me, certainty shining in his gaze.

Isa hopped up from her seat. "Well, that's perfect! Let's go, then, girls. I'm driving!"

"Oh, no you're not." Ellison snatched Isa's keys from her hands. "I don't feel like dying today."

"Fine, then I get the aux cord!" Her bubbly demeanor didn't change as she half-skipped to the passenger side.

"You have Bluetooth," Ellison muttered. "You don't even have an aux cord."

Amused by their banter, I followed, looking over my shoulder at the guys, who waved. Jake mouthed, *Good luck*, with a laugh.

I slid into the backseat as Ellison started the car. Isa's

phone connected immediately, and a girly pop song started playing through the speakers.

"What kind of music do you like, Juniper?" Ellison's eyes met mine in the rearview mirror as she backed up the car.

"Uh—" I forced out a laugh. "Not…whatever this is."

Ellison turned her head to Isa as if to say, *See?*

"Rude! My music is great," Isa protested, turning the music up even louder as she sang to the words at the top of her lungs.

"Has Reid ever said anything about your…singing abilities?" Ellison teased.

Isa was not a good singer. Not that I was any better, but there was a difference between just being a bad singer and being a bad singer and *knowing* you were a bad singer.

The pause in Ellison's joke didn't seem to phase her. "Nope! For all I know, he could think I sound like a dying cat. I think I'm better off not knowing."

"Well, you know what they say about cats and curiosity." Ellison bit her lip, holding back a laugh, and I did the same.

They weren't joking when they said Erin was tall. I considered myself to be slightly above average height at five-foot-seven, and I was taller than both Ellison and Isa, but Erin towered over all of us. She had to have been at least five-foot-eleven with a slim frame, light-brown hair, and mossy green eyes. While Ellison and I were alike in our mannerisms, Erin and Isa were almost identical in their personalities.

Isa and Erin immediately started chatting, but it wasn't something I could follow. It was like they picked up whatever conversation they had left off last time they spoke.

"Do you ever feel left out when other people come to hang out with you and Isa?" I asked Ellison, the question slipping out. I knew Isa and Ellison were best friends, but sometimes when Ava would invite other girls, I didn't know where I fit in the group.

She raised a brow. "What do you mean?"

Heat rushed to my cheeks, and I tucked my hair behind my ears to give my hands something to do. "It's stupid, but I was just wondering if you ever felt like a third wheel in the friendship." It sounded more ridiculous after verbalizing it.

"Honestly, not really." My stomach dropped, but she continued. "Isa's extremely extroverted, so she's always making friends. Everywhere we go it's like she runs into someone she knows. I'm content being alone and pretty secure in myself, so it's never bothered me before, but I think you're valid in having those worries. At a certain point, you just realize that the people who are meant for you will stick around. And if you're having to wonder, then maybe that person was never for you."

"I guess I've just always wanted people to like me, so I did what I could to keep them around."

"That's important, but so is how you feel about them. Your friends should make you the best version of yourself. I know Isa does for me. Her friendship serves me and my life as much as my friendship serves her. I wouldn't be where I'm at if it weren't for her." Ellison looked toward her friend and smiled.

I'd never looked at it that way. With Ava and Brady, all I'd wanted was to be seen, to be heard. But I shouldn't have to beg for someone to be in my life, to care about me. I saw that now, in the way Ellison interacted with Isa, Colter, and even the other guys.

Real friends saw your value in your true, authentic self.

After the second night of Colter and Reid's series, we headed back to the trailers, none of us wanting to go out.

"I think we're doing a good job of this whole fake relationship thing, don't you think?" Mikey lay on the pullout couch on his side, propping himself up on his elbow. From the beginning, I'd insisted that we not share the bed when he had a perfectly good couch that I could sleep on. It still didn't stop him from lying on it until he went to sleep, though.

I nodded as I took a sip of water. "I don't think anyone suspects a thing."

The media attention, though not ideal, had also been helping make our relationship seem more believable the past couple weeks. I wondered if Ava and Brady had been seeing it on social media at all. We were well over halfway through the rodeo, so I wouldn't be surprised, given Mikey being Brady's favorite bull rider, but what did shock me was that neither of them had tried to reach out. I'd blocked their numbers, but not all of their socials, so if they really wanted to talk to me, they could have.

Before I could say anything else, hushed voices from outside the trailer caught our attention.

"Who's that?" I whispered.

Mikey shook his head and raised his shoulders.

"The guys?"

"I don't think so. They wouldn't be quiet if it were them."

"Wait, I think I hear something. They're definitely in

there," one of the muffled voices from outside said, their voice attempting to be a whisper but failing.

"I need to get a statement about their relationship. Readers will eat it up," another one replied as footsteps approached the door.

"Quick! Moan!" Mikey hissed at me.

I pinched my brows. "Excuse me?"

"Pretend we're having sex and they won't try to come in," he explained. "They'll leave. There's nothing more awkward than walking in on someone."

You have no fucking idea.

"I can't just—" My protests were cut off by him grabbing my hand and pulling me toward his lap.

"Come on, Juniper," he rasped in my ear, his voice low and gravelly, as he tugged me down onto his lap. "Just grind on me a little."

"You can't be serious!" I whipped my head toward the door just as the reporter walked up the steps. Their silhouette was now right outside the window. "This isn't in the rules."

"Would you rather have to talk to them about our fake relationship and have them spin it in an unfavorable way?" he challenged.

"No. Fine." I huffed. I moved my hips a little against him, putting as little effort into it as possible.

Mikey grabbed my hips, holding me down slightly and adding more pressure. He was growing harder beneath me, and I inhaled a long, slow breath.

"That's it, Peach."

Before I could respond, he stood, flipping us so we were lying on the couch, him on top of me. He lifted one of my legs so it hooked around his torso. His hips rocked against mine and, through our clothes, his hard length brushed against my clit, dragging a moan from my lips.

I clamped my hand over my mouth, eyes widening at what I'd just done, but Mikey took my hand and pinned it over my head.

"Let it all out. Don't hold back. I want everyone outside to know exactly what I do to you, even without being inside you."

I knew the rules of our agreement, and this was explicitly against them, but at the same time, the reporters outside didn't know we were pretending, so technically this was within the rules to make it believable…right?

Shaking my head to dispel the thoughts, I pulled my arms out of Mikey's grasp and reached down to undo his belt and unzip his jeans. He pulled them down and kicked them off, leaving him in a T-shirt and his boxers. His cock strained against the fabric, and my core clenched. I palmed it through his shorts, and he groaned.

Even with the barrier of clothes between us, every roll of his hips against mine was heaven, sending waves of pleasure down my body to my toes. I tilted my body up toward his, so every time he grinded against me, a jolt wracked through me.

Mikey's chest rose and fell as he panted above me, rough grunts falling from his mouth with every thrust. His pace quickened, and I gasped, breathing heavily. The couch below us creaked along with our rhythm. He was going to make me come, and we weren't even naked.

My back arched from the couch, and stars clouded my vision as heat spread in my toes and I moaned. Loudly. If anyone outside hadn't heard us before, they did now. My legs shook around him, fingernails pulling at the fabric of his shirt, bunching it up behind his back.

"Fuck, Juniper. I'm going to come." Mikey's eyes closed as he bucked his hips. His arms trembled beside me as he let out a garbled breath then collapsed onto me. "The things you do to me, Peach. Look at me. You've made me come in my pants like a damn teenager."

I pulled my lip between my teeth, heat pooling in my core at the thought of being able to get him off just from dry humping. Then the silence hit me, and I looked toward the trailer door.

Laughing, I said, "I think they're gone now."

@therodeoroundup.official: Last night we tried to get a comment from Mikey Tucker on his relationship.

@thetipsycowgirl: @therodeoroundup.official Tried?

@therodeoroundup.official: @thetipsycowgirl Let's just say we CAN confirm that there's SOMETHING going on with Mikey Tucker and the girl he brought to Houston. If you know what we mean.

@texaswrangler2943: @therodeoroundup.official • •

CHAPTER SEVENTEEN

Everywhere we tried to go, people were holding up their phones, trying to take pictures of us in secret. None of them were particularly discreet about it, though. A few times, I was able to catch them in the act and shoot them a glare. I didn't know if it scared them off taking the photos or if it would bite me in the ass later, but that would be another bridge I'd cross when I got there.

After the night we faked having sex, a social media post went up "confirming" our relationship. Their only proof was overhearing us—not an actual statement—because neither of us had said anything, but the Internet was still going feral over it.

Travis hadn't said anything about it yet, probably wanting to wait to see how it played out. I'd recently started working with him in the hopes to secure some sponsorships. I'd made it to some of the biggest rodeos in the world, and I was also making six figures a year. It was time to expand my brand.

But my reputation wasn't a secret in the industry, and

sometimes it made it harder to secure deals. Nobody wanted the face of their company to be a man in his thirties who "couldn't settle down." It was possible my agent—like me—thought this relationship was the publicity stunt my career needed.

As long as the media didn't start twisting it and ruin Juniper's reputation in the process, I was willing to give anything a shot. I figured I'd keep doing what I was doing and ask for forgiveness later. If I was truly doing something wrong, Travis would have told me to knock it off. Since the main issue everyone had with me was that I couldn't settle down and was allegedly distracted by one-night stands, having Juniper on my arm on multiple occasions was working in my favor.

Colter and Reid won their SuperSeries, which wasn't a shock to anyone. They were the favorites this year for a World Championship. Things could change rapidly in this sport, but they were determined, just like I was. The difference was, no one had any doubts that they'd pull it off.

Jake and Hayden were set to compete in the final SuperSeries starting tonight, and then the competition would progress into the semifinals.

Colter, Reid, Ellison, Isa, Juniper, and I sat around a table at a little, family-owned diner here in town. They were famous for their burgers and milkshakes, but had other options as well.

"Welcome to The Legless Cow!" our server, a lively girl named Lauren, greeted us. "Nice to see you two again." She smiled at Colter and Ellison like she knew them.

"It's good to be back." Colter nodded as he put his arm around Ellison's shoulders.

"What can I get for y'all?"

Ellison ordered first, then Isa, and we went around the table listing off what we wanted.

"I'll take your Cowboy Burger." The half-pound burger with barbeque sauce and grilled onions sounded just right for me.

Juniper ordered a simple bacon cheeseburger, and everyone ordered milkshakes.

"You know the waitress?" I asked Ellison and Colter after she'd left.

A flush creeped into Ellison's cheeks.

"This was where our second date was. Ellison knows the owners," Colter explained.

I chuckled. "Ah, so this is where you went the day Reid cockblocked you, huh?"

Ellison reached over Colter to smack me on the arm, but Reid just grinned as he nodded.

"Do you have a favorite restaurant back at home?" I asked Juniper.

"My hometown in Michigan has this place where you can get the best deep-dish pizza. But my favorite place in Goldfinch is called Marco's. They're not better than the pizza back home, but they're a close second."

"Yeah, we know Marco's! That place is still open?" Reid jumped into the conversation.

"Well, now you just make us sound old." Colter elbowed him in the ribs.

He just shrugged. "You know how much that town changes."

Juniper smiled. "Yeah, it's still open. One of the few places that didn't change in the four years I was there. I'm sure if you went in today, they'd still have the black-and-white checkered floors, green countertops, and all the photos framed on the wall."

"Did you know we're up on that wall?" Colter asked me.

I shook my head. "I did not."

"Yeah! Reid, me, and a few other guys on the rodeo team back in the day made it up on the wall. Only the best of the best end up on the Marco's wall of fame. Even Coach Aaron's up there."

"I think I've seen that picture up there before," Juniper admitted, suddenly acting shy. "Maybe that's where I recognized you guys from."

Reid's eyebrows shot up. "Oh, yeah?"

There was a hint of skepticism in his voice, but I couldn't pinpoint why. I thought I'd recognized her from somewhere, too, but I chalked it up to seeing so many people and the faces all blending together. Besides, I wouldn't have thought I'd forget a face like Juniper's.

I rested my hand on her knee, giving it a light squeeze. Instead of moving it off her leg because no one would actually be paying attention to what was happening under the table, her lips curled up in a soft smile.

Our food came out surprisingly fast, and our chatter lulled as we dug in.

"This is probably the best burger I've ever had." A few heads bobbed with my compliment. "You've got good taste, Firecracker. In food and company, clearly." My brows wiggled.

"That's probably the nicest thing you've said to me all year, Michael," she teased.

Juniper gave me a confused look as she listened to us. Ellison and I had our fair share of banter, but it was all platonic—honestly more sibling-like than anything. Sure, I gave her a lot of shit, but she gave it right back.

My hand found Juniper's and gently squeezed, my thumb brushing over hers, rubbing small circles on her skin. For whatever reason, I liked the subtle intimacy. Pretend or not, it was comforting. Especially when she returned the gesture.

After we'd finished our meal, Reid flagged down Lauren so we could all pay.

"Suppose we should get a move on so we don't miss Jake and Hayden's performance." Reid stood then pulled out Isa's chair for her. "Shall we?"

One by one, we got up. As we headed toward the exit, Ellison and Colter shared a heartfelt goodbye with the older woman behind the counter and then we were on our way.

The moment we got to our seats, a couple of girls approached us.

"Are you Mikey Tucker?" one of them, a blonde, asked.

"Sure am." I looked up.

"I'm a *huge* fan of yours." The other—a redhead with giant eyelashes and far too much makeup—squealed as she bent down, practically pushing her tits into my face.

"Thanks," I muttered, snaking my arm around Juniper's shoulders and leaning toward her so I could try to see around the girl.

"Will you sign?" the girl asked, and I realized she wanted me to sign her boobs.

"Give me your arm," I instructed after she handed me a Sharpie.

She pouted as I signed her forearm instead and mumbled an unenthusiastic, "Thanks, I guess."

"What was that for?" Juniper asked when the girls had left. She lowered her voice. "Was it because of the media?"

"You're my girlfriend. It's always a bad look to be signing another woman's tits. The only ones I want to see are yours, Peach." I winked. "I'm a one-woman man now. You've shown me the light." Dramatically, my hand waved in front of my face, like I was Buzz in the *Toy Story* movies.

She rolled her eyes, but appreciation still shone in her expression.

"Never thought we'd see the day that a woman would have Mikey whipped." Colter chuckled.

In the moment, I'd forgotten the others were there and they saw the whole thing.

"Looks like you can never leave this man, Juniper. We can actually sort of tolerate the guy now," he continued.

I waved him off as the announcer called out the last steer wrestler over the loudspeakers. The cowboy, who came from a small town out of New Mexico, clocked in a time of five-point-three seconds.

"All right, ladies and gents, first up in the tie-down roping, we've got a cowboy hailing from the state of Montana! Jake Flynn!"

Jake sat tall on his horse in the roping box, the calf he'd rope in the chute. As a tie-down roper, he held a small string of rope between his teeth.

Up on the screen, his horse spun in a few circles. Jake backed him up then nodded. The calf was released from the chute, and his horse took off after it in an explosive run as Jake swung the longer rope over his head. He threw his rope and caught the calf, the loop falling around its neck.

His horse came to a full stop as Jake jumped down, and the calf was jerked back, not quite falling on the ground. Jake ran over to the calf to flip it over then tied three of its legs together with the string. When he was done, he threw his hands in the air.

Running back to his horse, he mounted it then urged it forward to take the slack out of his rope.

If the calf broke free before six seconds was up, he would get a no time.

The judges nodded, and the calf was freed. Once it was up on its feet again, it was as though nothing had happened as it happily ran to the gate to exit the arena.

"Eight-point-two seconds!" the announcer called out. Jake could be seen up on the big screen nodding, happy with his time.

In between competitors, the cameras panned around the audience for different activities to engage the crowd like the muscle cam or the dance cam. I should have expected the kiss cam to land on me and Juniper.

"Look! You guys are up on the screen!" Isa squealed.

Sure enough, the six of us were projected up on the jumbotron for everyone to see. Ellison and Colter obviously kissed, as did Isa and Reid after her outburst, but my eyes widened.

"Are you sure?" Juniper asked in a low voice.

I didn't get to answer as chants of, "Kiss! Kiss! Kiss!" erupted around the arena.

I guess if we were doing this fake dating thing, we were going all in. After all, media sources had already "confirmed" our relationship, so not kissing would have raised more questions than anything.

I took off my hat and put it in front of our faces for some sense of privacy as I leaned in and kissed Juniper, giving her a quick peck on the lips, fully intending to pull back. Instead, she grabbed the back of my head and pulled me back to her. Her taste invaded my mouth, and my dick twitched in my jeans. Everyone around us cheered, and as we pulled apart and I lowered the hat, the camera picked up the pink flush in her cheeks.

CHAPTER EIGHTEEN

After the second semifinal round—the one that Mikey, Colter, Reid, and Jake competed in—concluded, we piled into another bar downtown. This one had a mechanical bull, and Mikey was hell-bent on convincing me to get on it. The boys were all up at the bar grabbing us drinks, and Isa, Ellison, and I sat at a table in the corner away from the entrance.

At this point, people recognized me from social media and all the public displays of our relationship, even without Mikey by my side, and I was either being gawked at or glared at.

I had to make my social media accounts private, because I was also getting an influx of random followers, some of which were not kind in their comments on my old posts.

"Do you guys have people spamming your social media all the time?" I groaned as I removed yet another account who was lucky enough to follow me before I went private.

"My account has been private since I created it." Ellison laughed.

Isa shrugged. "I get the occasional person. However, Reid and Colter aren't as…controversial as Mikey."

"I think Isa just secretly likes the attention," Ellison teased, prompting Isa to lightly smack her on the arm before mumbling, "God forbid a girl wants recognition."

"I didn't sign up for this."

Ellison and Isa both raised their brows at my complaint. Which was fair. I may not have explicitly asked for the recognition and attention and everything that came with it, but I was with a world-famous bull rider. One whose notoriety wasn't exactly positive.

My mouth gaped, my brain trying to come up with something to say, but any excuse I could have come up with would have been disputed. I couldn't claim that I didn't know who he was; everyone in the near vicinity of Miles City knew who he was. I couldn't say I didn't know his reputation, either; it was obvious just looking at him and the way everyone talked about him.

I decided on, "Okay, technically, I signed up for this when I started dating him, but that doesn't mean I wanted this!"

The girls' response was to giggle at how flustered I'd gotten.

"You'll get used to it." Ellison patted my arm in reassurance.

I pulled my bottom lip between my teeth. No one knew that Mikey and I wouldn't be together long enough for me to get used to it.

And no one could.

"What are you three talking about?" Jake asked as the boys set down all the drinks they'd ordered.

"Oh, you know. Just the life of a rodeo WAG." Isa grinned.

"Well, I wouldn't know," he replied, a touch of humor in his voice. "Kind of missing an important part of that."

"What part? Having a girlfriend or *being* a girlfriend?" Ellison poked his arm as she joked with him.

"Technically both."

"Nothing's stopping you from fixing that, man," Reid pointed out.

Jake hesitated, like he was debating whether he wanted to say something.

"Are you kidding? Jake's had the hots for Colter's sister for *years*," Mikey cut in.

Jake glared at him. "Yeah, and she's married."

Mikey scoffed. "Just because there's a goalie, doesn't mean you can't score. Besides, I never liked the guy. No offense, Colter, given that she's your sister and all, but I'm betting they'll break up in the next year or so."

I hit him on the arm, protesting with a, "That's rude!" But no one else spoke up. I tilted my head, confused.

"It's a lot of backstory. Trust me, you don't want to have to listen to all of it," Ellison muttered when she noticed the look on my face.

"As long as she's happy, I'm happy. Let's change the subject, yeah?" Colter took a big swig of his beer, and the topic of his sister's relationship died right there on the spot.

"Hey, bet you can't stay on that bull for eight seconds." Jake elbowed Hayden, pointing to the mechanical bull in the middle of the bar.

Hayden raised his hands in defense. "I'm not betting you anything."

Mikey perked up. "I'll take you up on that."

"Nah, nah, you do that shit for a living. How about this, though. If your girl can stay on for eight seconds, I'll give you twenty bucks." Jake grinned. "Shouldn't be an issue, all things considered, am I right?"

"Make it thirty and you've got yourself a deal." Mikey stuck out his hand for Jake to shake on it.

"Hold on, what?" I interrupted. "Why are you betting on me?"

Colter shrugged. "It's kind of our thing. We make bets on all sorts of things, you know."

My eyes narrowed. "Like what?"

Mikey answered quickly. A bit too quick, but I wasn't sure why. "It's usually just stupid shit. It's not a big deal."

Everyone around the table fell silent.

"Am I missing something?" Suspicion rolled through my mind. I didn't like this.

"Here, I'll bet you, too." Reid pulled out his wallet, throwing out a twenty-dollar bill. "Isa's damn good at the mechanical bull."

The energy shifted, and suddenly everyone was back to their normal selves, joking and messing around. I still had a weird feeling in my gut, but I let it go as Mikey led me over to the mechanical bull, whispering tips as we walked.

"Make sure you're comfortable up there. If you start in a bad position, it's going to be hard to stay on. Focus on your balance and use your legs to hold on. Move with the bull, not against it. It's not real, but even so, you're teammates."

I couldn't help but choke out a laugh at how ridiculous this all was. "All right, Coach."

"Hey, can't blame a guy for wanting to win a bet, right?"

Shaking my head in amusement, I replied, "Guess not. Don't worry, I won't let you down."

His eyes shone with some emotion I couldn't quite

place. He quickly snapped out of it, though, not letting me in on what he was thinking. "I know you won't."

We stood in line for the bull, and when it was my turn, I climbed up into the inflatable ring and pulled myself up on the bull.

Mikey patted the operator on the arm and looked at me as he said, "Don't go easy on her."

"Wait, what?" I screeched as the machine turned on and slowly started to turn. I gripped the rope like a vise, knuckles turning white as the bull sped up and whipped me around. My hair flew into my face, but I held my position, moving my torso with the bull like Mikey told me.

Hoots and hollers from the boys erupted from the sidelines, and a few cameras flashed in the bar. My ears rang, and I mentally counted down until I could be done with this ride.

I didn't think it was possible, but the bull spun even faster, changing directions and whipping me back and forth.

Was this what Mikey dealt with every night? At least with the fake bull there was no risk of dying. A buzzer went off, signaling that my eight seconds was up, but out of the corner of my eye, Mikey told the operator to keep going.

"What the hell are you doing?" I yelled at him.

"Jake and I doubled it! For every additional four seconds, I get fifteen more dollars!"

The rest of the group cackled as I mentally cursed Mikey. I'd get back at him for this.

Around what had to be the twelve-second mark, I was almost thrown off, my legs losing their grip with each turn. Somehow, I managed to hold my ground, even though I almost slid off the back.

"Sixteen seconds!" the operator called out, and I decided I'd had enough.

In a dramatic show, I flung myself off the bull when it spun, landing near the wall of the inflatable.

"Hell yeah! Pay up, Jakey-poo, you owe me *sixty bucks*!" Mikey celebrated as he helped me out.

"I think I deserve at least half of that," I muttered.

"Don't worry, baby, I've got you." Mikey winked, and I tried to ignore the feeling in my stomach that arose at the nickname.

He was just pretending because he won the bet.

The way he was looking at me right now—like he wanted to devour me—wasn't real.

It was all pretend.

Fake.

But what if it wasn't?

CHAPTER NINETEEN

Tonight is Championship Night, folks! Let these cowboys and cowgirls hear you!" The announcer's voice echoed throughout the arena.

I sat behind the bucking chutes, doing whatever I could to get in the zone for my ride. I closed my eyes and let the rest of the world around me disappear, fading away to background noise, as I visualized my upcoming ride. From mounting the bull to the nod to the eight-second buzzer going off, I pictured every movement, envisioning perfect execution.

For a few short moments, it was just me and the bull.

No media, no fans, no competition, no pressure.

For the first time in weeks, it felt like I could finally breathe. Ironic, considering tonight was the most important ride of the Houston Rodeo.

But my thoughts were broken apart as the announcer called for the prayer, said before each rodeo to wish safety on the animals and athletes, and the national anthem.

When the anthem concluded, I squatted back down, closing my eyes.

"Getting in the zone?" Maverick's voice behind me got my attention, and my eyes fluttered open.

I nodded but didn't stand.

"Got room for another?" He squatted next to me. "You've been putting on quite a show for the reporters lately."

My eyes flicked toward him, and I clocked the amused expression on his face.

"I just want to get them off my back, man." The admission slipped out easily.

His shoulders shook as his chest rumbled with a low laugh. "And how's that been working out for you?"

I rolled my eyes. "Man, maybe you should start up a relationship so they'll focus their attention on you instead. I can see the headlines now. *Maverick Oakes: World Champion Bachelor No More.*"

He shook his head as he looked down with a wide grin. "Nah, it'd probably be something on the lines of *Buckles or Babies: Which One is in Maverick Oakes's Future.*" He laughed, and suddenly the weight of the competition didn't feel as heavy.

Maverick dealt with the media just as much as I did, but sometimes it was hard to see that when they were always in my face. He was under just as much pressure, but he handled it better. Respectfully and calmly and all that.

"No, but I, uh…" He looked back down at the ground, drawing his lip between his teeth.

"You telling me there's a girl, Mav?" I elbowed him. "And you're keeping it a secret?"

"It's not serious yet. I don't want to scare her away, you know. Or have it be blown up into something it's not."

"Yeah, I get that." I snorted. He had no idea that was

the situation I'd gotten myself into. I knew too well what a relationship getting blown up looked and felt like.

He stood, extending a hand to help me up.

"I'm going to sit here for a little while longer. Thanks, though, man. Good luck tonight."

He nodded. "Yeah, you, too."

I shook out my limbs before climbing onto the platform behind the chute, taking some deep breaths to ground myself. The bull I was matched up against for the night grunted in the chute, huffing hot air from his nostrils like smoke clouds billowing into the air. He pawed the ground, body banging against the metal gates.

"This is *the* matchup of the night, ladies and gentlemen. We've seen this cowboy successfully ride several bulls over the course of the rodeo, and tonight he's back again on the bull they call Rampage. Mikey Tucker!"

I tried to tune out the announcer as I settled on the back of the bull, rosining my rope then wrapping it securely around my hand. This particular bull was *mean*. But like I'd always said, *the meaner the bull, the better the score.*

"Watch him, folks. This is one you do *not* want to miss."

I nodded, and the gate swung open. The bull exploded out of the chute, whipping his hind legs around. I'd watched several others ride this bull, though, and I knew what he liked to do straight out of the gate.

I'd prepared myself for this.

When the bull spun, I adjusted my body to counter his movement, so I stayed centered and wouldn't be thrown off. Keeping my hips square to

Rampage's shoulders, I used my free hand to balance. My thighs clenched around the bull as he bucked and whirled around, but I held my position, working with him.

The audience yelled in the background over the bass of a country rock song, but my mind was locked in on the ride. My only focus was the bull and the eight seconds that were slowly winding down.

This is it, Tucker.

Prove them wrong. All of them.

If you win tonight, there's no way they can call you distracted anymore.

On the bull's final spin, he switched directions on me, trying a last-ditch effort to throw me off, but I managed to hold on and the eight second buzzer went off, signaling the end of the ride.

I let the bull buck me off, then I got the hell out of the arena.

Once I had made it to safety, I trained my gaze on the big screen where my score would be displayed.

"Now that's how you do it, folks! Ninety-three points!" the announcer called out just as the numbers flashed on the screen.

I pumped my fist as the score came in, pride washing over me. Now I just needed to take this momentum through the entire year and to the NFR.

The minute I stepped out of the arena after the buckle ceremony, press and media flocked to me.

"Mikey! How does it feel to be the RodeoHouston bull riding champion?"

"Was your girlfriend in the audience?"

"How serious is your relationship?"

"Is she going to come on the road with you?"

"Do you think you're going to be competing at the NFR this year?"

Question upon question was fired at me, but all I wanted to do was get to Juniper and the rest of my friends. I pushed through the reporters, ignoring them as they demanded answers.

"Nice ride out there, buddy." Jake clapped me on the back when I finally got to them.

Colter and Reid were nowhere to be seen, probably doing a few interviews of their own. They were much better at handling the press than I was, but then again, they didn't have reporters and influencers hounding them every two seconds. And the ones who did talk to them weren't out for blood with personal attacks and ammunition for their gossip websites.

"Thanks, Flynn." I nodded at him before turning to Juniper and saying, "Just stay with me, all right? They'll have to go through me first to get to you, and I'm not going to let that happen."

She nodded, pulling her bottom lip between her teeth as I wrapped the dark-gray leather jacket I'd gotten from the NFR last year around her shoulders.

"Let's go." I grabbed her hand and started to walk through the sea of cameras, Jake and Hayden flanking our sides.

"Juniper! Tell us more about you! How did you meet Mikey?"

"Mikey, why does it seem like you're keeping her a secret? Are you embarrassed by her? What is this going to do to your playboy image?"

I bit my tongue, fighting back a response. I wasn't going to give them the satisfaction of blowing up. I couldn't. Not when all attention was on me after the championship win.

"I hate that this is happening to you," Juniper whispered. "What can I do?"

"Just keep your head down. They'll have to leave us alone eventually." I shook my head, trying to ignore the flashes and questions coming from all directions, engulfing us like flames.

"What if they don't?" she asked.

I couldn't admit it, but that was what I was afraid of. I was worried the media wouldn't stop until they got answers, or would start speculating themselves, spreading rumors around until there wasn't a single speck of truth remaining.

"I'm willing to do whatever it takes to get them to leave you alone," Juniper said, again in a low voice.

Fuck it, then.

I stopped in my tracks, much to the confusion of everyone around me. Loudly, I announced to whoever would listen, "I'm not embarrassed of her. She's my girlfriend, and I don't care what it does to my *playboy image*, so please leave us alone."

I pulled Juniper to me, cupping her face in my hands and pressing my lips against hers.

Once the shock wore off, she kissed me back, our mouths fitting together like puzzle pieces. Juniper's fingers tangled in my hair as photographers snapped images, the flashes of their cameras going off like fireworks.

That was what this kiss, even if it was mostly for show, felt like. Fireworks.

Electricity hummed within my body, creeping up my spine and through my limbs to the tips of my fingers.

I slid my tongue past her lips, deepening the kiss, not

stopping to come up for air, even when she let out a gentle moan.

Seemingly satisfied, the reporters and media slowly started to dwindle, heading off to find their next victims.

I broke the kiss, although I still held Juniper's face in my hands. Looking deep into her icy blue eyes, I murmured, "You're trouble, you know that, Peach?"

"What's going to happen?" Her eyes widened, like the realization of what we'd gotten ourselves into had just sunk in.

"I don't know, Juniper, but it looks like we're going to be stuck with each other for a while longer."

CHAPTER TWENTY

The next morning, we hooked up our trailers to get back on the road. Our next destination was a rodeo in Arizona, but it was also a seventeen-hour drive to get there. We'd most likely split it in two and stop along the way in Amarillo.

"We all packed up and ready to go?" I called out to the guys.

"Yeah, let's get out of here." Colter nodded as he picked up the last lawn chair and put it in the back of his pickup.

"After you, milady." I opened the passenger side door and gestured for Juniper to climb in.

She looked unimpressed as she hoisted herself up into the pickup, grabbing the "oh shit handle" to help give herself a boost. Once she was safely inside, I shut the door and ran over to the driver's side.

I turned the key in the ignition, and the radio turned on to a country western station. The A/C was blowing through the vents, and the sun was shining. I didn't know if it was the combination of everything, but I reached for

Juniper, lacing our fingers together and resting our hands on the center console.

We drove out of Houston in a convoy of pickup trucks and horse trailers, leaving behind the rodeo, media, and the fans that changed everything about our fake-dating arrangement.

At the end of the day, I'd proven the boys—and the media—wrong. Juniper and I had been together for a little over a month *and* I'd won the championship buckle.

Technically, we could quietly end our relationship once we got back home. Lay low for a bit while it blew over on social media. It was what everyone expected, after all. A whirlwind fling. The Mikey Tucker special. But a part of me wanted to ride this out a bit longer.

I couldn't deny that I'd been happier in Houston than I'd ever been at a rodeo. Having Juniper by my side made me feel lighter somehow. I didn't want to get used to it, though. This thing wouldn't last. I had to remind myself of that. Nothing about our relationship was real.

"What are you thinking about?" Juniper asked about thirty minutes into our drive.

"Hm?" I snapped out of my trance.

"You looked deep in thought over there. Just wondering what's on your mind."

"Not a whole lot," I lied.

Bringing up whatever feelings I thought I had would just make this whole thing more complicated. How was I supposed to tell my fake girlfriend that she made me forget the pressures of being a professional bull rider? That when I was with her, a lot of my worries melted away, and I was able to just be myself.

She hummed like she didn't quite believe me, but at the same time, she didn't pry.

An old song from the late nineties came up on the radio, and I turned up the volume, tapping my hand on the steering wheel to the beat as Joe Diffie serenaded us.

"What kind of music do you like?" I asked as the song ended.

"I kind of just listen to whatever's on. I don't think I have a favorite genre or anything."

"Really? Not even a go-to station to listen to on the radio?"

Her cheeks flushed red. "Honestly, I don't really listen to the radio unless I'm at work. I don't know, I'm not the type of person to have music playing all the time."

"You like the quiet?"

"I wouldn't say I like the quiet per se, but at the same time I don't need something filling the silence all the time, if that makes sense."

I nodded, even though I didn't really understand. Music was a nice distraction for me when my thoughts got a little too loud. If I was able to focus on the lyrics, my fears of being forgotten seemed to fade a bit.

"Why does everyone care so much about who you're dating?" The question was barely above a whisper, like she was afraid to ask. "Or who you've been with in the past?"

"I wish I knew." I huffed out a laugh without humor. "I guess it's easier to focus on someone else's problems rather than their own. And that kind of stuff sells. It never used to bother me, the attention."

"How come you let it bother you now, then? Why do you let them continue to do it?"

While I'd normally have a different reaction to those questions—take it personally or get defensive—they didn't frustrate me coming from Juniper. I thought she was genuinely curious, so I answered.

"It was easier to go with it rather than fight it at first. I liked to think that any publicity was good publicity if it got my name out there. Then I think it just got to a point where I couldn't stop it. Now it's all anyone cares about. If I could change it, I would. Even on my best days of riding—the days *I* feel like I'm on top of the world—it seems like the only thing that matters to them is who I take home at the end of the night."

"I'm sorry that people can't see you for who you are."

Juniper didn't say it aloud, but she didn't need to. I understood the hidden message.

I see you for who you are.

"Okay, okay. Would you rather have hands for feet or feet for hands?" Juniper asked in between bites of the fast food we'd gotten on the road.

"Hands for feet. I could always use more hands." I winked, and she smacked my arm with a laugh. "What would you do?"

"Hands for feet also." She shot me a look when I laughed at her because she chose the same answer as me. "Without the sexual comment!"

"Who said it was for sexual reasons?" I teased, knowing damn well it was for sexual reasons.

She ignored me, instead waving me on. "Your turn, Casanova."

"Would you rather travel to space or to the bottom of the ocean?"

"Oh, that's a good one, actually. I'm terrified of open

water, but I don't know if I like the odds of going to space, either."

"I mean, either way there's a risk of dying. Don't you remember the people who died in that submarine?" I pointed out.

"Yeah, but think of how many people have also died in space!" she protested. "Space. I'd go to space."

"I think I'd go to the bottom of the ocean. I feel like it'd be cooler. We already know what space looks like, but there's so much of the ocean that hasn't been discovered."

She shuddered next to me. "Horrifying. Would you rather be able to read people's minds or see the future?"

I tapped my lips with my finger for a moment. "See the future. I don't think I need to know what people think about me. I already know too much."

"I don't know, I think it would be nice to know what people thought. Might prevent a lot of heartache." Juniper paused, going silent for a little too long. She snapped out of it, though, looking to me to ask the next question.

"Would you rather ride a horse on a two-day trip or ride a bull for eight seconds?"

"Of course, that would be your question." She snorted. "I value my life, so I would take the horse. Wouldn't you? If money wasn't involved?"

"Absolutely not. I wouldn't be caught dead on a horse."

"What? Why?"

I didn't answer, avoiding eye contact and gluing my gaze on the road.

"What, are you afraid of horses or something?"

"Of course not!" I didn't sound too convincing.

Laughter filled the cab. "Oh, that's good. Imagine that. A bull rider who's afraid of a horse." Her body shook as she tried to compose herself, but each time she came close, she burst into a fit of cackles again.

"Shut up." I rolled my eyes playfully. "Ask your next question, Peach."

"Would you rather be on a reality dating show or a reality competition show?"

"What kind of competition show?" I asked, because that was important. There was a difference between a show like *The Great British Baking Show* and *Survivor*. It was also important to note that I would much rather be on *Survivor*.

"Something where you have to do challenges. Maybe deceive people, too."

"See, I think I could win a dating show. But a competition show would be fun, too."

"I saw this reality show recently that combined the dating show element with a singing competition. It was actually really interesting. This country singer, maybe you know him, had to choose ten women from thirty singers to compete for his heart, but he wasn't able to see them when they sang. Just hear their voices. I'd never listened to his music before, but he was pretty good. The winner was good, too! There was this one girl, though, who drove me *insane*. I was so glad when she got eliminated." Her eyes lit up when she explained the show, and the way she described it almost had me convinced to start watching reality TV.

"Is this the guy?" After scrolling through my music app —one hand still on the wheel—I found his name, Dusty Wilder, and clicked on the most popular song. A catchy guitar riff started playing. The rest of the guys probably wouldn't have liked it, but I was vibing with it.

"Yeah, this is the one. I think he just released the album that he recorded with the girl who won and they're planning to go on tour soon."

"That's cool. Do you think you'll try to go?"

She shrugged. "Maybe. I probably don't have anyone to go with, though."

"I'm sure you'll find someone…" My voice trailed off. I didn't want to say I'd go with her, because we weren't going to last that long. And making promises on a fake relationship seemed like a recipe for disaster.

"Anyway, answer the question. You didn't pick one."

Right. "Uh, let's go with the competition show. How about you?"

"I think I'd be ruthless in a competition show." Gone was the uncertainty in her expression, replaced by a wicked grin. "I'm great at deception and manipulation, and I'm not afraid to get what I want."

"Damn, Peach. Scaring me a little there," I joked. "Don't go manipulating me to get what you want, now."

Her face flushed red. "Right. Yeah." She yawned as her eyes fluttered shut.

"Take a nap. We're not too far away from our stop for tonight."

After a good night's rest and another eight-hour stretch of driving, we arrived in Arizona where the next rodeo would be. Juniper napped in the cab most of the way, but when she was awake, we talked about anything and everything under the sun.

Her favorite type of candy was saltwater taffy, she loved autumn, and her favorite type of chewing gum was Wrigley's Big Red.

When she was six years old, she broke her arm falling out of a tree that she tried to climb, she hated horror movies but watched them in college anyway to make her friends happy, and most of the time she'd rather spend nights at home instead of going out to the bars.

That last point mostly had to do with the fact that she wanted to graduate early, so she'd taken as many credits as possible in the most challenging classes she could find.

When I caught her scrolling on her phone looking at jobs outside of Montana, I tried to untie the knots in my chest, reminding myself that she was most likely going to leave once this was over. What I still couldn't figure out, though, was why she ended up in Silver Creek anyway.

She looked up from her phone, giving me a curious glance. "What's up?"

"Nothing, just snooping," I admitted, caught in the act.

"Oh." She awkwardly put her phone away. "I was just looking at jobs. I don't know if I'll apply for any of them, because most of them require experience that I don't have."

I shrugged. "Doesn't hurt to look."

"Right, well…" She cleared her throat. "Are you ready for your ride?"

I nodded, taking a seat next to her and putting my hand on her knee. It'd become second nature at this point, but it was all for appearances.

At least that was what I kept telling myself.

"Nervous? Excited?"

"A bit nervous, but I think that's normal. It's all about

how you channel the nerves. You can either take advantage of them to fuel your ride or let them control you. The goal is always to stay on top."

"Well, I'm sure it'll go great." She smiled at me, and I could only hope she was right.

juniper

Mikey didn't make it to eight seconds. He was thrown off the bull around seven, meaning he wouldn't take home any prize money to add to his yearly earnings. It may not have seemed like a big deal, with it being a smaller rodeo, but every little bit counted when it came to a World Championship.

"Let's get out of here. Sorry it took me so long," he apologized.

A chorus of *No worries*, and *That's all right* rose from the group before they all started to walk to the trucks and trailers.

"I call shotgun!" Jake yelled to Colter and Reid. "Let's get food, I'm starving."

Ellison gave him a funny look. "You made me buy you three hot dogs at the rodeo." She held them up in her hands, and he snatched one.

"Yeah, and I'll eat these, too." He took a big bite out of one, and they disappeared around the corner toward the parking lot.

I stayed behind, squeezing Mikey's shoulder. "I'm sorry about your ride."

He smiled, but it didn't reach his eyes. "It's all right. Not that big of a deal." His posture stiffened as he stood a bit straighter, but his jaw ticked with tension. "Come on, we need to catch up with the group." Resorting to humor like he always did, he made a self-deprecating joke. "They can't just hold on for eight seconds to wait for us. But clearly we have that in common."

He started to walk toward the group, who was a short distance in front of us, but I stepped in front of him, stopping him.

"What're you doing? What's up?" Concern painted his features.

"You don't have to do that, you know."

"Do what?"

"Make those jokes. Pretend to be okay when you're not."

"It's all good, Peach." His eyes didn't meet mine, and his tone was almost too cheery. Strained. Like he was forcing himself to stay upbeat and not act upset about the ride. "I don't want to bring down the group. Come on." This time he took a hold of my hand, lacing his fingers with mine. His body language was still stiff, though, his grip squeezing a bit tighter than usual, like he didn't want me to let go.

Our walk to the vehicles was silent, but I gave his hand a reassuring squeeze if only to let him know that I was there for him.

"No, no, saddle bronc is not easier than bareback!" Jake argued.

"I'm just saying, anyone using a saddle has nothing on me." Mikey put his hands up.

"Try riding a horse at high speeds *and* needing good aim, though. It takes a lot of coordination," Colter pointed out, throwing his hat into the ring of whatever this conversation was.

"Mikey's never even tried to ride a horse before, so I don't know that he actually has any say here," Ellison teased.

"I have! I did last year!" Mikey protested.

At the same time I started laughing, about to reveal his secret, Ellison retorted with, "Not sober!"

I finally got a word in. "It's because he's—"

Mikey quickly threw his hand over my mouth, the rest of my sentence coming out muffled. My tongue darted out, licking his palm.

He squealed, ripping his hand away. "What was *that* for?" He wiped the spot I licked on his jeans, shaking his head but unable to contain a smile.

"Come on now, Juniper, don't leave us hanging." Reid chuckled.

"Don't you dare!" Mikey protested as my eyes scanned over the group.

"It's not that big a deal, he's just…" I paused.

Mikey beat me to it, blurting out, "I'm scared of horses, okay!"

A wave of laughter erupted around the table.

"You don't think we knew that already?" Colter wheezed.

Hayden even threw out a joke. "Dude, every time you go near a horse, your face pales like you just saw a ghost."

"Bullet huffed in his face a couple months ago, and I thought his soul was about to leave his body," Colter teased.

"They're *terrifying!*" Mikey's voice rose an octave, coming out shrill and not helping his case.

"Mikey, you go face to face with death every time you sit on a bull. You've tried to ride a fucking bison!" Jake was almost incomprehensible, his giggles uncontrollable at this point.

While most of the time Mikey's facial expression would go blank or dark, this time his eyes sparkled with amusement, telling me that he was playing along with it. I think he knew how irrational his fear was considering his career, and he was just having fun with his friends.

"If you think about it, horses aren't the worst thing to be afraid of. They can weigh thousands of pounds. At least I'm not afraid of mannequins." He gave Jake a pointed look.

"Excuse me? Explain yourself." Ellison howled, causing a few tables to look over in our direction, in concern or annoyance, I wasn't sure.

"That was *one time!*" Jake elbowed Mikey in the ribs.

Hayden shook his head. "No, it was more than one time. It's every time we go into a clothing store."

Jake shrugged. "They just come out of nowhere."

"They're inanimate objects!" Ellison had doubled over in her chair, tears staining her cheeks.

"Yeah, well, what are you afraid of then, Ellison?" he retorted.

"Not being in control," Colter coughed out under his breath.

She just rolled her lips between her teeth, shrugging a shoulder. "Pretty much. I talk to my therapist about it a lot, actually. Might do some of you guys good. Colter goes."

Colter nodded, while a few rumbles went around the group, some of the guys saying they'd looked into it and others completely disregarding it.

I tuned out their conversation as the topic switched, my mind latching onto the fear of not having control. For the first time in my life, I felt like I didn't have a grip on my life. Catching Brady and Ava together derailed my plans—my well-thought-out plans. Part of me wanted to claw my way back and take the reins again with a death grip, and the other part wanted to go with the flow and see what happened. After all, hooking up with and fake dating Mikey Tucker was not something I'd planned for. Neither was kissing him in front of hundreds of thousands of people.

"Where'd you go there?" Mikey leaned in to whisper at me.

I turned my head toward him, regarding his expression. Concern, maybe a bit of curiosity, shone in his eyes.

"Just thinking." I patted his leg.

"Just wanted to make sure you're good."

"I am. Thanks." Shooting a soft smile his way, I turned my attention back to the larger group, who were currently getting into another heated debate about the correct way to put toilet paper on the holder.

CHAPTER TWENTY-TWO

mikey

The temperature in southern Utah was unseasonably warm, and sweat dripped down the back of my neck. The rodeo wouldn't start for another hour or so, and instead of making Juniper sit in the stands until it started, I was giving her a tour of the arena. I'd offered to let her stand behind the chutes during my ride, but she said she preferred to sit in the stands with Ellison.

We'd said goodbye to Isabelle in Houston, but she'd be back in Montana for the Bucking Horse Sale. Juniper probably just didn't want to make Ellison sit alone. She would have been fine, but I understood the sentiment.

"These are the bucking chutes." I gestured to the four chutes next to us that led out into the arena. "Back here are the stock pens where animals are held before the events. On the other side of the arena are the timed event boxes and roping chute as well as the alleyway for barrel racing."

"They're a lot smaller than I would have expected." Juniper's head was turned, her attention focused on the chutes. "Doesn't seem like a lot of room for the bull."

"Gotta be able to contain the bull somehow. If the chute is too big, there's a greater chance of it escaping or trying to turn around before an athlete mounts," I explained. "Also protects the crew that's working back here and ensures a fair start for everyone."

"What would be considered an unfair start?" she asked.

"There's something called a re-ride in roughstock events. It's pretty self-explanatory, but there's certain criteria that must be met to be granted a re-ride. If a bull's performance isn't up to par you could get a re-ride, or if there's an unfair advantage for the bull, like if it hits the chute or stumbles, you could also get a re-ride. But it's all up to the judges' discretion. So something that grants you a re-ride for one judge, might not be the same for another."

Juniper hummed. "Interesting. Do you know any of the competitors here?"

"A few. I'm not super close with many of them, though."

Outside of Colter, Reid, Jake, and Hayden, I tended to keep to myself. Sometimes it was easier that way. I was less likely to be disappointed later if I didn't open up too much. And the media would have less material if there were less people to talk to them about me.

Clearly, that hadn't worked out in the grand scheme of things with the women I'd been with in the past, but there was only so much I could do to control that.

"This was cool. I'm glad you showed me all of this."

"Are you sure you don't want to come behind the chutes? I don't know that you'll have another opportunity given that the other rodeos we go to are bigger."

I also tried to ignore the fact that this would probably be the last rodeo she'd come to with me. The event she needed me to go to was in late May over Memorial Day and none of us competed in the Bucking Horse Sale. Once we got back home, we'd have a break between now and the summer run starting in June.

A small part of me hoped that we'd still be together when our next travel stint started, but a more rational part of me reminded me once again that this whole thing was pretend.

A flush creeped into her cheeks, and she shook her head. "No, that's all right. I think I'm okay not being so up close. If that's okay?"

As much as I wanted her close, I didn't want to pressure her into something she wasn't comfortable with. I also selfishly didn't want there to be any distractions during my ride. After a no score in Arizona, it was important to perform well tonight.

I planted a kiss on her temple. "Of course, that's okay. I'm just happy to have you here with me."

"There's a storm rolling in," one of the other bull riders to my left muttered, looking up at the sky. "I can feel it in my joints."

"Looks like a big one." The one to my right nodded.

A few menacing clouds covered the sky in the distance, but I hoped we'd be out of here by the time the rain started.

"Rain or shine, boys." I patted them on the backs.

The loudspeaker in the arena crackled as the announcer began talking. "Ladies and gentlemen, it looks like we might run into some inclement weather, but it hasn't hit yet! We've still got a night full of rodeo ahead of us! Let's kick it off with the bareback riding."

Bull riding was generally always the last event of the night. I understood why they did it; bull riding was the event that people got most excited for, but sometimes I just wanted to get the ride out of the way so I couldn't get too deep in my head.

Thankfully, this rodeo didn't have a lot of media presence, either. But there were always a few people in attendance who would post videos of rides on social media later. On good days, the praise and response from fans energized me, but on bad ones, I avoided the Internet as much as possible.

Unfortunately for me, the attention hadn't fizzled out after Houston. Juniper and I had thrown gasoline on the flames that the media had started in the beginning, and it had turned into a whole inferno. I had to have been tagged in at least fifteen posts a day since the end of the rodeo.

By the time the breakaway roping started, thunder rolled in the distance. There hadn't been any sight of lightning, so it was looking like we'd ride out the storm.

Colter and Reid had roped a good enough time to win the buckles tonight, and Jake had performed well, too. My turn was coming up soon, whether I was ready or not.

Rain poured over the arena as I climbed onto the side of the bucking chute. The bull I'd drawn tonight was named Down on Your Luck, and I prayed to God that wasn't an omen for my ride.

"This one's a mean motherfucker." I couldn't tell if the

man helping pull my rope was muttering at me or to himself.

I still replied confidently, holding my chin high. "Good. I like 'em mean."

Taking a few deep breaths, I kneeled down on the bull's back, then I dropped my legs so I was sitting. I corrected my seat a bit, getting in a comfortable position, then adjusted the bull rope to my liking. After rosining the rope and adjusting my grip, I let the helper know he was good to pull it tighter.

A few seconds later, my free hand was in the air and I was nodding the signal to open the gate.

"Here's Mikey Tucker!" The announcer's voice boomed throughout the arena, even louder than the thunder.

The sound of raindrops falling and hooves hitting the dirt created a symphony with the cheers of the crowd and the rock music backdrop. My heartbeat pounded in my ears, and I could hear my own breathing.

My teeth ground together as I rocked my body back and forth with the bull. Spit flew from its mouth, and I imagined steam blowing out of its nostrils.

They were right. This bull was mean.

Its muscles coiled with tension underneath me as it unleashed its fury in a series of spins and kicks. My own muscles screamed at me as I attempted to become one with the beast, like lightning coursing through my veins, each movement jarring my bones.

The eight-second buzzer went off, the sharp noise reverberating through the arena. I thrusted myself off the back of the bull, hitting the muddy ground with the thud.

Get up!

Get up!

Get up!

My brain screamed at me as the bull pawed the ground with its giant hooves. Its horns—although filed down—seemed to shine in the arena lighting, the steady drops of rain sparkling as they fell.

I scrambled backward on my palms and feet like a crab as the bullfighters stepped in front of me. The bull dipped its head and hunched its shoulders, ready to charge.

My heart pounded in my chest as fear rushed through me for the first time in a long time.

When the bull was distracted, I rolled over onto my knees and used my arms to push myself up to run to safety.

"Look out!" someone yelled from the sidelines, and I looked over my shoulder, darting out of the way just as the bull came barreling toward me. A rush of air knocked me further to the side, and I sprinted like a bat out of hell. Mud caked my jeans and covered my hands, and I did my best not to slip before jumping onto the fence as the bull turned around and came running back.

When the bull was out of the arena and I was able to catch my breath, I put a hand over my heart, feeling the erratic rhythm. Then I climbed over the fence, and collapsed onto the ground, sitting with my eyes closed.

"Damn, Tucker, that was a close one. But it damn sure paid off."

I looked up just as the announcer called out my score. "Eighty-six points!"

Thank fuck.

CHAPTER TWENTY-THREE

I held my jacket over my head, attempting to keep myself out of the downpour. Turned out, neither Ellison nor I had umbrellas, so instead of waiting for the guys, we immediately beelined it for the trailers so we didn't get soaked.

As if the rain wasn't enough, my heart was still thundering in my chest after Mikey's ride. Seeing him scramble away from the bull on his hands and knees, not being able to do anything from the stands, killed me. My brain kept coming up with scenarios where he didn't get out of the arena in time.

Not that I should have cared. At least, not in the way that I did.

Of course, a normal human being with compassion would be scared for him, but it felt like I couldn't *breathe* until he was safe.

"This way!" Ellison gasped as she gestured for me to follow her, cutting through a crowd of people trying to get out of the rain.

She lead me to a shortcut that would not only prevent

us from getting stuck in the slow-moving foot traffic, but would take us directly to the trailers so we wouldn't have to go around. She just didn't tell me that it required hopping a fence.

"Are you crazy?"

Ellison rolled her eyes. "It's *fine*. Would you rather stand in the rain?"

I hesitated, not making a move toward the fence, even though I shook my head.

"I mean, if you want to walk all the way around, be my guest, but I'm cold and want to get out of these wet clothes." She climbed the fence and hopped down to the other side much quicker than I would have expected.

I sighed, dropping my jacket from its position covering my head, and grabbed the fence, hoisting myself up and placing my feet in the mesh of the chain link. If I was dry before, I definitely wasn't now, water dripping down my face from my hair and my clothes soaked through.

"See? That wasn't so bad. You did better than Isa would have. She would have grumbled the entire time." She shook her head in amusement. "Come on, let's go. We'll be back to the trailers in no time."

I had to hand it to her, it was a lot quicker than I imagined walking all the way around would have been. Illegal? Probably. Practical? Meh. Efficient? Yes.

"I don't anticipate this rain stopping anytime soon, so I probably won't come back out tonight," Ellison said when we got to the lot. "We've got an early morning tomorrow, though, anyway. We need to get back on the road."

"All right, well goodnight, then." I waved to her as I approached Mikey's trailer. "See you in the morning."

Ellison dipped her chin. "See ya."

For someone living in the trailer year-round, Mikey

didn't have a lot of food. It looked like he had a bunch of protein powder, whole wheat bread, and a hell of a lot of meat.

I managed to scrounge up some noodles, tomato sauce, and ground beef to make spaghetti. I knew he'd be hungry after riding, and it looked like the food vendors had packed up early to get out of the rain, so it was unlikely that he would have been able to get anything. And he needed a big meal with carbs and protein to help replenish his muscles, not instant ramen or a granola bar.

Even though it needed some tidying, the trailer was really nice. I had a hunch that Mikey really only used it for sleeping, sleeping *with* women, and storage. In the short time I'd been around him in Silver Creek, it seemed like he was always at the gym, Colter's place, or the bar.

After defrosting the beef, I filled a pot with water and set it on the stove to boil. While I waited, I picked up some things, leaving the questionable-looking stuff for Mikey to take care of. When the water was ready, I tossed in the noodles and started browning the meat, seasoning it with what he had: salt, pepper, garlic powder, and onion powder. I would have liked some Italian seasoning in there, too, but it didn't look like he had any.

After adding tomato sauce, I covered the meat sauce and waited for the spaghetti to finish cooking. Right around the time that I started to drain them was when Mikey opened the door.

He sniffed the air. "What's going on here?"

I turned around, pot in one hand, strainer in the other. "I'm making you dinner. When was the last time you cooked in here?"

He shrugged, tugging off his boots and leaving them on the step. He started to pull off his muddy jeans, too, and I spun around, a bit of water splashing out of the pot onto my fingers.

"Ow, fuck." I hissed, immediately setting the pot down to bring my finger up to my mouth.

"What happened?" Audible panic laced in his tone, and he rushed over to me, wearing only boxers and his socks.

My eyes swept up and down his body, from his toned abs to the bulge in his underwear. Shaking my head to snap out of it, I dismissed the concern. "I'm fine. I just burnt myself."

Mikey grabbed my hand, inspecting my fingers. "Looks like you got yourself good. Run that under some cold water. I'll finish the rest of this."

"It's fine, I—"

Before I could finish protesting, he gently set his hands on my hips, moving me aside as he grabbed the boiling pot. He drained the pasta before setting it back on the stove and reached to turn on the cold water for the sink.

"Baby, it's going to hurt worse if you don't do something about it."

I tried to ignore the way the pet name made my toes tingle. Still taken aback by the entire interaction, I reluctantly ran my hand under the tap. The coolness instantly relieved the angry welt on my fingers.

"I wanted to do something *for you*," I whined.

"All I did was drain the pasta and mix it in the sauce. Don't worry about it." He handed me a bowl of spaghetti and a fork.

He dished his up next and took a seat at the table, moving the stacks of mail closer to the window to make room.

I slid in the booth on the side across from him,

spinning my fork in the pasta before blowing on it to cool it down. I didn't need to burn the inside of my mouth tonight, too.

A low groan rose from Mikey's throat after he took his first bite. "Damn, Peach, this is some good stuff. Don't tell Ellison, but I think you've got her beat."

Warmth spread throughout my cheeks, and I brushed a strand of hair out of my face. "Thanks. It's just a simple recipe, but it's a good source of carbs that I figured you'd need."

"I appreciate it. A lot. Nobody's ever done something this thoughtful for me after a rodeo. I'm usually left to fend for myself." He looked away for a second, as though he was embarrassed by the admission.

"I don't mind at all. It's the least I could do."

We finished eating in silence. Mikey kissed the top of my hand before setting our bowls in the sink and heading toward the bathroom.

"I need to take a shower. I probably stink."

I chuckled to myself, thinking it wasn't that bad all things considered. "I'll be here."

I'd scrolled on my phone for about twenty minutes when Mikey stepped out of the bathroom, a towel wrapped around his waist and water rolling down the planes of his chest. His hair was damp and spiky, as though he'd scrubbed his head with a towel.

My eyes may have wandered to the V-line just above his hips, under the guise that I was still looking at my phone. Unfortunately, I didn't think I was being subtle enough about it, because right before he disappeared into the bedroom, he shot me a wink.

In the time it took for him to get dressed, I pulled out the couch and started to make the bed, thinking the whole time that this was the last night Mikey and I had to pretend to be together, at least for a while.

Mikey walked out in a pair of athletic shorts and a fitted cotton T-shirt and plopped down on the couch, disrupting my process of putting on the sheets.

"Hey!"

"Whoops, sorry." He rolled off, and helped me finish what I was doing. Then he gently lay down on top of the sheets.

I crawled on the other side of the makeshift bed, propping myself up on the pillows.

"I was scared for you tonight," I murmured, turning my head toward his.

"I was scared, too."

I couldn't lie, the admission threw me off.

"Those eight seconds feel like forever, but somehow what happens after those eight seconds makes the ride feel like a blur. Especially in cases like tonight. I'm not going to lie, worst-case scenarios flooded my mind after the fact, and I realized how lucky I had been. Especially with the rain and the mud…" His voice trailed off, and I wondered what exactly he had thought about.

"Well, I'm glad you're okay."

His eyes bore into mine as his hand lightly skimmed my cheek until his fingers were under my chin. My brain screamed for him to stop before lines were crossed, but my heart was fighting back, hoping that he'd kiss me, even though there was no reason for him to. Unlike in Houston, this time we didn't have an excuse to fake hooking up.

No one was outside the trailer.

Not in the rain.

He cleared his throat, retreating and putting distance

between us. "We've got an early morning. We should both probably get to bed."

I nodded. "You're right. Sleep is…good."

"Yeah. Well, goodnight, then." He hesitated before he got up, heading to the bedroom.

"Goodnight," I replied before rolling over to face the opposite side of the trailer.

I heard the soft thud of him getting in bed. The dim light in the bedroom area flicked off, leaving us in darkness with only the light rumble of the air conditioner running and the soft pitter patter of rain hitting the roof. I closed my eyes, willing myself to fall asleep quickly.

"June?"

For a moment, I questioned if I was imagining things or if my name was actually being called. Mikey spoke so quietly, the word was hardly audible even with the short distance between the bed and the couch.

"Yeah?"

"Will you lay with me?" His voice cracked in the silence. Gone was the lighthearted, animated man I'd come to know over the last couple months. Tonight, that man was replaced by a softer one. "Please. I don't want to be alone."

"Yeah."

I slid out from under the covers, the fabric rustling under me. I tiptoed across the wood panel flooring to the steps leading up to the bed. The moment I crawled under the covers and the comforter, he pulled me close until my back was flush with his chest. His warmth enveloped my body, drawing me into an embrace.

Within seconds, his snores filled the space, and sleep overtook me.

CHAPTER TWENTY-FOUR

I can take that, thanks." Juniper grabbed the handle of her suitcase as I pulled it out of the backseat of my pickup.

She walked up the steps, and I followed her to the base of them, despite the look she gave me over her shoulder. She turned the door handle and turned around to face me as I shifted on my feet.

"Thanks for driving me home," she said at the same time I said, "Well, thanks for coming with me."

We both let out awkward laughs.

"I'll, uh, see you around?" I asked, a bit unsure. Now that we were back home out of the bubble we'd been in for the past month and a half on the road, we didn't really have to see each other anymore. If we needed to—if anyone asked —we could pretend to hang out without ever being together. This town, although small, was still big enough for that.

She nodded slowly, as though she was still deciding. "Yeah, I'll see you around."

I watched as Juniper stepped through the front door,

closing and locking it behind her. Then I trudged back to my truck, heading home to the small RV park I'd been living in. If I was being honest with myself, I was ready for that plot of land Colter had promised.

When I pulled into the horseshoe court, my closest neighbor was outside sitting in a lawn chair.

"Hi, Leroy." I waved as I got out of the truck to unhook the trailer.

Leroy was an older, retired gentleman. Sometimes he could be a bit grouchy, but I didn't mind. He didn't bother me, and I didn't bother him.

He grunted, his form of saying hello, and went back to reading his magazine. Upon closer inspection, I realized the front cover looked familiar.

Approaching him warily, kind of like he was a stray dog, I asked, "Hey, Leroy, can I borrow that magazine from you?"

"Whaddya need it for?" he grumbled.

"Just real quick, I'll give it right back. I promise."

After huffing out a breath, he thrusted the magazine in my direction. After mumbling a brief, "Thanks," I took a good look at the front cover.

Just as I suspected, a photo of me and Juniper at the Houston Rodeo was plastered on the front page.

MIKEY TUCKER, BULL RIDING BAD BOY HAS A BADDIE?

My face contorted at the headline.

God, was that the best they could come up with?

I flipped through the pages until I could find the brief article and skimmed what they wrote about me.

Has resident playboy bull rider, Mikey Tucker, finally met his match?

Tucker, one of the leading bull riders in the nation, was spotted several times with a new woman in Houston, Texas. During one instance, she made a point to say she was his girlfriend and the relationship was not a fling. After his championship win, a first for Tucker, fans crowded him as he locked lips with the lucky lady.

So, who is she?

An anonymous source told us that her name is Juniper Ray, age twenty-two, and she resides in Montana. Ray recently graduated from Sapphire Gulch University in the Molecular Biology program, which brings up questions of whether she's telling the truth.

Is their relationship truly real? Is she being paid to be seen with him? Or is it just another one of Tucker's flings that will fizzle out before it has the chance to burn? The coming weeks will be telling of whether this wild mustang has finally been tamed.

A representative of Mikey Tucker was contacted, but we have not received a response.

A resigned sigh escaped my lips as I handed the magazine back to Leroy.

"All this bull crap they're sayin' 'bout you true?"

"Depends on what part you're calling bullshit."

"That girl you're with in the photo. She's the one who works at Rudy's." His words came out more matter of fact than questioning.

I nodded.

Leroy pouted, seemingly in approval, as he nodded. "I like 'er. Don't fuck that up."

I chuckled, ready to brush him off, but he continued.

"I see you bringin' in those women all the time, and I gotta say, I think that whole skirt chaser thing you got goin' on is a big ol' steaming pile of horse shit."

"I—"

"Y'wanna know what I think?" He paused as he stood, his rickety knees shaking as he pointed a gnarled finger at me. "I think you just want someone to love you. And you're lookin' for it in all the wrong places, boy." Without giving me a second glance, he went back to flipping through the tabloid, leaving me utterly speechless.

I went into my trailer and immediately dialed my agent's number. He picked up on the second ring.

"This is Travis."

"Have you seen the magazine article that came out about me and Juniper?" I demanded.

"I have."

Annoyance prickled at my skin. "And? What are we going to do about it?"

"We'll stay on top of it, I promise. Just keep laying low, and it should blow over. It wouldn't hurt to spend more time with the girl. I know it looks bad, but if people continue to see you together, they might accept it and back off."

My brows furrowed. Was he implying that he didn't believe it was real, either?

"We'll handle it, Mikey. I've gotta go, but we'll talk soon, okay?"

My phone beeped in my ear as the call ended, and I huffed out a deep breath.

"Where's your girlyfriend?" Jake asked me as he took a seat at the dining table in Ellison and Colter's place.

Shrugging, I pulled out a chair for myself.

"What, you win the bet then drop her already?" Colter laughed.

"No." I glared at him. "We're in a relationship, not attached at the hip. We can spend time without each other."

"Yeah, Colt. It's actually healthy not to spend every waking hour with your significant other." Reid nudged him in the ribs.

"Yeah, yeah. Can't blame a man for being obsessed with his wife." Colter gazed longingly at Ellison, who was across the room.

"Give him a break, guys. It's only been a few days since we got back. I'd need a break from Mikey, too, if I had to spend six weeks with him," Ellison teased, sticking out her tongue when I rolled my eyes.

"You should bring her over for dinner again. A bit of a redo of the first time." Colter scratched the back of his head.

Ellison nodded, her smile beaming. "That's a great idea! Next week?"

"Yeah, that sounds great, Ellie," Reid agreed, followed by Hayden and Jake nodding their approval.

"Maybe we can have a potluck-style dinner?" Hayden suggested. "I always feel bad that you're the only one who cooks."

"I'll have to see what she's doing, but I'm sure that'll be fine." I was all for the idea of spending more time with Juniper, especially after my conversation with Travis. I just didn't know how she felt about spending time with me outside our agreed upon timeframe.

"Hey, next time Isa's in town, you guys should host. Give Ellison a break," Jake added.

It was subtle, but Reid cringed. "Isa may be good at baking, but she's an awful cook. We can host, but it won't be her doing the cooking, it'll be me. Probably throw something on the grill."

"She makes the *best* cookies, but I had to learn the hard way when we were in college that the girl cannot make a meal to save her life. If I didn't learn how to make more dishes, we'd have been living off buttered noodles, microwave meals, and sourdough bread." She laughed, and the rest of us let out a chuckle, too, knowing Isa well enough to know Ellison's recollection was probably accurate.

"Did you guys see that stupid article they had about me in that one gossip magazine?" I asked once the chatter had quieted down.

Jake snorted. "Yeah, *Bull Riding Bad Boy has a Baddie?* That shit's gold."

I rolled my eyes. "Man, they can't just leave me in peace."

"Maybe when you're dead, Michael." Ellison patted me on the back in mock reassurance. "Just imagine how much buzz they'll make at your wedding one day." She raised a brow then looked at each of the guys' expressions then flicked her gaze back to me. "You do want to get married one day, right? Settle down?"

I thought about what old Leroy said to me.

"Maybe. Probably." *Yes. Not right now, but someday, yes.*

"Well, shit, I mean, you and Juniper looked good together in Houston," Colter noted. "She's a nice girl."

"She's cool, Mike," Hayden added in agreement before he disappeared into the kitchen to help Ellison and Colter bring out plates, silverware, and food.

I grinned, and all the emotions swirling through my head—relief…longing—were completely genuine. "I think she's pretty cool, too."

juniper

We'd been back in Silver Creek for about a week after our small stint on the road. The minute I stepped back into Rudy's, I was able to pick my position up right where I left off. The way Liv and Nico looked at me, however, was the biggest indication that things had changed. As were the questions I got from them.

"Do you realize that you're literally rodeo royalty?" Liv squealed the second she saw me. She pulled me in for a hug, despite my protests, and Nico bounced right into the conversation, sidling up close—shoulder-to-shoulder close—to Liv when we broke apart from our hug.

I'd only been gone a month and a half, but the dynamic between them seemed different. Flirtatious almost.

"You were on the local news like five times, and you're all over social media. They can't get enough of you."

I rolled my eyes. "I'm sure they're not interested in *me*. They just want the inside scoop on Mikey's life."

"Which you are now a part of," Liv pointed out.

I sighed. Our agreement was supposed to be over, save

for the day or two we'd spend together next month, but there was no way we could end it now with all the media attention we were getting. Mikey's status was higher than ever, and it was looking to be just the publicity boost he needed to get people off his back.

I hadn't seen him in person, or even really talked to him other than the odd text every now and then, since we'd gotten back to Silver Creek. I wasn't sure if it was because he didn't have time or didn't want to see me. Surprisingly, no questions from Natalie, Ellison, or his other friends had come up, although Ellison did forward me the link to an article that media sources and social media influencers were calling "juicy." It was all the same thing Mikey'd been dealing with since before I came into the picture, except this time I was also involved.

Is it just another one of Tucker's flings that will fizzle out before it has the chance to burn? the article had asked.

I rolled my eyes, clenching my jaw just thinking about the salacious article. I wondered who the "anonymous source" was that gave them my full name. Not that it was really a secret to the droves of people who had followed me before I made my account private and changed my username. The source could be *anyone*, but I was afraid they were closer to me than I thought.

I finally replied, "I suppose I am."

"I want to know all the details. Where did you sleep? What did you do when Mikey wasn't competing? Was the rodeo ah-may-zing?" Liv fired off all her questions all at once, and I recoiled a bit.

"Livvy, give the girl some space." Nico chuckled, nudging her playfully with his elbow.

She rolled her eyes at him, but her cheeks flushed, too.

Before I could make a comment about the two of

them, he continued. "Just kidding. I also want to know things. Did you meet any other famous bull riders?"

"I slept in his trailer?" My response to Liv's question came out more like a question, because how was I supposed to answer that? It wasn't like I could say I slept on the pullout couch because the relationship—like the tabloids suspected—was never real. "We went to the bars a lot, and then Mikey and I went mini golfing one day, which sounds a lot worse than it actually was. The rodeo was actually really fun. I didn't meet any other famous bull riders. To be completely honest, I couldn't tell you the name of a single bull rider other than Mikey."

"Aw, that's sweet! It's like you're only focused on him." Liv swooned so hard I thought she might fall over into Nico's arms. "What else happened? Anything scary?"

"Actually, the night in Utah it stormed, and it rained so hard I was surprised they didn't stop the rodeo. Mikey made it to eight seconds, but the bull charged after him, and I don't think I took a breath until he was out of the arena."

"Whoa." Nico's eyes widened, and Liv threw her hand over her mouth.

I was sure they'd asked me more questions, but the only thing I could think about was cooking dinner in the trailer and everything that happened after. It wasn't sex, but the small intimate gestures filled my stomach with butterflies.

"Did something *else* happen?" Liv gaped. "You're *blushing!*"

"What? No!" Even though I denied it, Nico and Liv's faces told me I was caught in the act.

Guilty.

But by the grace of God, before they could interrogate

me some more, a customer—a man I'd never seen before —walked through the front doors of the bar.

"I'll help this gentleman," I quickly rattled out, despite Liv's, "June, wait," before they could double team me and have one of them actually work while the other continued to grill me. "Hello, sir. What can I do for you?"

"Are you Juniper Ray?" he asked, standing a few feet from the bar, not bothering to sit.

"I, uh…" I hesitated, stumbling over my words.

"Is that Juniper Ray over there?" He pointed at Liv.

I tilted my head, confusion rushing through me. This whole interaction was raising red flags for me, especially with the article that just came out.

"I'm not comfortable giving out that information, sir. Is there anything I can get for you?" I politely stated, trying to recover from my speech mishap.

"You sure you're not Juniper Ray?" The man continued to push as he walked directly up to the bar.

"Sir, this isn't appropriate, and if this continues, I'm going to have to ask you to leave." Even though my words were intended to sound firm, they came out a bit wobbly and unsure.

Instead of leaving like any normal person would, he reached over the bar and grabbed my wrist.

"Hey!" Nico yelled, storming over to my defense. "I don't know who you are, man, but you need to leave right now."

The man relented, yelling in Nico's face, "I'm not leaving until I find out the information I need about Juniper Ray and Mikey Tucker!"

I flinched, jumping back as the few patrons in the bar got up from their seats to help.

All I could do was stand there frozen as it turned into a

full-on screaming match, the man, who I now assumed was a reporter of some kind—or a crazed fan—flinging his arms around to avoid the gentlemen who were trying to lead him out of the bar.

In the midst of the chaos, Nico wrapped his arm around Liv, guiding her to the back office out of harm's way and presumably to call the police.

The disruption must have been loud enough to hear from the street, because the front door flung open and the Silver Creek boys barged through. Where they'd come from, I wasn't entirely sure, but what I did know was that Mikey's face was written with murder, anger painting his features.

"Hackett, you need to get out of here right now before I do something I'll regret."

I'd seen Mikey get annoyed with reporters and cameramen before, but that was nothing compared to this. His nostrils flared and reddish-pink streaks crept into his cheeks. His strides had an urgency to them, wasting no time getting to me.

"Oh, yeah? I'd like to see you—"

Hackett's response was cut short by Mikey's fist connecting with his nose.

"Ow! What the fuck?" Blood ran from Hackett's nose, and he brought up his sleeve to wipe it away.

The split second he was dazed gave Colter and Reid enough time to grab hold of his arm and lead him out of the bar.

"Mikey!" I gasped. Mikey was shaking out his hand. "What the hell? Why was your first thought to punch him instead of, I don't know, calling the police?"

"They were already on the way. Liv called." Nico appeared around the corner at the same time Mikey blurted out, "Juniper, he was harassing you. He wouldn't shut his mouth, and I warned him."

I glanced back and forth between the two guys.

"Let me get you some ice for that," Nico offered, pointing at Mikey's hand, like this was a normal occurrence.

"Thanks, man." Mikey nodded in acknowledgment.

My jaw dropped. In what world was this normal? "Can someone explain to me what's going on? How do you know him?"

A sigh slipped from Mikey's mouth. "He's slimy. Used to work for a newspaper in Billings, but they caught him doing shady practices, so now he's trying to do whatever he can to get back in good graces. No one will hire him, so he thinks his best bet is finding the most scandalous story out there to do an exposé on."

Understanding hit me. "And you just happen to be the hottest topic in Montana right now."

"Yep." Shooting me a reassuring glance, he added, "Don't worry about him, I'll take care of it. He won't bother you again. By the way, Ellison invited us over for dinner tomorrow."

"Both of us?" My eyes widened.

Nico came back, handing Mikey a small bag of ice, which he quickly grabbed before placing a kiss on my cheek.

"Of course. We're a package deal, don't you know?" He winked and followed Colter and Reid to the door, turning around at the last minute to announce, "I'll pick you up at six!"

Nico and Liv both said they could handle the bar and told me to go home after the scene Hackett made, so I packed up my stuff and drove back to Natalie's house.

She was waiting for me when I walked through the front door, arms folded across her chest.

"Hi," I greeted her.

She gave me a blank look in return.

"What's up?" I asked, acting as cool, calm, and collected as I could.

"Are you sure this whole thing is worth it? I mean, why are you going through all this trouble of being in the public eye just to get back at your shitty ex? You're getting assaulted by reporters—"

I cut in. "I got assaulted by *a* reporter."

"You shouldn't be getting assaulted at all!"

Well, she had a point there.

"Mikey took care of it." I shrugged her off, heading toward my bedroom.

"Took care of it, how? By punching him?"

I looked over my shoulder, a sarcastic grin on my face. "Exactly."

CHAPTER TWENTY-SIX

Normally, Miles City and Silver Creek were pretty quiet. Everyone respected others' privacy. But with the stir that Juniper and I caused in Houston, I wasn't necessarily surprised that people were talking about us. I didn't think any other reporters would bother coming out to Montana, but I'd be keeping a watchful eye.

Luckily, word about me clocking Hackett didn't get out, but I'd informed Travis about the situation in case something did arise. I thought Hackett was too scared he'd be run out of town, though, if he published anything or went to other news sources—not that they'd believe him anyway. He was trouble, and everyone in town knew it. I may have gotten into a few squabbles myself, but they were always in defense of myself or someone else, never as the initial aggressor.

Ellison had teased me once about how violence was never the answer and I should think with my brain before my fists, but we all knew she'd do the same thing. The girl was ruthless.

Dinner was tonight, but I had a few hours before I'd

need to go pick up Juniper, so I headed to the gym to work off some of my pent-up emotions.

Instead of hitting the weights, though, I wanted to focus on endurance. I didn't work out to get big and bulky like most guys. Believe it or not, size actually did matter when it came to riding bulls. Being smaller was an advantage in controlling the animal. Sure, a small number of guys were tall, but they were thin and didn't weigh much.

At five-foot-eight, I weighed in at around one hundred fifty pounds.

While roughstock riders typically were on the lighter side, athletes in other events—especially bulldoggers—were usually bulkier. That's why, while our workouts were similar in some ways, Colter, Reid, Hayden, and Jake had different focus areas when they were in the gym.

I also did a lot of cardio—inside and outside of the gym. While I wasn't a big fan of running, I occasionally did a HIIT program or cycling workout.

Today, the gym was a bit busier than normal with some college kids occupying the weights and machines. A few eyes latched on me when I walked in the door, but I ignored them as I walked toward one of the studio rooms where they occasionally had fitness classes.

After warming up, I started interval training, rotating between squats, planks, pushups, box jumps, and jump rope. Sweat dripped down my back as I ran through a few cycles of exercises.

To finish out the day, I hopped on a stationary bike, cycling at various speeds and resistance levels.

Muscles spent, I hopped in the shower to get ready to pick up Juniper for dinner. Steam enveloped my body as I stood in the stream of water, a heavy sigh leaving my lips.

A picture of her naked flashed through my mind, and I leaned forward, resting one of my forearms on the tile wall as my other hand reached for my hardening cock.

As I gripped the shaft, I pictured her pretty, pink lips wrapped around me and stroked the length, desperate to relieve the want for her building in my chest. I imagined myself thrusting into her mouth, the tip hitting the back of her throat, and the sounds she'd make.

God, she would look perfect choking on my cock. I regretted not letting her suck my dick the first time we hooked up, now knowing the fantasy may never actually happen. I wanted to take a fistful of her hair and tug on the strands until she was moaning my name around me.

There were so many things I wanted to do to her in so many places.

I squeezed tighter, wishing it was Juniper's pussy wrapped around me instead of my hand.

My head dipped until my forehead was also pressed against the wall.

The pressure in my balls built as I started climbing closer and closer to coming, my breathing coming out in low, desperate pants combined with her name falling off my lips. In my daydream, Juniper threw her head back as I fucked her, her tight, wet pussy clenching around me until she came undone. Hot, sticky cum shot into my hand, dripping down onto the floor, and my eyes rolled back.

I kept fucking my hand until every last drop was spent and I came back to reality, chest heaving harder now than it was during my workout.

When I got to Juniper's house, Natalie let me in, although she did frown, narrowing her eyes when she first saw me.

"She's in her room. Down the hall to the left." Her monotone voice caught me off guard a bit—I wasn't sure what I'd done to get that response—but I was determined to win Natalie over.

I dipped my chin in gratitude. "Thanks."

She eyed me up and down as I stepped past her, taking off my boots and heading down the hallway where she told me Juniper's room was.

I paused outside the door, ready to knock as to not startle her, when a soft noise from inside caught me off guard. A noise that sounded a lot like buzzing followed by a moan.

"Mmm." Juniper hummed.

I debated in my head whether or not to open the door. I didn't want to embarrass her or intrude, or break any of our pre-established rules, but when my name fell off her lips next, I turned the handle, finding Juniper with a neon pink vibrator between her legs.

Her eyes widened, and she shut off the toy while also moving to cover herself, but I stopped her, closing the door behind me.

"Don't stop on my account." A smirk tugged on my lips. The fact she was thinking about me stroked my ego a little. I leaned against the wall, my dick swelling in my jeans.

For the first time ever, she looked almost shy, like she was ashamed to have been caught.

"I—" she stumbled, as though she wasn't sure what to say.

Instead of letting her sit there any longer, I walked over to the bed, threw the covers off her, and admired her naked body, something I hadn't been able to do since the first night we got together.

Her mouth opened and closed, then opened again. "What are you doing?"

"Don't play, Peach. I heard you say my name."

She rolled her eyes, crossing her arms. "What about the rules? And I didn't think you wanted to see—"

I cut her off. "Fuck the rules." I took a deep breath. "Of course, I wanted to see you. I'm taking you to dinner with my friends tonight. I wanted to give you time, though. We'd just spent a month and a half together."

"Oh." She pulled her bottom lip between her teeth. "I guess, I just thought…I don't know. We have rules in place and…"

I picked up the vibrator, turning it on and crawling onto the bed in front of her. "Juniper, baby, I can't stand not having you. That first night wasn't enough for me, will never be enough for me." I laid my hand on her knee, gently pushing her legs apart. "If you don't want this, tell me. I'll stop. But I'd be damned if I said I didn't want to make you come right here, right now. Let me make you feel good."

She was silent, and for a second I worried I was pushing too far. Maybe I was being reckless, but I needed to know if she wanted me as much as I wanted her.

"Tell me what you want, Juniper."

She sighed, like she was fighting a battle within herself, but her eyes—shining with want—gave her away. "You. I want you."

That was all the confirmation I needed as I brought the tip of the vibrator to her clit, her head falling back with the contact. I applied more pressure, turning up the intensity of the vibration, and she let out a moan, her legs squeezing together.

Placing one knee on the inside of her thigh and my hand on the other, I separated her legs, holding them apart to restrain their movement.

Her thighs trembled under my grasp, and her hands fisted the sheets as a breathy mess of words fell from her lips.

"Hold this right there and don't move it," I commanded as I gave her the toy and got up from the bed to discard my clothes. My cock was rock hard in my pants, and I needed to ease some of the pressure. I pulled my shirt over my head and unbuttoned my jeans, letting them fall to the floor. My boxers went next, my cock springing out of them. By the time I crawled back up to the bed, Juniper looked like she was on the verge of an orgasm, her toes curling and expletives coming out of her mouth.

With one hand, I took the vibrator back, rubbing circles with it over her slick entrance, her arousal coating the tip. The other hand wrapped around my length, stroking it as I watched her squirm beneath me.

"I-I'm going to c-come," she stammered before moaning loud enough that I was sure her roommate heard.

"Let go, Peach." All it took were those three words and she fell apart, liquid flooding into a pool between her legs.

"F-fuck," she gasped. "I've never done that before."

I shut off the vibrator, tossing it aside as I brought my hand up to my mouth, spitting into it. I rubbed it up and down my cock, even though I was sure she was wet enough that we wouldn't need the extra lube.

"It was hot as fuck. But I want you to come on my cock. Bare. Can you do that for me?"

She nodded, pulling her bottom lip between her teeth.

"You know I'm clear. I haven't been with anyone since we started our arrangement and I got tested shortly after as well. Please, can I have you bare?"

"Yes. Yes, I want that. I haven't been with anyone but you in a while. And I'm on birth control."

A strangled noise rose from my throat as I guided my tip toward her slit, her pussy still dripping from her orgasm. My cock slid in with ease, and we both moaned at the sensation of me filling her. I thrust my hips forward until I buried myself to the hilt then paused, catching my breath and planting a gentle kiss on her lips.

"What's wrong, Casanova? I wouldn't think you'd be out of breath so easily," she taunted.

"Just getting started." I grabbed her hands, pinning them above her head as I pulled back then slammed myself inside her again and again.

The sound of skin against skin filled the room, and she became even wetter and slick as I pounded into her.

She wrapped her legs around my middle, creating an even deeper angle. Her eyes rolled back as I hit her G-spot, and she begged for more.

I released her hands from my grip and turned her body to the side, hooking one ankle over my shoulder and slamming into her at an angle. The pressure building in my balls was almost too much, but I wasn't going to come until she did. I willed myself not to, even as her pussy clenched around me, tight and hot and wet.

"Fuck me harder, faster, please." The plea fell from her lips like a prayer, and I almost came from her words alone. Flipping her over completely so her ass was in the air, I grabbed her hips and pulled her closer to me with each thrust.

"Soak my cock, Peach. Drown me. Let everyone in this town know you're mine."

Three more strokes and she detonated around me as my cock twitched and I spilled inside her, still pistoning my hips as she cried out my name.

Once I was spent, I collapsed on top of her, sweat dripping down my temples. I pressed my lips to her forehead.

"What are we doing, Mikey?" she sighed.

Not answering her question, I kissed her, nibbling on her bottom lip. She let out a soft breath, parting her lips and allowing me to slip my tongue in her mouth.

"What are the odds your roommate will catch us walking to the shower?" I mumbled against her mouth.

"She probably left the moment you walked in the bedroom." She giggled.

"Perfect." After getting off the bed, I scooped her up into my arms and walked her into the bathroom, where I got on my knees and worshipped her again until she fell apart under the hot spray of the shower.

juniper

Whatever stability our set of rules had provided us in this arrangement just crumbled to the ground. The no-sex rule was put into place for a reason—a good one, in my opinion. We'd just opened a new door, one I knew would be impossible to completely close again.

The only rules we had left—the only ones we hadn't thrown to the wind—were our exclusivity and not developing feelings. And I was starting to worry that the fake feelings wouldn't be so fake anymore after what happened today.

I toweled off my hair then took a comb to it, attempting to get out all of the tangles and knots.

"Fuck!" I grumbled, tossing the comb onto the bathroom counter after ripping out a few chunks of hair.

"Let me," Mikey offered, picking up the hair tool I'd discarded and standing behind me.

"How would you know how to—" I quickly ate my words as he gently raked the comb through my hair, being careful not to tug on the strands too hard. I closed my eyes as he worked on all of the tangled parts, the teeth blissfully massaging my head.

When he was satisfied, he ran the comb through the silky locks a few times, making it look nice and neat.

"Don't tell me you can braid hair next." I snorted, wondering what the odds were.

"Nah, I know my limits, but if you wanted me to, I would learn." He winked, handing me back the comb before he left the bathroom.

I quickly threw my hair in a loose braid then went into my room to change for dinner. For whatever reason, I turned around when I dropped my towel to put on undergarments, but Mikey grabbed my hips, spinning me around to face him.

"Mmm," he hummed, wetting his lips as he took me in. "Fuck, my girlfriend is hot."

I laughed, not bothering to correct him as I lightly pushed him away. "Let me get dressed or we'll never make it to dinner in time."

"Fine, fine. Ellison will have my head if we're late." That still didn't stop him from reaching out to give my boobs a squeeze, flicking a nipple as he pulled his hand away.

A jolt traveled up my body to the space between my legs, but I shook myself out of it.

Dinner. We're going to dinner.

Colter and Ellison's place was as rowdy as I remembered it, but it would be out of character for the Silver Creek boys not to be loud and make their presence known.

"Hi! Good to see you again." Ellison, to my surprise, pulled me into a hug when we walked through the front door. She didn't strike me as a hugger, though from the stories I'd heard, she definitely softened up a bit when she met Colter.

"Thanks for having me back."

"Sorry for the way the last one went. I promise we're all cool now." She let out a biting laugh, seemingly an attempt at a self-deprecating joke.

"Where do you want me to put this?" I held out the case of beer and a box of cookies Mikey had picked up from the store.

"I can take those from you, Juniper." Colter appeared behind Ellison, dropping a kiss on her shoulder before throwing out a teasing, "Damn, Mikey, you make these cookies yourself?"

"Yeah, I spent all morning on them, so you better be nice about it," he joked right back. "Wanna go sit on the couch?"

I nodded, kicking off my shoes at the door before following him to the living room. I hadn't really been able to get a close look at the Carson house when I was here the first time. I was a bit more focused on making a decent impression.

They had a nice home, one I knew they'd done several renovations on over the past couple years. The living room was pretty spacious, with a big L-shaped couch in front of a TV stand and some small bookshelves housing only a handful of books.

Mikey plopped down on the couch next to Hayden and Jake, who had a baseball game on the TV.

"Man, my team is ass this year," Jake grumbled.

"Who's your team?" I asked. I wasn't a baseball fan, so I didn't even know the teams that were playing right now.

"The Wranglers."

"Ah."

Well, he wasn't wrong. The Warden Wranglers were currently losing eight to one in the seventh inning.

"I mean, that's what you get for rooting for a team like Warden, Wyoming." Mikey leaned his weight onto Jake to nudge him.

"It's called team loyalty. You should try it sometime." Jake nudged him back. "At least I don't switch teams every season based on who's winning. I've been a Wranglers fan since they were good."

"Yeah, and that was, what? Fifteen years ago?" Reid piped up from the kitchen.

"They'll make a comeback."

"Yeah, and hell will freeze over." Hayden chuckled.

"Aye, well you guys were saying that about Mikey finding a girlfriend, too, and look what happened there," Jake rebutted, pointing at me with his thumb. "Hey, I guess you won the——"

"Shut up about it." Mikey glared at Jake as though he didn't want him to finish his sentence.

"Won what?" I asked out of curiosity, even though I probably didn't want to know.

"It's nothing, don't worry about it. Jake's just mad because his team is ass and hasn't had a winning season since he was in middle school."

I hummed, not quite believing what Mikey was saying, but before I could say anything, something happened on the TV that had Jake jumping up from his seat and yelling.

"Let's goooo!" He fist pumped in the air. "Home run, baby!"

"Are you a big sports fan?" Hayden asked me.

I wrinkled my nose. "Not really."

They all laughed.

"Well, that's going to change if you keep hanging out with us," Colter stated, a bit too confidently.

"Yeah, we'll see about that." I gritted my teeth at the thought.

"Y'all ready for dinner yet?" Ellison called. "My stomach feels like it's going to eat itself."

"We'd better go, then." Colter laughed. "Come on, guys, we all know Warden's not going to win."

"They could make a comeback!" Jake protested right as the team the Wranglers were playing hit a home run with a player on every base, scoring four more points. He clamped his mouth shut, snapping off the TV. "Uh, never mind, that's enough of that for today."

Mikey patted him on the back before standing and extending a hand. "It's okay, Jakey. Maybe one day when pigs fly the Wranglers will have a winning season."

Jake grumbled as we all found our seats at the table. Having a potluck dinner was the right move, because there was plenty of food for all seven of us.

Colter had grilled burgers and hot dogs, someone brought a few bags of chips, Reid—I think—brought some kind of baked mac and cheese, and we also had an assortment of fruit and vegetables. Oh, and several cases of beer.

Around the table, cans of beer were cracked open and plates were passed around. I grabbed a hamburger bun and patty, loading it up with lettuce, pickles, tomato, ketchup, and mustard.

"We doing the horse racing again this year?" Jake grinned from ear to ear.

"What do you mean *we*? And *again*? If I remember correctly, you didn't do shit last year." Colter gave him a pointed look.

"Horse racing?" I asked.

"*Wild* horse racing," Ellison answered. "Last year, Colter, Reid and Mikey won it."

"What exactly is it?" I asked.

"Here, let me show you." Jake grabbed his phone and pulled up a video of the wild horse racing.

My eyes widened. "Oh?"

Jake smirked. "Looks fun, doesn't it?"

"You and Hayden can do it with Mikey this year, then. I'm not doing that shit again." Reid shook his head, raising his hands in defense.

Hayden also shook his head. "I'm good."

"Aw, come on, guys. You're no fun!" Mikey whined. "We could win the whole thing again!"

"Easy for you to say, you didn't have to try to hold a horse last time." Reid paused. "That's what I don't understand. You said you're afraid of horses, but last year you rode one!"

"To be fair, I was pretty drunk." Mikey shrugged.

Ellison and I exchanged amused looks as the men engaged in a back and forth debate of why they should or should not participate in the Bucking Horse Sale tradition.

"I think I have to work anyway, so I won't get to witness it." I spoke the realization out loud.

"There you go, then." Reid gestured with his hand. "No need to show off for your girlfriend."

"I'm sure ol' Rudy would let you leave for an hour," Mikey protested.

I shook my head. "I'm not going to do that to them. It's all right, I'll see it next time."

Mikey's head snapped toward me, surprise flaring in his eyes. We both knew there probably wouldn't be a next time, but we could at least pretend, right?

"Anyway, no one's really filled me in on this event, other than it gets rowdy and I can expect the bar to be packed." I changed the subject.

"Rowdy's an understatement." Ellison rolled her lips. "How many times have you been arrested during it, Mikey?"

"Pfft. Only once…or twice…or thrice."

My mouth gaped. "Three times?"

"In my defense, two of those times were because I was defending my friends. I can't really speak for the other one, though." He laughed, and the other guys snickered under their breath, clearly recalling whatever inside joke they had.

"Do I even want to know?"

"Probably not," Hayden admitted with a soft smile.

CHAPTER TWENTY-EIGHT

Don't feel pressured to get on a horse or anything today." I squeezed Juniper's hand as we drove out to Reid's place.

"What if I say I'll only get on a horse if you do?" she teased with a wicked grin on her face.

"Then there *definitely* won't be any horseback riding from either of us."

She scoffed. "That's so lame. I thought riding horses was good for bull riders. I read that it helps with rhythm."

My brows rose. "You've been researching bull riding?"

"Just to understand it better. Don't let it go to your head, tough guy."

Oh, I was *absolutely* letting it go to my head. Both of them, actually. I'd never known anyone else to show that level of interest, not enough to go out of their way to learn more about the sport. Most girls were just interested in the fact that *I* was a bull rider, not the actual act of bull riding. And coming from Juniper, a girl who was probably the least sports fan I knew, it meant the world.

"Tough guy, huh? That's a new one."

Juniper tapped her lips with her finger as she tilted her head to the side. "You know, I take that back. A tough guy would face his fear of horses and get on the back of one."

"You don't think riding bulls is tough enough?" I teased, and her entire face flushed.

"Well, yes, but I just think if you can ride bulls, then a horse should be nothing."

"The day you get on a bull, Peach, will be the day I get on a horse. Deal?" I dared. "And not a mechanical one."

"Are you sure you want to wager that? I'm braver than you think, Tucker."

"I don't doubt it for a second."

When we took the turn onto Reid's property, I could already hear them bantering in the arena, throwing around playful insults.

I parked the pickup behind Colter's and killed the ignition. "Ready?"

Juniper nodded, and I hopped out of the truck, locking the doors before she had the opportunity to open it herself.

"You still haven't learned, have you, Peach?" I teased as I grabbed the door for her, helping her out of the truck, even though I knew she was fully capable.

She shrugged. "Guess I'm just not used to it."

I shook my head. Who was the asshole who let her open her own door? Didn't matter who she was, if I was pissed at her, or what she'd done to me. I was still holding the door for a lady.

"Well"—I planted a kiss on her cheek—"better get used to it."

I reached for her hand as we walked over to the arena where Reid and Colter were getting in a run. Colter roped the head as we stepped up to the arena fence, and Reid quickly caught the legs.

"Damn," Juniper whispered. "They're good at that."

I nodded. "They're in the top fifteen in the world for a reason."

Even though we competed in different events, I found myself in awe of Colter and Reid often. I knew they didn't like to talk about it—just like I didn't like to talk about my feelings—but they had shit that they'd dealt with in the past five years and still managed to come out on top and win gold buckles. And they were able to do it with the support of Ellison and Isabelle by their sides.

I knew there wasn't a rush or a perfect timeline on settling down. There wasn't a magical age to get married and start having babies. I also didn't think I was ready for it yet—felt like I still had a lot of life left to live on my own—but the past couple months with Juniper had me thinking it was at least possible.

More and more, I was wanting that future to be possible with *her*.

But I also knew she was young and had a lot of life ahead of her, too. I knew at twenty-two that I didn't want to get married yet. That obviously still rang true at thirty-one. Juniper was smart, damn smart, and I didn't want to get in the way of her goals. I had a feeling she wouldn't expect me to give up bull riding for her if we were in a real relationship, and I sure as hell wasn't expecting her to uproot her life for me any more than she already had for this arrangement.

"What are you thinking about?" She squeezed my hand, breaking me out of my thoughts.

"Oh, you know, deep shit like existence and the meaning of life."

Juniper rolled her eyes, and I winked, knowing it was all bullshit but not quite wanting to let her into that corner of my brain. Those would stay inside thoughts. For the sake of both her heart and mine.

I told myself it was because I didn't want her to get her hopes up, but really, I think it was just a reminder for me.

Rule number four. Absolutely no—under any circumstances—falling in love.

Too bad that ship had already begun to sail.

"Ready!" Hayden called from atop his horse. Ellison was in the box on the other side of him, and I was manning the chute. He nodded, and I released the steer, its feet pounding against the dirt as it sprinted toward the other end of the arena. Juniper stood next to me, watching in awe as Hayden and Ellison expertly roped the steer.

"That was about nine-point-six seconds." Colter looked at his stopwatch. "Truly, that's not bad, honey," he reassured her as disappointment fell over her face.

"You have to remember, we do this for a living. You're just doing it for fun and practice," Reid reminded her.

Ellison was as competitive as they came. She hated being bad at things, and she hated losing even more. It made beating her in pool and darts even more fun.

"I know. I just want to be able to keep up with you guys."

"No, you just want to be able to say you kicked our asses." Colter chuckled, to which she pushed her lips outward and bobbed her head to the side in agreement.

"Mikey, your turn?" Ellison grinned as she rode her horse over to the fence line.

I shook my head. "When are you gonna learn, woman? The answer is and always will be no."

"I've become accustomed to saying, 'Never say never,' Michael. I figure if I bother you enough about it, you'll get sick of me asking and finally just do it."

"I've been trying to get him to do it, too." Juniper sighed. "What if you just *touch* one?"

I made a dramatic show of shaking my head, yet again. "Nope. I'm good right here, at least ten feet away from that thing."

Juniper looked to Colter, Ellison, and Reid. "Can I ride one?"

"Uh, yeah. Come here." Reid gestured for her to follow him over to where one of Colter's horses, Trigger, was.

She looked over her shoulder at me, a beaming smile plastered onto her features.

"I like her a lot." Ellison had moved to stand by me. "I think she's good for you."

"I do, too."

That was what I was most afraid of.

From afar, I watched as Reid taught Juniper all the basics. How to approach a horse, what not to do around them, and basic safety things. Juniper slowly reached out her hand to let Trigger sniff it, letting him become familiar with her.

Soon, she was hoisting herself up into the saddle. Reid walked a lap around the arena with her, just to make sure nothing happened, but she looked more and more confident with every turn.

"Come on, Mikey! This is fun!" She giggled.

I waved her off, still not convinced about the horse. I was just glad he was taking care of my girl and that she was happy.

After Juniper had her fill of horseback riding and I'd opened the chute a few more times for Colter, Reid, and Hayden, we set up some chairs on Reid's back porch. The sun was just starting to set, casting hues of orange, pink, and yellow across the western sky.

I pulled Juniper up on my lap, and she leaned back against me, her long hair tickling my jaw.

"How's working at Rudy's been for you?" Hayden asked.

"I actually really enjoy it. It's pretty laid back compared to some of the bars I've worked at in the past," she stated. "I also love working with Liv and Nico. They're fun. What do you think you guys would be doing if you weren't competing in the rodeo?"

"Ranching," Colter promptly declared. "My degree was in Farm and Ranch Management, so I was always going to end up back here."

"I probably would have ended up doing something similar," Reid replied. "But I don't know, I can't really see myself doing anything other than rodeo right now."

I waited for the others to answer, because I wasn't sure what I'd be doing.

Hayden mentioned that although he went to school to rodeo, he also got a degree in Business Management and Economics. Jake probably would have ended up in some blue collar field like construction or auto mechanics.

I didn't go to college, a fact that not many people knew. I graduated high school, but quickly started riding bulls, and the thought to get a degree never occurred to me. I wasn't sure where I'd be without bull riding. Maybe I'd still be roaming around, trying to find a purpose.

I was good with my hands, so I probably still would have found my way to a ranch or farm. Or I'd be working in a shop. I could have seen myself welding or being a carpenter for a living. Leather crafting also sounded interesting. I was also good with finances, having taken care of my own for the past decade or so.

I had options, should the bull riding thing not work out. I had to make it work out, though. If not for myself, then to prove everyone who'd ever doubted me wrong.

juniper

The weekend was quickly approaching, which meant the population of Miles City was about to double in size. Liv and Nico had started to mentally prepare me for the Bucking Horse Sale festivities. Based on what everyone had told me, I wasn't sure if I'd ever be ready for what I was about to witness.

With the Bucking Horse Sale this weekend, and Gulch Days the next, I had an action-packed week ahead.

Gulch Days was considered the summer kickoff celebration for my college town. It consisted of live music, trade shows, and food vendors, and occasionally they'd bring in a Ferris wheel and other carnival rides. It was like a smaller scale county fair—without the 4-H shows and exhibits, since that took place in mid to late August.

Today was my last day off for about five days. I'd work the weekend closing shifts before switching to day shifts, ending my week with a double right before we'd leave for Goldfinch.

Originally, I'd planned to have a day of doing

absolutely nothing, but then my phone buzzed on the kitchen counter.

TUCKER

I'm outside

What? Why?

TUCKER

Kidnapping you

Come outside

I walked over to the window to see if he was telling the truth, and sure enough, he was standing outside…in a pair of swim trunks.

Not bothering to put on a pair of shoes, I stepped outside, shielding my eyes from the sun as I exited the house.

"What are you doing here, and why are you wearing a swimsuit?"

"I'm kidnapping you so we can go spend the day by the creek. Go get dressed, unless you prefer skinny dipping." He wiggled his eyebrows suggestively. "You know I wouldn't mind either."

"I wasn't planning on doing anything today."

"Well, now you have plans. Come on, it'll be fun. Why relax at home when you can lay out in the sun, get a tan, and spend time with me?"

It was a fair point. Besides, I hadn't been down to the creek—the namesake of the place he lived—yet.

"Okay, be right back." I disappeared into the house. I slipped on my favorite purple bikini, some denim cutoffs, and flipflops, grabbing a towel and sunglasses before leaving Natalie a note and heading out the door.

Mikey whistled when I descended the stairs, and I shook my head at him.

"You look good, Peachy."

This time, I didn't bother trying to open my own door, remembering what he had said earlier in the week. It seemed to make him happy, and call me a romantic, but I liked seeing him that way. Mikey deserved good things, too.

The Silver Creek was exactly how I had imagined it, but when we drove past the pullout where several vehicles were parked, I looked at Mikey confused.

"I know a secret spot." He winked. "Trust me, this is going to be way better than the normal place people go."

About ten minutes later, we drove down a narrow gravel road surrounded by trees. The creek ran parallel to the trail, the soothing sound of water filling my ears.

We parked in a small clearing deep in the woods. When I took a good look around, I understood exactly why Mikey drove here. Trees loomed overhead, blocking out the harsh sun rays, while still allowing light to dapple on the ground. The creek widened into a swimming hole beneath, the water rippling, but not moving swiftly like the current downstream. Large, flat rocks lay near the bank, providing a peaceful area to sunbathe. A larger, ledge-like rock jutted out over the water, and on the other side stood a tree with a rope swing hanging from its wide branches.

"How did you find this place?" I spun around in awe, taking in everything. The birds chirped and the breeze rustled the trees, a natural orchestra for the breathtaking view.

"I was heading down to the creek one day to fish and ended up going too far. I might have even taken a wrong turn, but it led me here. I don't think Colter, Reid, and the others even know about this place. Colter might, but I've never seen him here, so I like to think it's my best-kept secret."

"You've never brought anyone here?" I didn't mean to sound surprised, but my mind immediately went to this being one of his hookup spots.

"No, never. You're the first."

"Well, I appreciate you showing me." I swayed on my feet.

Mikey's mouth curled up in a smirk as though a thought just dawned on him. "I'll race you to the rope swing."

"What do I get if I win?" One of my eyebrows shot up.

He thought about it for a minute. "Whatever you want."

I challenged his statement, for that could mean a lot of things. "*Anything?*"

"Within reason," he backpedaled.

"Mm, I think if I win, you have to get on a horse."

He dipped his chin, shaking his head. "You're relentless."

"So, is that a deal?"

"Fine." He huffed out a breath.

"Perfect!" I laughed as I shoved him to the side, making him lose his balance as I took off, sprinting around the edge of the water to the other side where the rope swing was. I unbuttoned my shorts in the process, discarding them on the ground so I was only in my swimsuit.

I looked over my shoulder as Mikey gained on me, his feet pounding against the earth.

Almost there.

I pushed forward, lungs burning as I extended my hand out, only a couple feet away from the rope swing.

"Oof!" Before I could grab the rope, strong arms

cradled my body, spinning me in the opposite direction. "Hey! That's cheating!" I screeched.

Mikey laughed in response. "And what you did back there wasn't?" He adjusted so he was holding me in one arm as the other brushed the rope, finalizing him as the winner.

"What do you get as the winner, then?" I asked.

"This." The mischievous look on his face gave away his plan, and I clawed at his arm, trying to free myself.

He lifted me so I was in his arms bridal style and walked over to the water.

"No! Please! No!" My voice came out in a high-pitched shriek, but it was no use. He swung me in his arms and tossed me in the water.

It wasn't as cold as I was expecting, but the chill still shocked my system when I hit the surface. I held my breath as I sank into the cool, clear water.

A few seconds later, I emerged from the water, hair soaked and swirling around my face. "That was *dirty*!" I yelled at Mikey.

As if throwing me into the swimming hole wasn't bad enough, I heard his cheer as he swung from the tree, cannonballing into the water and splashing me in the process.

When he popped up again, his hair clung to his forehead, almost covering his eyebrows.

I swam toward him, closing the distance between us. My arm reached out, brushing the hair out of his face then running the back of my hand along the stubble on his jawline and my thumb through his mustache. His hand closed over mine, warmth radiating through my body.

"That wasn't fair, you know," I teased, my voice barely a whisper.

"I know." He tucked a wet strand of hair behind my ear. "I'm going to kiss you now," he murmured before he leaned in, lips gently skimming mine.

I kissed him back, our mouths melding together in a hot, frenzied kiss. His hands gripped my waist and he pulled me even closer to him. I wrapped my legs around his middle, his length hardening.

I took a breath, and Mikey inched his tongue in, licking my teeth and catching me off guard. His laugh rumbled against my mouth, and I felt him smile. Knotting his hair in my hands, I let him deepen the kiss, our tongues tangling together.

He broke the kiss, lips traveling down my jaw and neck to my collarbone before reaching the swell of my breasts.

With one hand on the small of my back, he used the other one to slide the straps of my bikini off my shoulders, baring my breasts and hardening nipples. His mouth latched onto one, teeth grazing the sensitive peak, and I gasped, jolts of pleasure traveling down between my legs. I ground my hips against him, his cock rock solid beneath me.

"Fuck, Juniper," he moaned. "You drive me insane, you know that?"

With my legs still wrapped around him, he brought us over to a grassy area on the bank. Water droplets clung to our bodies, but the sun quickly warmed my skin. The only thing keeping my bikini top on was the loose bow I'd tied in the back, and Mikey took the liberty in completely removing it as he crawled atop me.

He skimmed the fabric between my legs, teasing me slowly before his fingers hooked inside the tiny strings of my swimsuit bottoms. He pulled them down my legs, baring me to him.

After brushing his mustache out of the way, he lowered himself down, licking a broad stroke up my center, eyes trained on mine the whole time. Slowly sliding a finger inside me, he rubbed my clit with his thumb. My hips bucked with the pressure, and he added another finger, pumping his digits to create an intense pleasure coursing through me.

"You taste like trouble, Peach." He moaned, the vibration on my clit sending my head reeling.

Fire pooled low in my abdomen, and I bit out a quick, "Please don't stop." My toes curled, heat building throughout my body as I climbed toward my orgasm.

When I came down from my high, he withdrew his fingers, sucking my release from them.

"Stand up," I ordered.

He raised his brows but did as I asked, standing as I knelt before him. My hands found his waistband, and I tugged down his shorts, his bulging cock springing free. Precum glistened on the tip, and I wet my lips.

I gripped the base, wrapping my hand around to stroke it a few times before I licked a long line up the shaft, swirling my tongue around the head. Mikey moaned, urging me to take his cock in my mouth.

At first, I thought the size was too big, too wide, but I adjusted, using both my hands in tandem with my mouth to enhance the sensation. My head bobbed up and down, drool rolling down the sides of his length, creating more lubricant for my hands.

Looking up at him and batting my lashes, I forced his cock deeper, until the tip hit the back of my throat.

"Juniper," he rasped, his hands fisting my hair, tugging on the strands.

One pushed my head forward, and I grabbed his hips

as he bucked them against my face, not wanting to gag. I fondled his balls as he fucked my face, pleasure painting his features as he threw his head back.

"God, I've been imagining this for weeks, Juniper. You have no idea how much I've wanted this."

I pulled him out of my mouth, spit dripping off the tip of his cock and down the side of my lips. "Oh, yeah?"

"This is so much better," he panted as I went down on him again, hollowing out my cheeks and moving my tongue as quickly as my mouth.

I moaned around him as his breathing caught in his throat. His cock twitched in my mouth, throbbing between my lips. I wanted him to fall apart, to be at my mercy.

"Juniper, Juniper," he panted. "I'm going to come."

I moved faster then, flicking my tongue against the tip, moaning and slurping around him. Hot, sticky cum flooded my mouth, and I took his length in my fist. He pulled his cock from my lips, his release dripping from the tip down my chin as I swallowed what was left.

Mikey tugged on my hair with one hand, while the other replaced mine on his cock.

"Open your mouth," he instructed.

I did, sticking out my tongue, and he jerked his cock until the rest of his cum spilled over my lips, down my throat.

I stood, looking him in the eyes and drawing my lip between my teeth.

"You're fucking incredible," he whispered as he wiped his cum off my lips before kissing me.

When he pulled back, I shot him a cocky grin. "I know."

CHAPTER THIRTY

We ended up not signing up for the wild horse racing this year, but that didn't stop us from going to watch.

After the horse racing, we planned to head over to Rudy's before it got too swamped with people. We'd leave right before the mutton bustin' in an attempt to beat the rush heading to the street dance and, inevitably, the bars.

"Ladies and gentlemen, we're starting our final wild horse race of the night!" The rodeo announcer introduced all of the teams and shortly after called for the crowd to count them down.

"I'm telling you guys, we should have entered this year. I really think we'd have won again," I complained as the teams struggled to even get their horses steady.

Reid shook his head. "If there's ever a next time, and emphasis on *if*, you'd have to hold one of the horses."

I wrinkled my nose. Fat chance I'd do that.

If I was being honest, a lot of the Bucking Horse Sale last year was a series of blurs—I didn't remember much—but I didn't think any amount of liquor would give me the courage to hold a horse's head. I didn't know what it was about them. Maybe it was their faces or their eyes, or how tall they were, but horses gave me the heebie-jeebies.

"Yeah, I don't know, that might require you to get over your fear of horses first, buddy," Colter teased.

"Maybe we just need to give you a couple shots then send you and Bullet on a nice long trail ride," Jake teased. "By the time you get back, you'll have sobered up. Exposure therapy or whatever they call it."

"Not *my* horse," Colter protested.

"Not mine, either!" Reid added with a grumble.

"That's all right, guys, no one needs to sacrifice their horse for me. I get enough rides as it is." I winked suggestively. "Mustache rides, specifically."

"Ew," Ellison groaned, conveniently having returned to our seats at that moment. "Please stop."

"Oh, grow up, Ellison." I rolled my eyes. "Sex is normal. Everyone has sex. You and Colter—this I know, because I'm pretty sure I walked into Colter's house and interrupted something that one time. Reid and Isa, probably. Hell, I'm sure Jake and Hayden even have sex."

Hayden's face turned bright red, and Jake started sputtering, asking why I was bringing him into this.

"I didn't mean with each other, but if that's the kind of thing you're into, then hell yeah, brother...brothers?" I added.

"*Please* stop talking about sex," Ellison begged.

"Damn, never thought I'd see the day you begged for me, Firecracker," I joked, earning myself a death glare from Colter.

"You know I'd punch you, Mikey, but I also know Ellison, and I wouldn't take an opportunity to clock you away from her either."

"I'm *just joking*!"

When the wild horse racing ended, we packed up our belongings and beelined it out of the fairgrounds, leaving our vehicles to walk downtown. The entire street was blocked off for the dance, so there was no point in trying to find new places to park.

A good crowd of people had already gathered, and the cover band had started playing in the middle of Main Street.

Despite my plans—which I assumed were well thought out—Rudy's was already pretty busy. It wasn't quite at the level it'd be in a few hours, but there were a lot more people than their normal occupancy.

Juniper was busy flitting from one end of the bar to the other, taking drink orders and pouring shots. Liv and Nico were also working, but Rudy wasn't here tonight.

I sidled up to the bar, leaning against it while I waited for Juniper to finish serving a customer.

"What can I—" she started to ask, her customer service voice laid on thick. "Oh, hi." She huffed out a sigh like it was the first moment she'd had to breathe tonight.

"Hey, pretty girl." I reached out, twirling a long strand of her blonde hair around my finger.

"Can I get anything for you guys?"

Reid, Jake, and Hayden had walked up behind me.

"We'll just do a few Coors Banquets," Reid answered.

"You want something?" she asked me directly.

"Nah, I'm good."

Her eyes widened. "You sure?"

"Yeah, I had a couple at the rodeo, so I'm quitting for the night. I want to be able to drive you home tonight."

"You don't have to do that. Natalie said she'd pick me up after she dropped me off earlier."

"Tell her she doesn't have to worry," I assured her.

Her facial expression shifted from confusion to suspicion. "Okay," she said, drawing out the word.

"We're going to play a round of pool, but I'll be back." I leaned over the bar to give her a quick peck on the cheek before joining the boys.

"Colt and Ellie are dancing, so someone will have to play with Mikey." Reid tossed us all pool sticks.

"Nose goes." Jake placed his finger on the bridge of his nose. Reid quickly followed, leaving Hayden as the odd man out.

He groaned. "I always get paired with Mikey. No offense."

I waved him off. "Eh, none taken. I guess I can't be good at *everything*."

"We'll let you guys go first." Jake gestured to the table.

Hayden went first, taking the break shot and hitting a solid ball into one of the pockets. He hit another one in then missed his third shot.

"Juniper looks like she fits in here just fine," Reid mentioned as he took his shot.

I nodded. "I think so, too. She's made good friends with Liv and Nico. And then she's got her other friend, Natalie, who she's living with, too."

"I swear we've seen her before. You sure you don't remember that?" Reid asked.

I shook my head, and he shrugged before continuing.

"You think you'll ever ask her to live with you? You've

clearly proven us all wrong, so Colter's scoping out that plot of land for you."

I thought about it for a second. I didn't even know if she was going to stay here. The easy answer would be yes. I would love for Juniper to stay in the area and pursue a *real* relationship with her now that our fake one had almost run its course, but I didn't know how she felt about it. The idea of not holding her back still rang true.

I didn't know if she wanted to end the arrangement to find someone better.

I didn't know if she was only still with me for the benefits.

I didn't know if I was just *fun* for her.

But I didn't say any of that. I just settled on, "Not sure," then lined up my own shot after Jake had taken his turn.

"Please don't hit the eight ball in," Hayden muttered.

"That was *one time!*" I protested as I pulled back my stick before striking and making contact with the cue ball. It bounced around the table a few times, not hitting any of the targets I'd actually intended and nearly brushing the eight ball. "See, I didn't hit the eight ball in."

"Let's get out of here." I grabbed Juniper's hand a few hours later after her shift ended and pulled her along, not wanting to waste any more time to get to the pickup parked back at the fairgrounds.

"But we were having so much fun back there," she teased.

We'd listened to the music for a little bit, but most of our time was spent standing in the corner of the bar watching the guys play pool.

"I have an idea that'll be more fun." I turned my head to look at her and smirked.

The fairgrounds were deserted when we got there. The sun had started to go down, casting an orange glow over the land.

When we reached the pickup, instead of opening the passenger door for Juniper, I spun her around to face me then backed her up so she was leaning against the front of the pickup. As I ran my hands up and down her arms, the only thoughts filling my mind were the list of things I wanted to do to her tonight.

"What are you thinking about, Casanova?"

My eyes met hers as I replied, "Just you."

She raised an eyebrow like she didn't believe me.

"And maybe a little about fucking you."

"That sounds better." Her tongue darted out to wet her lips, and she pushed up on her toes to kiss me.

Her fingers tangled in my hair, and my hands wandered down to her waist as our mouths collided. She tasted sweet, like the cherries in her drink tonight, and all I wanted to do was savor the taste as long as possible.

I pulled her bottom lip between my teeth, and she gasped, opening her mouth ever so slightly so I could slide my tongue past her lips, deepening the kiss. My tongue flicked against hers, tangling together. We fit together so perfectly it was hard to believe this was ever fake.

My hands drifted up her arms to her neck and jaw. She broke the kiss, pulling back slightly and looking at me with those icy blue eyes. I traced her lips with my thumb, taking the time to admire her, then leaning in to press a gentle kiss to her lips.

"You're being…sweet tonight."

"Is that a problem?" I grinned.

She shook her head. "No, it's just, I'm surprised. Normally, I'd be undressed by now." She let out a small laugh.

"Can't a man take time to appreciate his woman?"

"I—"

"Wait, don't answer that."

Before she could say anything more, I kissed her again, this time more aggressively, more passionately. As though she sensed the shift in emotion, her kisses became sloppier, like she was caught in the heat of the moment. Soon enough, I was hoisting her up onto the hood of the truck, then running my hands over her bare, gooseflesh-covered legs. One strap of her tank top had slipped off her shoulder, and her legs wrapped around my middle.

"How do you want me, Peach?" I asked between kisses.

"I want your tongue, and then I want you inside me. And I want you now."

I chuckled. "Can't even wait until we get home? What if someone sees?"

She glared at me. "That's never stopped you before. Besides, there's no one here."

Can't argue with that.

"Scoot forward," I told her, and she did, moving so she was sitting on the very edge of the hood.

I moved quickly, unbuttoning her denim shorts and pulling them down her thighs, past her cowboy boots, and let them fall to the ground. I dragged a finger up the fabric that covered her, and she shuddered.

I groaned at the wetness seeping through the fabric. "Fuck, Juniper, you're already soaked."

I circled her clit with my thumb, eliciting a moan from her lips before hooking my fingers in the waistband of her panties and pulling them down, baring her to me. I swiped a finger through her slit, bringing it up to my lips and sucking her arousal off. "So sweet."

"Please, I need—" she pleaded.

In response, I inserted a finger, pumping it inside her. Her head fell back as a moan escaped her lips, and I added another and then a third, using my thumb to apply pressure to her clit. I curled my fingers inside her as she tightened around them. I fucked her with my fingers until she squirmed, then I pulled them away before she could reach her high.

"Why did you stop?" she demanded, but I wasn't listening.

I took off my cowboy hat, setting it on the hood next to her. Bending forward, I lowered my face between her thighs and wrapped her legs around me. My tongue swiped up her center once in a broad stroke before I swirled it around her clit. I was a man starving, and Juniper was my next meal.

Her legs trembled around me as I lapped at her pussy, devouring her. Her hands gripped the top of my head, pushing it down, holding it against her as pleasure took over her body.

I pulled back for a second to say, "Let go. Come on my face," before sliding two fingers into her pussy and using my tongue on her.

She cried out my name as she pulled at the hair on my scalp.

"That's it, baby."

"Fuck," she whimpered after she came down from her high.

"Oh, I'm not done with you yet. That was just the beginning."

CHAPTER THIRTY-ONE

My legs shook, still wrapped around Mikey's head. Just when I thought sex couldn't get better, it did. It was a miracle if Brady could get me to come with his tongue and fingers, much less his dick, but it felt like Mikey could just touch me and I'd fall apart at his fingertips.

I unhooked my legs and moved to hop down, ready to return the favor, but Mikey stopped me.

"What are you doing?" He squeezed my leg to hold me still.

"Returning the favor?"

"Uh-uh, I'm not waiting a second longer to be inside you." He moved my hand to the front of his jeans to feel him.

His cock was hard, painfully hard, and I pulled my bottom lip between my teeth, pressing my thighs together to relieve the ache that formed so soon after his tongue was inside me.

"How badly do you want my cock?" he taunted. "How do you want me to fuck you, baby?"

"Rough. I want you rough. I want you to use me, to

fuck me like you hate me." I couldn't believe the words that came out of my mouth. I was a woman possessed.

"I'll have you screaming my name so loud there will be no questioning who you belong to." With the hiss of a zipper, Mikey pulled down his pants and boxers, letting his cock spring free.

He brought his hand up to his mouth, spitting into it and massaging his cock before sliding me even further off the pickup.

"Wrap your legs around me and hold on."

I did what he asked, and he grabbed my ass as I slid off the truck. I was wet enough that he slid into me with ease, my pussy swallowing his cock as the sensation of him filling me rushed through my body.

"Fuck, you are so tight"—he trusted his hips up—"and wet. I'm not going to last long like this." He carried me to the side of the pickup, somehow opening the backdoor while still inside me. He slipped out of me as he set me on the backseat then climbed over me, leaving our legs hanging out.

Mikey lifted my legs as he guided his cock back into me, his head lolling back for a moment. "Is this all right?"

I nodded then adjusted my legs so they were on his shoulders, and the angle was pure bliss. Holding on to the backs of my thighs, he pounded into me, sending shockwaves up my body as his cock brushed against my clit with each thrust.

"God," I moaned, my eyes rolling back. My hands fumbled around, trying to find something to hold on to. Heat licked at my body, and my toes curled from the pleasurable burn.

"Look at me, baby." His voice was all gravel and grit, deep and wanting.

My eyes fluttered open, and we held eye contact. Normally, the intimacy would make me uncomfortable, but with Mikey, it was sensual.

He lowered my legs so they were wrapped around his waist again and leaned forward so his chest was pressing against mine. His hands snaked around my back, pulling me closer to him as his lips found my neck.

He was rough and soft at the same time.

Dominant, yet I knew if I said the word, I'd be in control. He'd be at my mercy if I wanted him to be.

In the beginning, I worried that he'd be the type of guy who was only concerned about his own needs. His playboy reputation gave me the impression that he'd get what he needed and not focus on his partner, but I was wrong. If anything, he got off on my satisfaction, making sure I got what I needed, even if it meant his release was put on hold.

Mikey flipped me over, bringing me out of my thoughts as he lifted my body so I was on my hands and knees. He did his best to kneel behind me, entering from behind.

"I'm close, Juniper." He gasped, gripping my hips. His pace quickened, and soon I was on the brink of my orgasm, crying out his name.

My pussy clenched around him, and a tremor moved through my body as I saw stars. Mikey's cock twitched as he spilled inside me, and he brought his mouth down to my shoulder, his teeth applying the lightest bit of pressure.

"You." He kissed the spot he had bitten. "Are." His lips found the nape of my neck. "My." My head turned toward him, and he murmured against my lips, "Undoing."

There was no going back. I'd completely fallen off the ledge, plunging into the feelings I was scared to admit aloud.

I was falling for Mikey Tucker.

And there was no way this would end well.

I sat on the couch in Natalie's living room, leisurely scrolling job search sites. Most of them were going to be out of my level of experience, but it didn't hurt to look.

The biggest issue I had was most of the jobs that would hire me were out of state. I knew my original plan was always to leave Montana once I got a better footing and was able to find a job, regardless of where that career took me.

However, over the past couple months, I'd found a sense of place here. I'd made friendships that would be hard to leave behind, and Mikey and I had grown closer. We hadn't talked about our arrangement, but things were starting to feel more real than fake lately.

I knew better now than to sacrifice my goals and future for a man. I'd been there and done that before. But I couldn't deny that Mikey and his friends were now a factor in my search.

For a while, I scrolled mindlessly, not really looking too deeply into the listings. I stifled a yawn, not wanting to fall asleep on the couch before my shift, but I was exhausted. The weekend festivities had sucked the energy out of me.

I nearly missed it, but my eyes caught on the job title and description. The words *research assistant, biotechnology,* and *cancer research* stuck out to me, and I skimmed the rest of the listing. The position fit my education and experience perfectly, going as far to say it was designed for a recent college graduate. The only experience needed was working in academic research labs, techniques we were taught in school, and familiarity with software that I used in my daily studies.

The kicker? The job was located in Minnesota.

Honestly, the location was ideal. It was close to my home state of Michigan, without being too close, and the weather was similar to what I was already used to here in Montana and back at home. But it would require me to pack up my life and start over once again.

I spent a few minutes staring at my computer screen, hovering my mouse over the "Apply Now" button then moving it all the way over to the other side of the screen, and again, and again, and again.

"Ugh!" I let out an exaggerated groan.

Natalie stepped out of the bathroom in the world's most inconvenient, or perhaps most perfect, timing. "Whoa, what's going on?" She quickly sat on the couch next to me. "You found a job?"

"Kind of." I sighed, closing the laptop. "It's just…"

She tilted her head in confusion. "Just what?"

"It's in Minnesota."

"Okay…"

I didn't think she understood my hesitation.

"Well, I—" My throat made an *uh* sound as I paused. "I'm thinking of staying?"

"Here?"

"Montana, yes."

She furrowed her brows but quickly righted them, as though she was trying not to look disappointed. "Are you doing this because of—"

"Mikey? No…" I cut her off, but even I wasn't convinced by my own voice. "I want to stay because I don't want to uproot my life twice in six months."

"I mean, that's reasonable, but, June, this is what you've

been working for. From the brief two-second glance I got at your computer before you shut it, this job looks like exactly what you've been looking for."

"It is." I nodded, but my eyes met the floor.

"But?"

"But what if I can find this job somewhere closer? Somewhere here. Where I don't have to start over?"

"It's up to you, but this is your chance. You said it yourself, you spent the last four years planning your life around Brady."

I narrowed my eyes. "What are you getting at?"

She let out a resigned breath. "I would just hate for you to be disappointed again, June."

I didn't respond, so she got up, heading to the front door.

Looking over her shoulder one last time, she said, "I'm going to the store. Text me if you need anything, okay?"

I nodded, but she was already gone, the front door shut, leaving me alone to simmer in my thoughts.

After grabbing my laptop again, I opened it, letting the job listing stare back at me once again. I could just apply for the job, and if I got it, I wouldn't have to take it. Maybe nothing would come of it.

Besides, my resume was already done, and I'd just have to adjust my cover letter. The work was practically done. What did I have to lose?

Taking a deep breath, I hovered over the "Apply Now" button, closed my eyes, and clicked on it.

ELLISON'S HUSBAND

Congrats man

I never thought I'd say this, but you won

Land's all yours buddy

She's a keeper btw

What's that?" Juniper looked over my shoulder at my phone just as I swiped out of the messages.

"Nothing." I slid my phone back into my pocket.

She narrowed her eyes in suspicion. "Okay…"

"Come on, we've gotta get on the road." I changed the subject, opening the passenger door for her.

We were heading to Goldfinch this weekend for Gulch Days, the last condition of our fake-dating arrangement. I didn't really understand why she needed me to come with her to this event, what she needed from me in the first place, but I also didn't question it or think about it too deeply. She didn't ask why *I* needed a fake girlfriend, so I didn't ask her, either.

I thought some things were better off not knowing.

Eventually, we'd have to talk about our plans. We'd have to figure out how we wanted to end things, or if we wanted to end things at all. When Juniper and I first made the agreement, we knew this would have an expiration date, but we never really discussed what would happen when we reached that date.

Not to mention, we'd already broken nearly every single rule we'd agreed to.

An hour into the drive, the cab fell silent as though both of us were deep in thought.

"I—" I broke the silence at the same time she took a deep breath and said, "So…"

Both of us huffed out shallow laughs.

"You first," I urged her on.

"So, I, uh…" She stumbled over her words. "What's going to happen?"

"Well, we're going to go to this festival," I teased, and she glared at me.

"Mikey."

"Juniper."

"We should really talk about what this is. What we want to do."

My chest heaved as I thought about how to respond. On one hand, it was nice to know we were on the same page, or at least half on the same page. On the other, I was afraid of what she might want. If she'd decided this relationship had run its course and wanted an exit strategy.

"What do you want to do?" I asked, wanting to hear her answer first.

She rolled her lips. "I'm not sure."

Nervous energy swirled in my stomach. Her hesitation

could mean she wanted to see what happened, or it could just mean she wanted to let me down easy.

"What if we just see how the weekend goes then decide from there?" I suggested.

She paused for a moment, as though contemplating and weighing her options. "I don't see the harm in that. This…agreement has been mutually beneficial."

A devilish grin pulled at my cheeks. "Damn, Peach, would it kill you to admit you like me?"

Juniper rolled her eyes. "How do you know I'm not just pretending to like you?"

I didn't know. Not for certain at least. But I wanted to believe the glint in her eyes gave her away.

"Just a hunch." I winked, taking her hand and lifting it to my lips to kiss her knuckles. "Who wouldn't like me?"

She laughed, the sound like sunshine peeking through the clouds after a storm, breaking up the nervous energy in the air. "That's the real question, isn't it, Casanova."

The streets of Goldfinch, Montana, were filled with people milling about for the festivities. Much like the Bucking Horse Sale, the fairgrounds were used as an event space as well as the main road running through town.

Businesses had their doors open, welcoming visitors inside, but many also had tents set up on the sidewalk to attract people passing by. Hanging from light poles above each intersection were decorations attached to cables. Some had signs reading *Gulch Days Annual Summer Kick-Off* or *Welcome to Goldfinch, Home of the SGU Miners*.

I drove to the fairgrounds, deciding that would be the best place to park.

"They did bring in a Ferris wheel this year." Juniper craned her neck as we turned the corner. "It's always a bit hit or miss whether that happens."

I'd never been to Gulch Days, even though I'd lived in Montana for years now. We were always either on the road, helping Colter on the ranch, or, in the case of last year, participating in wedding festivities.

"Do you come to this every year?" I asked, pulling to a stop in the parking lot.

"Almost every year. One time I went home for the summer, but I'd spent nearly every break between the school year here." She unbuckled her seatbelt, but sat, waiting for me to get out and open her door.

I suppressed a smile, but on the inside, my heart was screaming.

When I opened my door, the smell of fried food hit my nostrils immediately. I opened June's door and helped her out of the pickup, keeping her hand in mine as we walked toward the entrance gates.

"What do you want to do first?"

She knew more about this than I did, so I was more than willing to let her take the reins.

"I say let's grab some food to snack on while we look at vendor tables first. They've got some carnival games that I want to kick your ass in"—she winked—"and then we can either ride the Ferris wheel or take a walk downtown. We've also got all day tomorrow, so we don't have to do everything all at once."

We'd planned to stay the night in a hotel to really make the most out of the weekend.

"I'm along for the ride. Show me around, Peach." I let

her lead me to the food trucks as she pointed out her favorites.

"We're going to have to eat it all, you know." She pulled her bottom lip between her teeth.

"Good thing I haven't eaten much today." I chuckled as she pulled me up to a food truck selling stir-fried noodles.

Ten minutes later, our arms were full with noodles, mini corndogs, funnel cake, a snow cone, apple cider donuts, fried Oreos, and fried pickles. We laid out our spread on a picnic table—instead of walking through the vendors—and dug in, sharing plates and ranking our favorites.

"Apple cider donuts are my favorite, hands down," Juniper mumbled through a mouthful. "They have my number one spot every time."

I took a bite of the fried Oreo, immediately pushing the pickles away.

"You don't like fried pickles?" Her jaw dropped, mouth gaping.

Wrinkling my nose, I shook my head. "I don't like pickles at all."

"That's a criminal offense. Those are my second favorite."

"I just can't. Okay, my number one is the funnel cake. Last place is obviously the pickles. These Oreos aren't bad, though."

"Are there any other foods you don't like? I'm prepared for my heart to break," she teased, taking a sip of the peach mango snow cone that had already melted.

"I hate bananas. I love pear flavor, but I don't like the taste of actual pears. I also don't like corn."

"What do you have against corn?" she cried out.

"I just don't see the point? It gets stuck in my teeth and

doesn't taste good, so it's more of an annoyance than anything. What about you?"

"All of the normal things. Brussels sprouts, licorice, mushrooms, blue cheese." She started to list things off.

"Hold on, mushrooms?"

She narrowed her eyes. "Yes, I do not like mushrooms. Before you judge me, Mr. I-Don't-Like-Corn, it's the texture."

"Fair enough. Can't argue with that."

We finished our food, my final ranking being funnel cake, fried Oreos, stir-fried noodles, apple cider donuts, mini corndogs, snow cone (it was too sweet), and pickles. Her ranking was apple cider donuts, fried pickles, funnel cake, stir-fried noodles, snow cone, corn dogs, then Oreos last, to my surprise.

I accidentally let out a long, loud burp, immediately covering my mouth as heat rushed into my cheeks.

"Excuse you!" She giggled, and I was starting to think the sugar was going to her head.

I shook my head, a smile tugging on my lips, as we stood and I wrapped my arm around her shoulders. "Where to next? Please don't say rides. I don't know if my stomach can handle that."

"What, you don't want to go on the Tilt-A-Whirl?"

My face contorted into a grimace. "Not if you don't want it to be a Puke-A-Whirl."

She pursed her lips. "Noted. Shall we go look at the vendors or play carnival games?"

"How about let's do the vendors here and go downtown, then I can kick your ass in carnival games tomorrow." I winked, grabbing her hand and giving it a squeeze.

Juniper scowled, but I knew it was all in good fun when

she muttered, "Good luck with that. I'm the best at carnival games."

The vendors here at the fairgrounds were set up in one of the large exhibition buildings. The air conditioning hit us with a cool blast when we stepped inside, and Juniper let out a content sigh. I didn't think it was that hot outside with it only being the end of May, but it brought relief, nonetheless.

This trade show wasn't too large, with four different rows to walk down and about fifteen businesses in each one. The products ranged from paintings to handmade crafts to sourdough bread.

I had to admit, I wasn't a big patron of trade shows or farmers markets. A lot of the big rodeos we went to offered them as events, but I tended to avoid them because of the crowds.

This one was nice, though.

Juniper stopped at almost every booth, meticulously looking at what everyone had to offer. Occasionally, she'd strike up a conversation with the vendors like they were old friends.

"Pick out something that you want," I told her after we'd walked through two of the rows. I'd caught her staring at some silver jewelry, looking like she was debating whether or not she wanted to get it.

"What do you mean?"

"Can't I buy something for my girl?" I flashed her a smile.

Juniper put her hands on her hips, leaning her weight on one side of her body. "I seem to recall you saying you didn't want to spend money on me."

"What can I say? I'm a changed man," I joked, but then added more seriously, "You're worth it. You could tell me you wanted one of everything, and I'd gladly spend every penny."

She snorted, rolling her eyes. "Okay, Romeo, no need to get ahead of yourself. Thank you, that's very nice of you, but you don't have to do that. I truly don't need anything."

When she wasn't paying attention, I ended up buying some of the things she spent the most time admiring. A simple silver necklace with a small sapphire pendant and a handmade copper bracelet. I threw them in my pocket for safekeeping until I wanted to surprise her with them.

That night we went to Lucky Sevens, the college bar that Juniper worked at when she was in school. It wasn't the same one the boys and I had gone to last year for Colter's bachelor party, but it was fairly close by.

Goldfinch had three main college bars, all nestled in the same triangular area of downtown. Each bar was a point of the triangle, and it made for an easy way to bar hop.

Of course, there were other bars, but Lucky Sevens, Sippers, and The Sapphire Bar were the big three and very popular with the students at SGU.

The DJ was playing the classic nightclub selection—a mix of hip-hop, rap, and top twenty pop hits. A few bold people were on top of the bar shaking their hips, and the small dance floor was packed with bodies.

"Wanna brave the dance floor with me?" I asked, extending a hand.

She playfully slapped it away with a laugh. "No, not really." Taking a sip of her drink, she surveyed the room.

Beer in hand, I watched her look around, scoping everything out.

"See anyone you know?"

Something flickered in her eyes at that. I wasn't sure what it was, but her entire demeanor shifted.

"W-why do you ask that?"

I shrugged. "You just keep looking around like you're trying to find someone."

"Actually, I changed my mind. Let's dance." After throwing back the rest of her drink, she hopped down from her barstool, grabbing my hand to drag me onto the dance floor.

The bass thumped, echoing off the walls as she turned her back to me and I pulled her close. She ground her hips against my front, and blood rushed to my cock. Leaning in, I brushed my lips along the crook of her neck, breathing in her peachy floral perfume.

She tilted her head to look at me, and I gave her a quick peck, brushing her hair out of her face.

Still, despite being here with me, she seemed distracted, like her mind was preoccupied.

I didn't have to be a rocket scientist to sense that something was off with her, but I also wasn't sure I wanted to know what it was.

So, I tried to distract my mind, losing myself to the music and her body pressed against mine.

CHAPTER THIRTY-THREE

Lucky Sevens was Brady's favorite place to go on Saturdays. I knew he'd show up at some point, it was just a matter of when.

I tried to be discreet about my attempts to find him in the sea of people, but clearly I wasn't doing a good job, because every so often, Mikey would look at me with suspicion in his eyes. I didn't know what I was doing here, what I was trying to achieve. The chances that Brady had already seen us on television, a magazine cover, or social media were high, so there really was no need to try to make him jealous.

I'd never been one to let things go easily, though. I wanted to drive the knife in, really make it hurt. I wanted him to regret what he did, to feel as much pain as I felt when I caught him and Ava together.

The song changed from an upbeat melody to a slow, sensual beat. My intention was to get off the dance floor, but Mikey had other ideas. He grabbed my hand and pulled me toward him, wrapping my arms around his neck before running his hands down the sides of my body until they reached my waist.

"I didn't take you for a slow dancer," I teased as a flash of copper hair caught my attention out of the corner of my eye. Sure enough, it was Ava, and Brady followed her shortly after.

"Anything for my girl," he countered with an amused tone. "By the way, I got you something." He reached into his pocket, pulling out a silver necklace with a sapphire pendant and a copper bracelet.

"These are beautiful." I pouted my lips as I let him clasp the chain around my neck and slide the bracelet on my wrist. "Thank you."

"I can be a romantic sometimes."

I watched as Ava stopped near the bar, getting Brady's attention and pointing toward us.

This was my chance.

"Oh, yeah? Prove it, then. Kiss me." I pulled my lips between my teeth, flicking my gaze from his eyes down to his lips and back up.

With one smooth movement, Mikey crashed his lips onto mine, yanking me toward him with a passion. One hand stayed on my waist, while the other roamed down to my ass, giving it a squeeze.

I opened my eyes just a sliver, finding Ava with her mouth gaped open, right before it clamped into a thin line. Brady's eyes were narrowed, like he was trying to wrap his head around what was going on. Something like longing flickered in his gaze, but Ava seemed to snap at him and he shook his head, taking her hand to lead her to the back of the bar.

Returning my attention to the kiss, I closed my eyes, sliding my tongue past Mikey's lips and grabbing a fistful of hair from the back of his head. He moaned, and I felt him harden between us.

"Should we get out of here?" I whispered against his lips. I'd gotten what I needed, and Mikey would never have to know.

Easy and done.

"Yes, let's go." He pulled away, but when he looked at me again, his pupils grew. He smashed his lips against mine one more time for good measure then took my hand, practically dragging me out of the bar, adjusting himself as he went.

When we got outside, he scooped me up in his arms, drawing a squeal from my lips.

The fairgrounds were illuminated with lights from the carnival rides, and it reminded me that we still had one more thing to do.

"What about the Ferris wheel? We still have to ride the Ferris wheel!"

Mikey shook his head and put me down. "All right, then, come on." Hand in hand, we walked back to the fairgrounds and got in line for the ride.

About ten minutes later, the line moved and we loaded into the cart. On the first time around, we didn't say anything, just taking in the views. You could see the entire town of Goldfinch from the top—the college and football stadium, downtown's lights, and even the silhouette of the mountains.

On the second time up, the Ferris wheel jerked to a stop, leaving our cart swinging.

"Folks, we're experiencing some technical difficulties," the operator announced through a megaphone. "We're working as quickly as we can to get it running, but for now, just hang tight and relax."

"Oh no, oh, God." My heart raced in my chest as my breathing grew faster. I looked over at Mikey, but he wasn't panicking. No, he was actually *laughing*. "Why are you laughing? We're stuck up here!"

His lips curled. "I'm just thinking about how this will give us plenty of time to finish what we started at the bar."

I smacked him lightly on the arm. "Seriously? You're thinking about sex right now?"

He shrugged. "Might help take your mind off things."

As much as I hated to admit it, he did have a point.

Swallowing my pride, and irrational fear of being stuck up here forever, I kissed him, unbuttoning his jeans in the process. We were all the way at the top, so it was unlikely that anyone would see us, but we'd need to be quick in case the Ferris wheel started running again.

I palmed the bulge in the front of his boxers, wetting my lips. I moved to pull his boxers down, but Mikey stopped me.

"What are you doing?" I narrowed my eyes.

He didn't say anything, just reached for the buttons on my shorts, tugging the zipper down and sliding his hand inside the waistband of my panties. He swiped a finger up my center, and I let out a sharp breath.

"So wet already," he hummed, slipping one inside.

I wasn't sure how we were going to manage this, but I reached into his boxers to grip his length. It pulsed in my hand as I ran my finger along the tip, lightly brushing the crown of his cock.

Mikey pumped a finger inside me, and I bit back a moan. Letting go of him, I brought my hand up to my mouth, spitting in it to add some lubrication. This time, when I stroked his length, a low rumble left his throat.

"Fuck, I don't know if I'm going to last long," Mikey muttered.

"Good," I whispered in his ear. "Don't hold back."

Both of us picked up our pace, our pants filling the air around us. I wasn't sure if anyone else could hear us, but if they could, we were none the wiser.

Mikey's thumb brushed my clit as he added another finger. The sensations increased as he filled me, and I had to close my eyes to focus on what I was doing.

It turned into a sort of competition of who could make the other fall apart first, and we were neck and neck, climbing closer and closer to our highs together.

"Juniper, I-I'm going to—" Mikey groaned, and I lowered my mouth onto him, bobbing my head up and down until he came, exploding on my tongue.

Even though he'd finished, he didn't stop fingering me. If anything, it just motivated him more. He thrusted his fingers into me faster, pressure building and building inside of me. Heat radiated in my toes and my legs stiffened as I cried out his name, begging him not to stop. One of his hands came up to cover my mouth, and I bit down on it, though not hard enough to hurt.

Electricity coursed through my veins as my orgasm washed over me.

"Holy shit," I breathed out just as the Ferris wheel started moving again.

"Perfect timing." Mikey winked as the ride lowered us back down to the ground.

juniper

So, which game do you want me to kick your ass at first?" I teased as we entered the fairgrounds again the next day.

"Which one's your favorite?" he asked, not answering my question.

"Ooh." I thought about it for a moment. "Probably the ping-pong toss."

"Play a lot of beer pong while you were at SGU?"

Heat rose to my cheeks. I was the reigning champ of beer pong at my—Brady's—house. I could run the table all night. "A couple times here and there," I replied in a self-effacing manner.

"I'll take that as a yes, then." He smirked, nudging me with his elbow.

I stuck out my tongue. "I guess you'll just have to find out," I teased.

"What does the winner get?"

"What do you think the winner should get? Keep in mind, you're going to lose, so you're essentially choosing what *my* reward is. Choose wisely, because I'm still waiting for you to get on a horse sober."

He rolled his eyes. "You women and your horses."

"Well, then what do you think the winner should get?" I repeated my question. "I mean, from what I've heard, you all make a lot of bets. What kind of things are you wagering?"

A cloud suddenly passed over his gaze, but it was gone as quickly as it had appeared. "Money usually…"

I waited for him to continue, but was only met with silence. "All right, then. The winner of each game gets five bucks," I decided.

We stepped up to the first game, the ping-pong toss, where rows of shot glasses were set up and you had to sink as many ping-pong balls as possible.

"Okay, Peachy, show me what you've got." Mikey handed me a ball.

I gave him a smug look. "Please, I could do this in my sleep." I threw the first ball, and it bounced off the rim of one of the glasses but managed to land in a different one. "See?"

He raised his brows like he didn't believe me, and I grabbed the next ball, sinking another shot.

"I've gotta say, I'm impressed. If I ever need a pong partner in the future, I know who I'm going to call."

"Like I said, I'm a professional." I did miss the next shot, but I didn't have to eat my words quite yet because I made the next two. My percentage may not have been perfect, but it was good enough. By the end, I had made five out of six. "Your turn, Casanova."

Mikey only made three out of the six, and I shot him a cocky grin as I stuck out my hand. He paid up, handing me a crisp five-dollar bill.

"You can pick the next game. Are we upping the wager?"

"Hmm, tempting, but no. You're going to drain my pockets if we increase the reward." He laughed, and it almost made me forget the reason why we made this trip in the first place.

He led me over to the game where you hit a pad with a hammer and test your strength.

I let a boisterous laugh slip. "That's a low blow!"

After shrugging, he gave me a wink. "I've gotta win somehow. If playing dirty is how I have to do it, I'm not above that."

"I'll remember that the next time you want to make a bet with me," I teased.

This time, I made Mikey go first, so at least I had reasonable expectations for how hard I was going to have to swing the hammer.

He rubbed his hands together before stretching his arms and twisting his torso like he was about to compete in a boxing match. Then he took the hammer from the carnie and stepped up to the plate. His muscles rippled and the veins in his forearms popped as he reared back the hammer and brought it down onto the pad.

I brought my hand up to my mouth to make sure I wasn't drooling over the sight of him, but my eyes widened in shock when the weight only went about three quarters of the way up to the bell.

"I'm kind of shocked you didn't get it, but I definitely enjoyed watching." I bit my lip as he handed me the hammer.

"It's all in the technique."

I weighed the hammer in my hands. It wasn't very heavy, so I should have been able to lift it over my head easily and swing it with enough force. It was making sure I hit the target in the right spot that mattered.

I closed my eyes, taking a deep breath, then opened them, swinging the hammer with all my might. The ball shot up, hitting the bell ever so slightly, but still causing it to ring.

My jaw dropped, and so did the hammer in my hands. It fell to the ground as I spun to face Mikey. His smile reached ear to ear as I practically jumped in his arms from excitement.

"I did it! I can't believe I did it!"

He wrapped me in his arms, and I felt the vibration of his laughter in his chest as he stroked my hair. "You sure did."

We raced around the fairgrounds, playing every game we could find. I was sure he was letting me win some of them, but I didn't even care. It wasn't about the money, I just liked being around him.

Mikey wrapped his arm around me as we walked toward the food vendors. We'd be heading home tomorrow.

"I've had a lot of fun with you this weekend." I smiled.

"I have, too."

"Should we talk about…" My voice trailed off as a realization hit me.

Whether or not we talked about our relationship status now or later, I knew what I was going to do. I was going to tell him how I felt. How I *truly* felt. That even though this all started out as fake, everything now was real to me. That I cared about him. That I wanted to be with him.

My thoughts were cut short as we turned around the corner and I made contact with someone's shoulder.

"Oops…" I began to apologize until I realized who I had run into.

Ava's eyes widened. "Juniper? I didn't know you…" Her eyes flicked to Mikey's then down to our interlaced fingers. "Wow, I didn't realize you were still with him. I figured once you'd gotten what you wanted, you'd be satisfied."

Mikey's gaze also bounced back and forth between me and Ava. "What are *you* doing here? How do you know each other?"

"What, you didn't recognize her?" Ava crossed her arms, the corners of her lips dipping in a frown. "Juniper and I *used to* be best friends."

"Babe? Everything okay?"

I heard his voice before I saw him. Brady didn't realize it was me until after he'd put his arm around Ava's waist.

"Juniper," he muttered.

As though my true identity dawned on him when he saw Brady, Mikey's eyes widened then narrowed in suspicion. "What's going on here?"

"I-I can explain." I stumbled over my words at the same time Ava pointed at me with one hand placed on her hip.

"Why don't you ask her?"

"I—" Words failed me, and defensiveness boiled up in me. "You were my best friend until you decided to fuck my boyfriend, Ava."

She forced out a laugh, but there was no humor in it. "What? And you're so much better? You *knew* about me and him. You were there last year when he took me home from the bar." She pointed to Mikey, recognition flashing in his eyes for a brief moment. "You couldn't have chosen literally anyone else, Juniper?"

Brady piped up next. "Yeah, babe, if you wanted me back, all you had to do was say the word. You didn't have to use my favorite bull rider to make me jealous. Although, you did look damn good last night."

I didn't miss the way Ava glared at Brady, but my attention was torn away from them when Mikey snapped his head toward me. "What are they talking about?"

Ava scoffed, still giving Brady a look that said, *We'll talk about that later*, then continued without letting me explain or defend myself. "What, did you actually think she wanted you? You actually believed she liked you? She used you. I mean, what better way to get back at your ex and best friend than fucking around with the famous bull rider who just so happened to be my sloppy seconds. The media attention was just the cherry on top." Directing her attention to me, she asked with a laugh that sounded all too genuine, "How did you manage to do that one?"

I rolled my lips, prepared to argue, but Mikey beat me to it.

"That's why you agreed to be my girlfriend? You wanted the media's attention to do what? Make someone jealous? What, was defending me to the press part of your revenge plot, too?" Hurt—betrayal—flickered in his eyes.

"No, I—" The media attention was never part of my original plan, but he didn't give me time to explain. "That wasn't my intention, but—"

"You knew why I didn't want the media attention." His voice grew louder. "You *knew* it would drag things out longer, but you made it happen anyway."

"I wasn't planning on it being more than one night! *You're* the one who asked me to do this!" I retorted, not even realizing that Ava and Brady had already gone, leaving us to fire accusations at each other. "Why did you even need a fake girlfriend to begin with?"

He hesitated like he didn't want to tell me, but I wanted answers. I needed the answers to the questions I'd been so afraid to ask from the beginning.

A rational person would let the dust settle, come back to the topic when we were calmer, less emotional.

But neither of us had ever been rational when it came to this.

"Was it for your image? Did you do it so the fans would leave you alone? What was it?" I pushed and pushed, not letting up until he finally exploded.

"It was a bet, okay!" he yelled, even though it was drawing attention to us.

Bystanders paused in their tracks to see what was going on. When they realized who was getting in a fight, a few pulled out their phones. Mikey noticed and pulled me back around the corner, away from prying eyes. The social media trolls would have a heyday with this.

Lowering his voice, he growled, "Are you happy now? The guys bet me that I wouldn't be able to keep a girl for longer than two weeks. Then they bet me a month. Colter offered me a nice plot of land if I could stay with the same girl until the end of the Houston Rodeo."

I flinched, my body recoiling at his words as though he'd sucker punched me in the gut. "That's what those texts were. Why you didn't want me to see them. You *used me* for money." The words fell out of my mouth under my breath. Humiliation washed over me. "That's why you didn't want the media attention. You didn't want anyone to know."

Mikey scoffed, throwing his hands in the air. "Do you realize how hypocritical you sound? I wasn't the only one with an ulterior motive. And *I* wasn't the one who dragged it out longer. This was never supposed to last more than a month."

The irony of it all didn't escape me. No, I knew how it looked. But over the past few weeks, it became less about revenge and more about actually enjoying Mikey's company. I thought maybe he felt the same way, that this fake relationship was starting to feel real.

But, once again, I was a fool.

"You're right." I bit the inside of my cheek until I tasted blood. "*This*"—I gestured to the both of us—"should have ended a long time ago. None of this was real, and I should have never trusted you."

CHAPTER THIRTY-FIVE

Hurt flashed in her eyes, but her emotions didn't match what she was saying.

Even though I knew I would regret it later, I couldn't stop the words from falling from my mouth. "Well, then, we might as well end this 'relationship' while we're at it." I put air quotes around *relationship* because it was never real, was it?

It was always meant to be temporary. *Fake.* There was always a risk that someone would end up getting hurt, but I still went through with it.

Worse yet, I let myself fall.

My heart was screaming at me to stop, to explain. To say even though none of it was real, I *wished* it was.

But instead, poison dripped from my lips, tainting whatever was left of us. "You clearly got what you wanted, and I got what I needed out of this a long time ago, so there's no need to pretend anymore."

As though I drove the knife in further, ripping our chances to shreds, her shoulders fell.

"I guess not." Her jaw set in a hard line as she tore off

the silver chain of the necklace I bought her and threw it on the ground, the blue gem shimmering in the sunlight amongst the gravel.

Without another word, she walked away, leaving me behind.

I watched as she pulled out her phone and placed it against her ear. Even with the distance between us, I heard the break in her voice when she choked out, "Come pick me up. You were right all along."

It didn't take long for videos of our fight to pop up on social media. Less than twenty-four hours later, gossip accounts were talking about us.

@therodeoroundup.official: Trouble in paradise? Our sources say that bull rider Mikey Tucker and his girlfriend got in an explosive argument last week in Goldfinch, Montana.

> **@cowboy4lifee1423:** @therodeoroundup.official I heard their relationship was fake the entire time.
>
> **@kalee.marieee1:** @cowboy4lifee1423 It was fake. I was there. He used her to win a bet.
>
> **@codylbarton102:** @kalee.marieee1 That's rough.
>
> **@cowboy4lifee1423:** @kalee.marieee1 How embarrassing.

@connorridesbulls12: I knew it was too good to be true. There's no way he actually liked her.

@ranchandmoto123: @connorridesbulls12 I wonder what she got out of it.

@ttchance16: @ranchandmoto123 Fifteen minutes of fame probably 🌚 Typical buckle bunny shit.

@kalee.marieee1: @ranchandmoto123 She was using him to get back at her ex. It's all messy AF.

I threw my phone across the trailer. It wouldn't be long until the press caught wind of this and it was all anyone would talk about. My life would no longer be about my bull riding performance. It would once again be about my non-existent love life.

Old Leroy must have sensed something was wrong, because he didn't shoot me his usual scowl when I came tearing into the trailer park the other day. He just went back to reading his newspaper, a sad expression plastered on his face.

This morning, Colter had sent me the pin for the plot of land he owed me after the bet. I was going to take it, but I couldn't deny the twinge of guilt that pricked at my chest at the idea of it.

Sure, Juniper had used me to make her ex jealous, but I was no better. In fact, I was probably worse. The look of betrayal on her face replayed through my mind like a broken record. Every time I closed my eyes, I was teleported back to that moment.

I decided that moving would take my mind off things, at least temporarily, so I got dressed and headed outside to hook up the trailer and get out of this park for good.

"Whaddya do to that girl?" Leroy croaked. "I saw something about you two getting in a fight over the weekend."

I ignored him, resisting the urge to tell the old man to

shut up and get back to reading his paper. He didn't deserve that, even if he was a nosy, grouchy old fart.

"I told you not to mess it up." He tutted. "It's not every day you find someone like that. I thought you'd met your match."

"You thought wrong," I muttered as I opened the driver's door of my pickup to back it up to the trailer.

Before I could close the door, he raised his voice. "You skipping town now? Too embarrassed to show your face?"

The old man seriously was going to mock me after all this?

"Are you bored or something?" I finally gave in to his harassment.

He shook his head. "No, I just know a fuckup when I see one."

"Gee, thanks." I rolled my eyes. "And I'm not skipping town. I'm just moving to a plot of land my friend gave me."

"Ah, so the rumors are true."

"Don't you have anything better to do than speculate about my love life?"

"Clearly no." He shrugged.

I shut the door, slamming it a bit harder than I intended. Ignoring Leroy, I backed up the pickup, having to get out, pull forward and adjust, then back up again because I kept missing the spot where the hitch needed to be. Frustration churned in my gut, and I was about to get out yet *again*, but the old man had gotten up from his chair and hobbled over to the trailer.

"Come on, son." He waved me backward, putting a hand up when I needed to stop.

I hopped out to check, and sure enough, the hitch was perfectly lined up.

"Thanks," I muttered. I hooked up the trailer, removed the wood under the tires, and started to head back to the pickup to get the hell out of here when Leroy called my name.

I raised my brows at him, and he looked at me with empathy in his gaze.

"Mikey, I know happiness when I see it." He sighed, his breaths wobbling with age. "You love her, I can tell. Don't make the same mistake I made once. You can still make it right."

What was the point anymore in trying to prove everyone wrong? They had their idea of who I was, and I wasn't sure if I could change that. To them, I was the idiotic, womanizing bull rider who'd never be anything more than one night of fun. I was the guy who everyone laughed at, a distraction.

Juniper looked at me differently. She saw right through the bullshit, but all I'd done was prove everyone right. Even if I could fix this, I didn't deserve her.

So, what was the point in trying?

I pursed my lips, shaking my head to be stubborn. "I'm not sure I can, Leroy." Then I hopped in the truck, closed the door, and drove away, leaving the old man and my former home behind.

The acre of land Colter had set aside for me was nice. The plot was nestled at the base of the hills on the west end of the ranch. It wasn't too far from his place—fairly close to it, actually—but it was enough out of the way that we wouldn't be under each other's noses. Probably intentional on his part, but I wasn't complaining.

Then again, this part of the ranch had already been set up with a water well and septic system. I'd assumed the land was intended for one of Colter's siblings, but when they both left Silver Creek, it became vacant and they didn't have much use for it.

Dust plumed into the air about a half mile up the road while I was unhooking the trailer, and within a few minutes, Colter's pickup was pulling up.

"What do you think?" he asked as he hopped out of the truck.

I wiped my hands on my jeans after getting up from the ground. "It's nice. I really appreciate it, Carson."

He shrugged. "Figured it was about time you had somewhere to call your own. This land's just been sitting out here with no one to occupy it. If you decide to stay here and put down some roots, you can build on it." He hesitated. "Or if you want to leave, it can be a temporary thing."

I nodded tersely. "I'm guessing you've heard all about my *explosive break up*." Using air quotes, I relayed what the press had been babbling about online.

"Honestly, I don't know what exactly happened there. It's not my business, so I won't pry. Partially because I'm not sure if I *want* to know, but also because I know how it feels to have everyone obsessed about your relationships. No one's entitled to your personal life just because you're a professional athlete." His voice trailed off slightly, but he cleared his throat. "Anyway, if you need someone to talk to, I'm here."

"Thanks. I'm just waiting for it all to die down. They can't talk about me forever, right? Or maybe they'll just keep talking and I'll be the butt of everyone's jokes until I croak. Someone's gotta be the funny guy who everyone makes jokes at the expense of, am I right?" I forced out a laugh without humor. When Colter didn't laugh with me, I deflected. "Actually, it doesn't matter, I'm just—"

"No, man, don't do that. Talk to me. What's going on?" Colter's face was written with concern.

I shrugged. "I don't know, I guess I just deal with enough shit from the press. It's kind of the cherry on top for my closest friends to also give me shit about my personal life and bull riding career." I flicked my gaze away from Colter. I couldn't meet his eyes.

He sighed. "Man, fuck. Mikey, I'm sorry. I didn't realize it bothered you. That's on me, and I'm sure the others would understand, too. We love you, you know that, right? You're our brother, our family."

I nodded as I kicked the pebbles on the ground. "Yeah, yeah, I know. I try not to let it get to me because I give you all just as much shit, but sometimes it weighs on me. Especially this year with all the fans having opinions on my career being mediocre. I mean, shit, the whole reason I took that stupid bet was to hopefully get you all off my back for a little bit. Didn't think it would blow up in my face like it did."

Colter huffed out a breath. "Damn."

I pursed my lips in a tight smile. "Yeah."

"I...I can have a talk with the boys and Ellison and Isa. Eventually, they'll probably have to hear it from you, but I can try to get them to tone it down a bit."

"Thanks, Colt. I mean, I don't want you guys to treat me differently or for our friendship to change. I still want to shoot the shit with you guys, but maybe someone else can be the punchline for once. At least until the media dies down with all their bullshit."

He nodded in understanding then reached out his hand. I grabbed it, the firm handshake a symbol of solidarity between us.

"You know, I want to wish you'd talked to us about it sooner, but that would make me a hypocrite. I mean it, though, Mike, we're all here for you. We're not gonna leave you. We're family, and family has each other's backs."

It wasn't much, but a weight seemed to lift off my shoulders. I'd worried for so long that my friends wouldn't want to be my friends anymore if I'd confronted them, but Colter was right. We were brothers. We may not always have gotten along—as families do—but at the end of the day, we always had each other's backs. I'd go to war for those boys, and I knew they'd do the same for me.

Our hands unclasped, and Colter ran his fingers through his hair. "Well, I'll leave you to it. I just came to check on you and make sure everything's working right. Call me if you need anything."

"Thanks, man. I'll see you all later at Reid's."

CHAPTER THIRTY-SIX

juniper

Two weeks had passed since the blowup at Gulch Days. Two weeks of wallowing in bed, because for some godforsaken reason, Mikey's betrayal hurt worse than Brady's.

Perhaps it was because, deep down, I'd seen Brady and Ava's affair coming. I just didn't want to accept it as a possibility. I'd seen the way he looked at her when he thought I wasn't paying attention.

But Mikey wasn't like that. He looked at me like I was the only girl in the world, despite his long history of women. He looked at me like he was a changed man, like he *wanted* me. Like he *saw* me.

Within hours, social media was blowing up with speculation and posts about Mikey and our fake relationship. I couldn't deal with the fallout without spiraling, so I deleted my social apps and did my best to stay away from any rodeo news.

It was weird not being able to talk to Mikey about what was going on. He'd know exactly what to say or do in the situation. Technically, I could have reached out to Ellison or Isa, but I didn't think they'd like me too much after finding out what happened.

Tears pricked at my eyes, and I wiped them with my forearm, sniffling in the process.

Knuckles lightly tapped on my door.

I groaned, pulling the comforter higher over my head. "Please go away, Nat. I don't want to talk." I wasn't in the mood to hear *I told you so*. After she picked me up in Goldfinch, we'd managed to drift past each other the last two weeks—me because I didn't want to talk to *anyone*, and her because I was sure she didn't want to kick me while I was already down so she just let me have space. She'd sent occasional texts to check in or ask if I needed anything, but I admittedly kept my answers short.

"It's Liv." My coworker identified herself. "I'm coming in, okay, June?"

The door creaked as she stepped inside, her footsteps approaching my bed. The bed shifted with her weight when she sat, and I uncovered my head, revealing her soft expression.

"How are you?"

"Fine," I lied, fiddling with the bracelet Mikey had bought me.

I may have torn off the necklace he gave me in the heat of the moment, but I'd forgotten about the copper bangle. I didn't have the heart to get rid of it, so I'd put it on every day, if only to serve as my own sick form of punishment for catching feelings.

She looked down at my wrist then back up, pouting her lips. "He's an idiot."

"I'm not much better," I grumbled. "I was using him, too."

"You know, I was really skeptical of you guys at first."

I glared at her, but she scolded me, pointing out that she wasn't finished.

"I was skeptical at first, but the more I saw you two together, the more it made sense. He's not the type of guy I would have pictured you with, but it worked. I had no idea it was fake, and clearly neither did anyone else. Either you guys were really good at acting, or it wasn't really pretend."

"It became real to me." I had put a pillow over my face so my sentence came out muffled.

"Huh?"

I removed the pillow with a resigned sigh. "We had rules, and I broke the most important one. I told him that no matter what happened, we couldn't get feelings involved. No feelings meant no one got hurt. *And look what happened.*"

Liv gave me a sympathetic smile. "Hearts don't know the difference between what's real and what's fake, June."

I shook my head. "It was all temporary anyway. It was never going to last."

"If you say so. You just seemed really happy, and I hate to see you hurting."

"I'll be okay. I'll, uh, see you at work later." I waved her off.

Liv took the hint and pursed her lips into a soft smile as she stood to leave. Before she left the room, she turned over her shoulder. "We're all here for you. You don't have to go through anything alone, you know that, right?"

Her footsteps disappeared down the hallway and the front door opened and shut, temporarily leaving me in a blissful silence.

Nothing good ever lasted, though, and my phone buzzed on the bedside table. At first I didn't pick it up, but my curiosity got the better of me and I rolled onto my side, letting the lock screen light up.

I blinked a few times, wondering if my brain was processing what I was seeing correctly.

Right in front of me was an email notification requesting an interview for the job in Minnesota.

Holy shit.

I skimmed the email, rereading the first few lines just to make sure I wasn't imagining things.

Thank you so much for submitting your application for the Research Assistant position. We've reviewed your resume and cover letter and are very impressed by your background. We would love to set up an interview so we can tell you about the position and learn more about you.

After checking my schedule, I sent a reply with my availability, letting a squeak of excitement slip as I navigated to my messages.

> You'll never guess what

My heart lurched as I remembered that I couldn't text him that. We were over. I deleted the text, opening a new thread with Natalie instead. I'd have to talk to her eventually, and this felt like a better conversation starter than Mikey would be.

> Sorry I've been MIA.

> I have a job interview

NATALIE

That's amazing! For the job in Minnesota?

> Yep, I ended up applying the day we talked about it.

NATALIE

How do you feel about it?

Nervous but I think it'll be a good change

I love you and Liv and Nico but I think I
need to do this.

NATALIE

Do what's best for you

You didn't plan to stay, so this feels like par
for the course, you know?

Right…

The original plan was always to get my feet set and recover from the betrayal that got me here in the first place. I had a small detour, and now I was back on track to achieve my goals.

I snuck into the back office when I got to Rudy's for my shift, needing to catch my breath and compose myself a little before going out onto the floor.

I'd only worked a few shifts since we'd come back from Goldfinch, and they were all opening shifts instead of a mid-shift or closing. I knew Mikey and the other guys wouldn't come in during the early afternoon, and opening hours were slow enough that I didn't have to deal with many people. Today was my first closing shift since the Bucking Horse Sale.

When I finally stepped behind the bar, only Nico was working.

"Where'd Liv go?" I asked as I tied my apron around my waist.

"She left early. Some kind of family emergency."

"Oh. I hope everything's okay."

"I'm sure it will be. It didn't sound super urgent, but Liv would run herself into the ground worrying if she didn't go. She's…really caring. You know, like if there's a problem or you're sad, she always knows how to make people feel better." His eyes glazed over a bit as he talked about her.

I nodded in understanding.

"And if you try to lie to her and say everything's fine, she'll comfort you anyway and somehow figure out the problem. It's like it's second nature to her." He lowered his voice, so quiet I could barely hear. "It's sweet and kind of adorable, actually. Anyway, how are you holding up?" His question and the abrupt change of subject caught me a bit by surprise. Not to mention nearly every conversation I'd had with Nico in the past four months had been lighthearted.

I played coy, curious about where this was going. "What do you mean?"

"I mean, it sounds like you've gone through two pretty nasty breakups in less than six months. One breakup is heavy shit, let alone two. Just want to make sure you're okay, you know, since Liv isn't here to do it."

"Aww!" I cooed teasingly. "That's so sweet of you. I'm fine, though."

It wasn't a complete lie, but Nico still gave me a suspicious look.

"Seriously, I'm good. I don't have the time or the mental capacity to be sad anymore. If anything, this was a reminder of what my priorities need to be. I have a job interview for a position in Minnesota."

Nico perked up. "Really? That's awesome, Junie!"

"Don't call me that." I playfully rolled my eyes. "It is, though. I'm actually really excited. Nervous out of my mind, but excited." Changing the subject, I lowered my voice some. "So, can we rewind for a second? What's the deal with you and Liv? I've always known you guys were close, but it seemed like you were even closer when I got back from Houston."

It seemed like they thought they were being sneaky, but I noticed the way Nico protected her against the reporter that one day and the way he'd look at her from across the bar during a shift. Not to mention the way he was just talking about her.

"Huh?" He pretended to be confused, but I didn't miss the glint of longing in his eyes.

"Don't play dumb with me."

"She doesn't see me like that."

I raised a brow. "But you do?"

Shrugging, he mumbled, "She's cool. But I don't know. What would you do in this situation?"

"You're really asking *me* for relationship advice?" I cackled. "You sure I'm the best person for that?"

"I don't know. I never thought that bull rider guy would ever stay with someone for that long. From what I'd seen and heard, he keeps things very casual."

I scoffed. "All right, in that case then, strike up a fake-dating arrangement with her under the guise that you want to make your ex jealous. You'll both realize pretty quickly that the feelings you thought were just for show weren't so pretend." I caught myself at the end of my sentence and looked at Nico, who had a smug expression. "I—that's not what I meant."

"I think you know *exactly* what you meant, Junie. You said it yourself. It may have started as fake, but you *both* know you have feelings for each other. Thanks for the tip, though, I'll keep that in mind." He winked, heading around the corner to the back office.

Dammit. I walked right into that one.

CHAPTER THIRTY-SEVEN

A steady wind blew through the arena in a small town about forty-five minutes outside of Billings. It was a small rodeo—much smaller than the Fourth of July rodeo in a couple weeks. While some guys might have grumbled about the smaller crowd, I was grateful for it.

I wanted to lie low and keep the attention off myself for a couple weeks—give myself just enough time for people to forget about me and Juniper. That way I could come back swinging at the Home of Champions Rodeo and leave everyone no choice but to talk about my bull riding skills instead. It was a great idea in theory, but I didn't have high hopes for it in practice.

Travis had tried to talk to me about the situation, but really all he'd done was accuse me of ruining my chances at sponsorships. *This is the worst thing you could have done for your image*, he'd said.

My head probably wasn't on straight, but I'd told him if he ever talked to me like that again, he wouldn't be my agent anymore. He shut up real quick. I ended up calling him to say I was sorry, that I did appreciate his work, and he'd apologized, too, letting me know he'd be taking care of any media attention that came up.

Luckily, the press had been quiet lately, at least in terms of me and the persona they loved to bring up. I hadn't tried to replace Juniper by getting a new girl in my bed, so any claims of that would be blatant lies without proof. The guys could attest to that, too, because I'd spent nearly every second I could with them.

Each time we'd gone to Rudy's for a beer, I'd expected Juniper to be there, but she wasn't. The idea of her taking different shifts just to avoid me felt like a knife to the heart, but that was what I deserved. A few tourists had come up to me, wanting to take their chances on a one-night romp, but I didn't give them the time of day.

No one compared to Juniper. I was convinced that no one ever would.

I needed to focus on my ride tonight. Even though I wanted to believe that the competition wasn't fierce, anything could happen. Bull riding wasn't like football or hockey where you could predict the outcome based on who you were competing against. That alone was both a blessing and a curse.

After the national anthem played, I stayed behind the bucking chutes to focus and prepare myself for my ride. Normally I was able to let the world around me fade, but every time I closed my eyes, instead of a successful bull ride, the only thing I was able to visualize was Juniper.

A vision of her sitting next to me in my truck flashed through my brain, and my eyes flew open, the roar of the crowd and hooves pounding the dirt filling my ears.

Focus.

I closed my eyes again, the bucking chutes in front of me. In my brain, I straddled the chute gate where my four-legged opponent stood waiting. Taking a deep breath, I lowered my knees onto the bull's back, but then the scene changed and instead of a fifteen hundred pound beast beneath me, it was Juniper, her hair splayed out on the bed like a halo.

Frustration rippled through me as I opened my eyes once again. The sun beat down on my back and sweat pooled on my forehead, wet strands of hair sticking to my forehead.

Instead of forcing a visualization that clearly wasn't working, I stood, brushing the dirt off my jeans. Maybe music would help me. I quickly grabbed my headphones from my bag, replacing them with my baseball cap. I slid them over my head and ears then turned on my pre-competition playlist.

This is it.

Heavy bass drums thumped in my ears as an electric guitar played. I shook out my limbs then once again squatted to the ground, letting the world fall to the wayside.

I was on the back of the bull in the chute now, adjusting my rope to my preference. My hand gripped the bull rope and ran my hand up and down it, the pine smell of rosin filling my nostrils. After wrapping the rope around my hand to secure it, I looked to my spotter. My face contorted in confusion as my gaze focused on ice-blue eyes and blonde curls.

Fuck this.

She was everywhere. No matter what I tried, I couldn't escape her.

I wasn't sure if I wanted to.

"It's the matchup of the night, folks! Taking on Relentless Revenge, we've got a cowboy from up the road in Silver Creek, Montana. Put your hands together for Mikey Tucker!"

A feeling of dread settled in my chest the minute I sat on the bull, but I pushed it down, forcing it into the depths of my mind.

The bull thrashed in the chute and the metal rattled as I tried to control my breaths. I worked quickly to secure my hand and the rope, ready to get this over and done with.

Bells from an AC/DC song rang over the speaker as the announcer shouted his encouragement and wound up the crowd. Electric guitar started playing over the loud, deep ringing, and I tucked my chin before I nodded.

I threw my arm up as the gate opened, and the bull entered the arena with an explosive buck. The ride was going well. Even though he was working against me as a fierce competitor, I managed to move my body with him. We flowed together like a powerful river as dust flew up, surrounding us in a hazy cloud. The blinding arena lights overhead seemed to flicker as the bull spun, whirling around like a muscular, beastly tornado.

For a split second, the world around me froze, as if everything was moving in slow motion. A flash of blonde in the crowd was all it took to distract me, and my gaze settled on the crowd, ripping my focus away from the ride and the bull beneath me for a millisecond.

A distraction that would cost me.

The bull switched directions, breaking its bucking pattern and catching me off guard. One millisecond was all it took for me to lose my balance and grip on the bull's back.

He flung me off his back, but I couldn't get my hand loose from the rope to get to safety.

The arena fell silent. I couldn't tell if it was because a hush fell over the crowd or because my body had gone into flight mode. Either way, my ears were full of static, and my mind was full of panic.

I slammed against the side of the bull, his hooves coming dangerously close to my body as he continued to kick, hell-bent on making sure I didn't get out of this arena.

Men yelled from around me, and a wave of chaos surrounded me.

Get yourself loose, dammit.

I was finally able to free myself from the bull, but it was too late.

When I hit the ground, a shockwave went through my body and I couldn't scramble away fast enough.

Fuck.

Fuck.

Fuck.

Revenge came down on my leg—my ankle—and white-hot pain shot through my body.

My ankle.

The world around me spun as the bullfighters got the beast out of the arena. But I still couldn't move. I was frozen to the earth, my muscles weren't responding.

All I could feel was the burning pain.

Then an epiphany.

One day I wouldn't have bull riding anymore.

One day I'd be a prisoner to those stands.

One day I'd only have the memory of the thrill, the rush, the adrenaline.

And the only person I wanted by my side when that day came was her.

Her.

No matter what I did, no matter how hard I tried, I'd never be able to get away from her. Not now. Not after everything we'd been through.

Juniper was the only thought running through my mind when everything went black.

BREAKING: PROFESSIONAL BULL RIDER MIKEY TUCKER INJURED IN SMALL TOWN MONTANA RODEO

PRCA bull rider Michael "Mikey" Tucker was injured over the weekend after his matchup against Relentless Revenge, a bull from Triple Creek Cattle Ranch. He was taken to the nearest hospital in Billings, Montana, to undergo tests after the bull landed on his right ankle just seconds after being thrown.

Witnesses to the accident say he looked distracted during his ride, and after being thrown from the back of the animal, his hand got caught in the rope. After he freed himself, spectators recalled him trying to scramble away from the bull before the devastating injury.

Sources say that moment out of focus cost him a qualifying ride and potentially the rest of the rodeo season.

His timeline for return has not yet been determined.

Representatives for Tucker were unavailable for comment. We'll have updates on the bull rider and whether or not Tucker will return for the Home of Champions Rodeo in July.

CHAPTER THIRTY-EIGHT

EMAIL NOTIFICATION

SUBJECT: Research Assistant Job Offer

The grin that spread across my face made my cheeks hurt as I scanned the email Kelly Daniels, the hiring manager from the research lab, had just sent me. The starting wage was higher than I'd ever expected, and from everything I'd learned in the interview a couple weeks ago, the company seemed to have a great environment and atmosphere.

My mind wandered back to the interview.

Despite being nervous out of my mind for it, everything had gone well. I'd told them about the experience I'd gained at SGU, and when the time came for them to ask when I'd be able to relocate should I get the position, I'd told them I could as soon as I was able to secure a place to live.

I dialed Kelly's phone number and hit the call button, turning it on speaker phone.

My fingers tapped the kitchen counter as though they

had a mind of their own. No matter what I tried, I couldn't calm myself down. I didn't know why I was nervous. I had the job offer, I just needed to accept it.

If Mikey was here, he probably would have cracked a joke to ease my stress. He'd have known how to lighten the mood, even if it were at his own expense.

I shouldn't have been thinking about Mikey Tucker.

The phone rang three times before Kelly answered. "Hello?"

"Hi, Kelly, this is Juniper Ray." My voice shook a little, but I cleared my throat to compose myself and continue. "I got your email, and I would love to accept the job offer."

"Oh, that's wonderful to hear! We're thrilled to have you join the team."

My heart swelled a bit at the validation. "Thank you. I'm looking forward to working with you all. I've been looking at apartments, and I think I should be able to be out there within a few weeks."

"Good to know. Keep us updated, and we'll send over some onboarding information and documents to complete in the meantime."

"Sounds good. Thank you again. I'm very grateful for the opportunity."

"It's my pleasure, Juniper. Take care now, and we'll hopefully see you in a few weeks."

The low tone rang in my ear as the call ended, and I closed my eyes, sucking my lower lip between my teeth.

This was it. My ticket out. This was what I wanted. A brand new start away from Montana and all the pain it'd caused me in the last six months.

So, why did it feel like there was a gaping hole in my stomach?

I opened my laptop next, opening the website I'd saved

for an apartment complex located just outside of the city with single-bedroom units in my budget.

They still had units available, so I quickly submitted an application, taking a deep breath and letting the universe take care of the rest.

Needing some air, I drove downtown, planning to browse through businesses and clear my head.

Funny, because nearly five months ago, I was doing the same thing, albeit I was looking for a job instead of celebrating one.

I was perusing the racks at a clothing store when the bells on the front door jingled and the sound of boots clacking against the floor got my attention.

"Juniper?"

I recognized Ellison's voice and turned around. Sure enough, she was standing there in a black polo with the Veterinary Hospital's logo on it, denim jeans, and cowboy boots.

"Hi."

"What are you up to?" she asked, walking over to look through the same clothing rack. "This shirt is cute, do you think?" She held up a light-blue blouse with a tie front.

"Yeah, I like that. It'll look good with your eyes. I'm just clearing my head."

"Ah, retail therapy or whatever Isa likes to call it?"

I laughed. "Something like that."

"What's going on? I won't claim to be a therapist or anything, but I can listen."

"Oh, it's nothing bad, all things considered. I just…" I took a deep breath. "I got a job position at a research facility. For cancer research."

"That's amazing, June! Congrats! Why's that bad?"

I shifted awkwardly on my feet. "It's in Minnesota."

Her face fell a little, but she recovered quickly. "Oh."

"Yeah, I just put in a housing application. Once they approve it, I'll be leaving. Probably soon. In the next couple weeks, most likely."

"I'm happy for you. I'll be sad to see you leave, but it sounds like this is something you've wanted, right?"

I nodded.

"I'm glad you're sticking to it and following your dream." She hesitated for a moment, like she wanted to say something else, but then changed her mind. "Well, I've got to go, but it was good seeing you. Take care, June." She waved as she went to check out. When she left, the bells on the door once again jingling, I huffed out a long sigh.

I didn't know why I hoped she'd say something about Mikey, but I did.

I needed to stop thinking about him. If not for my own sanity, then for the fact that I was leaving.

Natalie parked the car in one of the few spaces on Main Street. Tonight, the entire town gathered in the community park for the Fourth of July fireworks show. Well, the entire town minus a group of rowdy cowboys who I knew would be out of town. That was one of the few reasons I agreed to come out to the festivities. If I'd seen Mikey, I would have caved.

A month had gone by and he hadn't reached out to me, so I felt like it was safe to assume we were over.

Truly over.

Liv and Nico both gave me a hug when we met up with them.

"I'm so glad you came out!" Liv exclaimed.

I plastered on a fake smile, hoping I was convincing enough. "I wouldn't have missed it."

"Well, we're glad you're here, Junie. Especially since you got that job offer and are going to be leaving us soon!" Nico pretended to pout.

"I know, I know. It'll be good, though, guys." I couldn't decide if I was trying to convince them or myself.

We chatted a little while longer, and before long, Liv started resting her head on Nico's shoulder. I guessed after our conversation, he finally gathered up the courage to say something to her. I was happy for them, really. At least one of us out of our friend group deserved to be happy and have a relationship go right.

Behind us, a few townspeople were gossiping about the Silver Creek cowboys. I managed to tune it out for a while, but curiosity got the better of me and I started to eavesdrop.

"Colter Carson and Reid Lawson will definitely win the world this year. Have you ever seen them in person? They're incredible."

"Colter's wife did a few lessons with my niece. They're good people."

"It's a shame about that bull rider. Nobody knows how long he'll be out for. He was having such a good season, too."

My brows scrunched in confusion as I turned my head, interrupting their conversation. "What do you mean?"

"You didn't hear? Mikey Tucker isn't competing. He got injured a couple weeks ago."

CHAPTER THIRTY-NINE

We've got an incredible night of rodeo ahead of us, folks! Thank you for choosing to spend your Fourth of July right here with us for the greatest sport in the world!"

Although the injury to my ankle wasn't severe—just a moderate sprain, a miracle considering the angle the bull had landed on me—it was enough to take me out for four to six weeks.

"Sorry about the injury, man." Maverick had patted me on the shoulder when we'd arrived earlier that afternoon.

He was leaning against one of the fences talking to another bull riding competitor. I'd debated going over there, but I didn't want to talk about my injury or whatever else the press was saying about me lately.

Colter and Reid were warming up their horses, and Hayden and Jake were nowhere to be seen, probably getting ready for competition themselves, so I was alone.

Since I wasn't competing, I had no reason to be back behind the chutes. But being in the stands felt wrong.

I pulled out my phone, opening my messages.

Happy Fourth

What the fuck are you doing? Happy Fourth? How pathetic are you?

I sighed, deleting the text. I wanted nothing more than to hear from Juniper, to ask her if she was okay and say that I was sorry. I wanted to tell her how badly I'd fucked up and how much I still thought about her, about us.

In the past month, I'd probably typed out at least five different texts, all of them having the same fate. Unsent and deleted.

I wondered if she'd heard about the injury.

A darker part of me convinced myself that she probably had and didn't care. Everyone had been talking about it online, so there was no way she hadn't seen it. And she would have reached out to say *something* if she cared.

I wandered around the rodeo grounds for a bit, not wanting to have to sit alone and watch as my friends and rivals competed.

When the team roping started, I headed back behind the chutes.

"Folks, you are not going to want to miss this next roping duo. They hail from Silver Creek, Montana. The four-time NFR qualifiers, and two years ago they were the average champions, Colter Carson and Reid Lawson!"

The crowd erupted into a chorus of whistles and claps. Colter and Reid were like rodeo royalty around here. The two of them were easy fan favorites in the state of Montana. Sometimes I caught envy crawling up my skin at the thought, but I always pushed it away. They were my brothers. My family.

My time would come. I just had to be patient.

Music played over the sound of hooves against the dirt as Colter and Reid roped. Colter's horse shot out of the box like lightning, and he was able to catch the steer's horns quickly, turning the animal so Reid could follow behind.

"How about a five-point-two for these cowboys!" the announcer called out their time.

Ellison and Isa were somewhere in the stands, and I was sure they were celebrating the time. Five-point-two would put them up at the top of the leaderboard for the day, so they were almost guaranteed to cut a nice check tonight.

Hayden and his partner ran a five-point-four, not quite putting them at the top. Hayden was young, so I was sure he'd get his shot at the NFR and a gold buckle one day. Luckily for him and the other guys, his event didn't have as great a toll on the body. He didn't have to worry about retiring at thirty-five like most bull riders.

I wasn't sure where Colter, Reid, Hayden, and Jake had gone off to after they'd competed, but the bull riding was about to begin.

I'd offered to help some of the guys pull their rope, because if I wasn't competing, it was the least I could do. I wasn't able to spot with my ankle, but being up there as support in the chutes was important to me all the same.

"He was your World Champion bull rider last year. Coming all the way from Oklahoma, he's here to show you how it's done! Let me hear you! His name is Maverick Oakes!"

Deafening cheers echoed throughout the entire rodeo grounds, drowning out nearly everything, even conversation with someone a foot away.

"Let's go, buddy," I encouraged him as he adjusted his seat on the back of the bull.

"Go ahead and pull it," he said when he got to the spot he wanted to be in.

I pulled the bull rope tight, and Maverick wrapped it around his hand, tucking the end of the rope between his ring finger and pinky.

"Suicide wrap?" I raised my brows. While that kind of wrap made the rope tighter and more secure, it could be risky if he got thrown off and was unable to get his hand free.

"Confident in this one today," he muttered back.

"Let 'er buck." I dipped my chin in support, and he focused his attention back on the bull, taking a few deep breaths before nodding.

The gatemen swung open the gate, and the bull burst out with a fire, bucking his legs out behind as he spun in a wild circle.

I glanced up at the clock.

Three seconds.

Four.

Five.

Maverick expertly held on, spurring the bull to let the judges know he was in full control.

The buzzer rang out at eight seconds, and he waited for the perfect time to let the bull sling him off his back. He landed on his feet and ran over to the arena fence, hopping up to get to safety.

"How about that! I bet that ride felt pretty good, and I'm sure it'll feel even better with ninety-three-point-five points! He's your number one bull rider tonight! Let's hear it one more time for Maverick Oakes!"

Once Maverick was back behind the chutes again, I gave him a fist pump.

"Hell of a ride out there."

He nodded at me. "Thanks, brother. Next time it'll be you."

Despite the warmth that spread through my chest at the compliment, I nodded back, keeping my cool. I said my goodbyes then went to find the rest of the crew to get out of here so the real fun could begin.

While most people stayed behind to watch the fireworks show, the boys, Ellison, Isa, and I found a table at one of the local bars.

"Good day out there today, eh, boys?" Jake raised a glass for a toast.

Colter and Reid nodded, offering their cheers, and everyone looked at me.

"Sorry you couldn't compete these last few weeks, Mike," Reid offered.

I shrugged. "Shit happens. I'll just come back stronger after this ankle heals."

"That's the spirit, buddy." Colter patted me on the back as he slid me a beer.

"So," Isa started. "What exactly happened between you and Juniper? I liked her!"

Ellison elbowed her in the ribs, earning her an *Ow!*

"We just decided it was best to end whatever it was we had." I rattled off the bullshit excuse I'd been giving everyone. "Everyone knows it was fake, so there's no use in lying about it. We had an agreement and those terms were met."

She tilted her head. "Are you sure it was fake?"

The rest of the guys paused their conversations and looked at us like they were interested in what I had to say. I raised my brows at her, and she continued.

"I mean, I'm just saying, it didn't *seem* fake to me. I know you want to seem all tough and nonchalant like you don't care, but you seemed to have something real together. And don't say it's just me being a romantic!"

I chuckled. "I wasn't going to say that. Yeah, maybe it felt real to me, but in the end it was always going to be temporary."

"If it was real, then why aren't you doing something about it?!" Isa groaned in frustration, and Reid laughed as he wrapped his arm around her, pulling her close to whisper something in her ear. Whatever he said must have calmed her down a bit, because she mumbled a quick apology.

"I don't know. I just figured if she wanted to work it out, she'd have reached out…" I knew I'd been thinking about it for a while, but it sounded ridiculous the moment I spoke it out loud.

Ellison pursed her lips. "Interesting. How would she know *you* want to make it work if you don't say anything? Maybe she's waiting for you to reach out?"

"She's right, man. If you want her, you're going to have to go get her," Colter added.

Even Hayden piped up. "The way I see it is you have two choices. Go after her, or do nothing and lose her, knowing that *you'll* always be in her orbit, but *she'll* always be just out of reach. There's always a risk, but at least if you go after her you'd know." His face fell slightly, a type of sadness glimmering in his eyes.

"It's up to you, brother, but from what I've seen, you two make each other better. Sometimes, that's all you can ask for." Reid kissed Isa on the temple, both of their smiles lighting up the room.

I looked around the table at my friends. My family.

Their words meant the world to me, and if they saw what I saw in my relationship with Juniper, too, then it was time to swallow my pride before I lost her for good.

"I wasn't sure if you knew, but I saw her last week. She's not going to be here for much longer," Ellison said, determination flaring in her gaze. "She got a job, so she's leaving soon."

Based on the information Ellison had, I needed to act fast. If what she said was true, I didn't have much time.

That night, as we left the bar, an idea hit me. I couldn't just ask her to take me back. I'd fucked up too badly for that. I had to prove to her that I wanted this. That I'd do whatever it took to keep her in my life.

The media may have been the reason we'd gotten into this mess, but I planned to make it the reason we made it out of this, too.

I just had to make some calls.

CHAPTER FORTY

My apartment application was approved a week after the Fourth of July holiday, so I told Kelly I'd be able to start by the end of the month. It didn't take me long to pack up the things I owned—I didn't have many belongings since Brady kept almost all of the furniture. My parents were going to bring a U-Haul over to Minnesota to furnish my new place, so I didn't have to worry about that at least.

Time sped by in a flash, and tomorrow was the day I was set to leave. I knew Mikey and his friends had been out of town for the holiday, and I'd heard around town that they wouldn't be back right away. I had no way of talking to him in person, but it was probably for the best. I could have sent him a text, but what was I supposed to say? *Hey, I'm leaving Montana. Have a nice life?*

I didn't think so.

When I heard that Mikey got injured, I redownloaded social media to see if it was true. It seemed as though the entire rodeo and western community was talking about it, and a pang hit my chest. I hoped he had someone to support him even if it wasn't—couldn't be—me. As much as I wanted it to be me, there wasn't enough time. We'd run out of that.

All throughout my shift at Rudy's, the regulars came up to me to congratulate me on my new job and express that they'd miss seeing me when they came in for a drink. I guess they'd heard about my departure, probably from Liv and Nico, possibly even Rudy himself.

"Oh, June, I'm going to miss you so much!" Liv cried when she arrived at the bar.

I was working the mid-shift so I could get out at a decent time to ensure the rest of my belongings were packed up and I was ready to leave bright and early in the morning.

"Yeah, Junie, who am I going to harass about going to bonfires and parties now?" Nico sighed, his shoulders slumping.

I let out a soft laugh. "I'm going to miss you guys, too. Coming to Miles City may not have been in my plan, but becoming friends with you guys was one of the best parts of working here. Maybe I'll come back to visit, and you can host a bonfire in my honor."

Nico smiled and nodded vigorously before a patron waved him over.

The three of us dispersed, working around each other at the bar, tossing around stories and memories in our downtime.

Before I knew it, my shift was over, and Rudy had come out of the back office to send me off.

"We're sure going to miss you around here, Juniper." The old man pulled me into a hug. "Even though we didn't have you here for long, you'll always have a place if you want to come back."

My eyes blurred, but I wasn't going to cry. I blinked a few times, forcing the tears back. "Thank you, Rudy. I'm sure I'll always have a soft spot for this bar."

I went to hang up my apron when the television caught my attention.

"Mikey, a few weeks ago you got injured. Do you mind telling us what happened out there during your ride? What was going through your head after your injury?"

"Honestly, I was unfocused and that moment of distraction cost me. But even if I could go back and change how everything shook out, I wouldn't, because I realized something."

The reporter didn't say anything, leaning in closer as though she was entirely engrossed in what he was saying.

"What the fuck?" I muttered as the video footage continued on the television.

"I was selfish. I hurt someone important to me. I know this whole bull riding thing won't last forever. Every cowboy has to hang up his hat eventually."

The reporter looked like she was about to cut in, but he held up a hand to stop her.

"No, I'm not retiring, if you think that's what this is about. I've still got a lot of fight left in me. But when that day comes—when I don't have the thrill anymore, when I don't have the fans or the glory—I want the people who I care about the most by my side. Right now, the most important person isn't here, and it's my fault. I fucked up. But I intend to do everything in my power to make it up to her."

"Would this happen to be about—" the reporter started, but Mikey just smirked and replied, "No comment."

Before the reporter on screen could respond, the TV

snapped off. I turned around to face the bar to see who turned off the TV, but my eyes caught on the entrance. Mikey was standing in the doorway, the sun behind him creating a silhouette of his frame.

mikey

Juniper started to walk toward the end of the bar, like she wanted to hide in the back office until I left, but I limped toward her.

"Peach, listen to me. Please," I pleaded.

"What was that?" She pointed to the television screen. "Was this just another act for you? Something to improve your image? Another bet?"

"No, God no. I meant every word I said. After the accident, when I was laying on the dirt, I was terrified. Not because of the injury, but because I realized if I can't have a future with bull riding, I also don't want a future without you. You make me feel whole, Juniper. The past few months have been some of the happiest of my life. I know whatever we had started out as fake, and I was a hypocrite for being upset when I lied to you, too. I broke your trust, and for that I'm sorry. We could have ended our arrangement right in the beginning, but you stuck with me. You *chose* me, and I took that for granted."

"I—"

I grabbed Juniper's hand across the bar, desperate for her to listen. "I've broken a lot of hearts, baby, but the one

I regret the most is yours. I can't promise I'll be perfect. If you haven't figured it out by now, I can be a fucking idiot, but I swear to you, if you give me the chance, as long as I'm still breathing, I'll do everything in my power not to hurt you again. I'd let you break my heart a million times if it meant I could use the fragments to make yours whole again."

"I-I'm leaving," she choked out. "I got a job and I'm moving. I'm going tomorrow."

I winced. Mustering up all the strength I could, I murmured, "Then we'll make your last night here in Silver Creek one to remember. We can figure out the rest later, Peach."

Her eyes widened. "You mean that?"

"Of course. I let you go once, but I'm not doing that again. Please, just give me a chance to make everything up to you."

"What about everything that happened? I was using you, too. How can you just let that go?" She looked down at the bar.

"Hey, look at me." My index finger and thumb found her chin and lifted it so she was looking at me again. "We both made mistakes, but I'd be a hypocrite if I asked you for forgiveness without also forgiving you."

She pulled her bottom lip between her teeth before nodding slowly. "Okay. I really am sorry."

"I know, baby. I am, too."

After hanging up her apron for the last time, Juniper followed me out of the bar, letting me take her hand and pull her along to my pickup truck, ironically just like the first night we got together.

The ride home was silent, but the cab of the truck still buzzed with anticipation and tension. I peeled into my makeshift driveway, not bothering to park straight as I threw open the driver door then ran to Juniper's side, practically ripping the door off.

I lifted her out of the cab, holding her in my arms as I carried her inside.

I kicked the front door of the trailer shut then set Juniper down, moving her so her back was flush against the wall by the entrance. My hips pinned her in place, and her hands fisted my shirt as she pulled me even closer.

"You have no idea how much I've missed you." My voice came out in a low groan as I thought about all of the nights I had to spend without her by my side.

Her eyes burned with desire. "Oh, yeah? Then show me."

My lips smashed against hers, and my hands cupped her cheeks. A quiet whimper fell from Juniper's mouth as her tongue darted out like she was asking for permission. The kiss deepened, but it was still patient. Neither of us were frantic, instead taking the time to explore each other as though we were strangers meeting for the first time.

Her hands roamed down my body until one cupped the front of my jeans. I sucked in a breath as she squeezed, and my cock sprung to attention.

I grabbed her hips and lifted her. Juniper wrapped her legs around my middle, and I carried her to the bedroom, laying her down on the bed gently.

My lips brushed against her collarbone as I kissed my way down her body before stopping at the top of her breasts.

A whine fell from Juniper's lips, and I looked up at her. "Please."

I shook my head. "No, baby. I plan to take my time. I

had to be without you for too long, and I'm going to make up for all the time we lost."

Her head lolled back as I pulled the top of her blouse down and flicked my tongue against her nipple. I sat up when she lifted her arms so I could pull the shirt over her head, leaving her chest bare.

After planting a line of kisses down to her navel, I unbuttoned her jeans, tugging down the zipper and hooking my fingers in the waistband. She shimmied out of them as I pulled the denim down her thighs.

"What do you want from me, Peach?" I asked as I blew a puff of air on the cotton covering the space between her legs.

She narrowed her eyes. "Don't make me beg for anything, Mikey Tucker. You know I won't."

"I wouldn't dream of it. Just tell me what you need, and I plan to give it to you."

"Just touch me. Please."

I gently ran my thumb along the apple of her cheek. "Like this? Or"—I swiped a finger up her cotton-covered center—"like this?"

Juniper sucked in a breath. "Stop teasing."

"As you wish." My lips melded with hers as I slid her panties off. Her entrance was slick with her arousal, and I curled a finger inside her, eliciting a moan.

My thumb circled her clit as my index finger brushed her walls. She clenched around me, and I added another, pumping them faster.

We kept kissing as I fucked her with my fingers, our mouths tangling together, exploring each other even though she already knew every inch of me and I her.

"Don't stop," she mumbled against my lips, and I picked up my pace.

Her hips bucked up against my hand, and I knew she was close. A few more strokes and she was falling apart at my fingertips.

Withdrawing my fingers, I brought them up to my lips for a taste.

My hands moved to unzip my pants, but she stopped me, sitting up to pull off my shirt. She moved to my jeans next, but paused as something caught her eye.

She leaned down, her top half disappearing next to the bed, before she popped back up. "What's this?" she grinned as she held up a strip of black, cotton rope.

I reached for it, but she pulled it away, making a clicking noise with her mouth.

"Uh-uh. If anyone's going to use this, it's going to be me."

Heat rushed to my cheeks as I nodded. "Do your worst."

Juniper moved behind me and took my hands, putting them behind my back. She quickly tied my hands together, making sure the rope wasn't cutting off my circulation or tightening with movement.

My heart raced at the idea of her taking control. When she placed her hand on my chest, pushing me down onto the bed, I knew that was exactly what she had in mind. She crawled over top of me, her hands on both sides of my body. I looked at her in awe as she hooked her finger under my chin and lifted it, sealing her lips over mine.

"My turn," she whispered in my ear, sending a shiver down my spine.

Her nails trailed down my chest, leaving a tingling sensation in their absence. She scooted down my body so her torso hovered just above my thighs. Juniper unbuttoned my jeans and pulled them off, taking my boxers with them.

My cock, already rock hard, lay flat against my stomach, the tip glistening with precum.

I was helpless with my hands bound as Juniper lowered her mouth onto the tip, swirling her tongue around it. The sensation was overwhelming and she'd hardly done anything. But with each gentle, teasing stroke of her tongue, a jolt shot through my body.

She looked up at me when she put my cock into her mouth, the length disappearing as she took me deeper. Her hands twisted around it, stroking in tandem with her head as it bobbed up and down.

"Fuck." I groaned, wishing I could hold on to her hair. "Juniper."

Spit dripped down my shaft and her chin as she kept going, nearly bringing me to the edge before stopping right after my cock twitched in her mouth. Just when I thought she might quit, she was back at it again. Each time I got closer to coming, though, she'd pause, relentless in her teasing.

"Dammit, Peach, come here and fuck me. I need to come inside you."

She batted her lashes. "What else do you say?"

"Please," I begged, hearing how desperate I sounded.

"Good boy."

She smirked as she crawled up my body again, guiding my cock as she lowered herself down onto it. A sigh left both of our lips as she adjusted to my size, then she started swiveling her hips. She was so tight, so wet. I moaned as she leaned forward, palms pressed into the mattress next to my shoulders, and started bouncing on my cock.

Her breasts bounced with the movement, and I resisted the urge to sit up and suck a nipple between my teeth.

"Ah, fuck," she cried as her pussy clenched around me.

Her movements started to slow, no doubt an effect of the pleasure that seemed to be rippling through her, and I bucked my hips, meeting her stroke for stroke as she continued to sink down onto me. Skin slapped against skin, and sweat glistened on her collarbone.

"Come for me. Come all over my cock. Take ownership, Juniper, because I'm all yours," I panted as her eyes widened.

Juniper leaned back then, placing a hand on my chest that she used for leverage as she swirled her hips and circled her clit with her fingers. I looked down to where our bodies joined, her pussy swallowing my cock, and bit my lip to hold back a moan.

"Mikey, I'm coming," she gasped as her face contorted in pleasure, warmth enveloping me. Her muscles tightened, and I followed her release shortly after, thrusting my hips up to ride out my orgasm.

Juniper cried out before collapsing onto me, her forehead pressing against my shoulder and her chest rising and falling with her rapid breaths.

Hot cum dripped down my shaft when she finally sat up, lifting herself off of me and reaching her arms around my back to untie my hands. She rolled next to me, laying her head on my chest, and I wrapped an arm around her shoulder, pulling her close.

We lay there for a moment without speaking. Then, after pressing a kiss to her forehead, I walked to the bathroom to grab a towel to clean us both up.

"What's going to happen now?" she whispered in the dark after we'd climbed into bed together.

"Whatever you want to happen. I'm yours, if you want me. The ball's in your court, baby."

"I still need to go. Working in a research lab has been a

goal of mine for years, and I…I can't just put that on the backburner."

I'd never expect her to. She didn't expect me to give up bull riding—and I wouldn't—so I would never expect her to sacrifice her dreams for me.

"I want to make this work. I'll take you however I can have you." She looked up at me with her big blue eyes, even as sadness clouded them.

"I meant what I said. I'm not going to lose you again. Whatever it takes, I'm with you. I'm all in. One day at a time."

"One day at a time," she repeated back.

Soon enough, soft snores alerted me that she was asleep.

I closed my eyes, but before drifting off, I whispered into the silence, "I love you, Peach."

I didn't think she heard, but I still noticed her lips curl up into a soft smile as she nuzzled her head against me. Even if she wasn't awake to say it back, that was all the confirmation I needed that this would work.

Whatever it took, we'd make it work.

It was nothing short of a miracle, but a few days after Juniper had left, I was cleared to compete again in Cheyenne. Missing the Fourth of July rodeo may have hurt my standings a little, but I was currently only seventeenth in the world. Performing well would put me in a good position and set me back on track to make it to the NFR in December, if not propel me into the top fifteen. It was a ten-day event, so there was an opportunity to bring home a large check as long as I didn't buck off and lose out of the tournament-style bracket.

Isa had gone home after the Fourth of July, so it was just the boys, me, and Ellison.

"You didn't hear it from me," Ellison whispered when the others were walking a little bit ahead of us, "but I'm glad you and Juniper worked it out. It was about time you found someone."

I gave her a look, and she waved her hands.

"Not in a 'you need to settle down' type of way, but in a 'I'm glad you're happy, you deserve that' kind of way.

Although, it does help that she's your match in every sense of the word."

I chuckled. "Thanks for the clarification, Firecracker."

"Too bad she couldn't be here."

"Yeah, it's too bad, but she's adjusting nicely to her new place and job. I've got plans to go see her."

"Mikey Tucker, taking a week off bull riding?" She feigned shock.

"You know I'd do anything for a woman." I winked.

Rolling her eyes, but still flashing me a grin, she corrected, "You'd do anything to get a woman in bed."

"I mean, yeah, but don't you know? I'm a changed man. Who would have thought all it would take is a bet for me to get my shit together, huh?"

"I'd expect nothing less." She laughed as she threw her arm around me, even though I was just tall enough that she had to stretch her arm up a little. "Bring her home a nice check tonight, why don't you?"

"That's the plan."

Colter looked over his shoulder. "What're you two getting into back there?"

Ellison waved him off. "None of your business, Sparky. Just keep walking."

"Don't try stealing my girl now," Colter teased.

I shook my head, lips curling up into a grin. "No thanks, Carson, I've got my own spitfire now."

"Atta boy." He winked as he faced forward again and started up a conversation with Reid and Jake.

"I'm telling you, though," I raised my voice a notch, "Jake and Hayden are next. It's gotta be Houston. There's some kind of weird magic in that city."

"Houston or the Ace in the Hole bar?" Ellison

laughed. "God, if I didn't have to step foot in that place ever again."

Hayden shook his head, laughing silently to himself.

"What's up, bud?" Reid asked.

"Ah, nothing. Just thinking to myself."

"You got a secret girl you haven't told us about?" I reached out my arm to smack him lightly on the shoulder.

He looked back at me over his shoulder. "Something like that." I could tell he was trying to be casual about it, but there was a longing—a yearning—in his eyes. The same type of longing as the night of the Fourth of July.

"Wait, have you ever had a girlfriend, Hayden?" Jake asked curiously.

He shrugged, spinning around to face forward again. "Sort of."

"Hayden!" Ellison drew out his name. "Tell us more!"

"Nah, guys, there's nothing to say. She…words don't do her justice. Come on, we need to get going so we're not late." He started walking faster, the conversation—if there ever was one—was clearly over.

"How's everything going?" Juniper asked on the other end of the line.

She'd called to check in a few times during the rodeo, especially when she knew she would be working and wasn't able to watch a broadcast. I'd also talked to her once before a performance, and it seemed to help calm my nerves a bit, just knowing she'd be watching from afar.

"Been good so far. If I compete well enough tonight in the semifinal, I'll be moving on to the Championship."

"I hope you do! I have to work today, so you've gotta make it so I can watch you win on Sunday. But I thought I would call, just to wish you a good ride."

"I'm glad you did. You're my good luck charm, you know." I grinned.

I could practically hear her rolling her eyes. "Glad I could be of service. I'm sure you don't need luck, though, you can do it all on your own."

"Nah, I definitely think having you in my corner has helped. Listen, I've gotta go, but I'll talk to you soon?"

"Talk to you soon. Good luck out there, Casanova. Don't fall off," she teased, the sarcastic nickname that had eventually transformed into a term of endearment rolling off her tongue.

"Don't plan on it, Peach."

The call ended, and a wide grin pulled at my cheeks.

"I guess the headlines should have read, *Mikey Tucker: Bull Riding Bachelor No More*," Maverick teased as he walked up behind me. "Guess the rumors are true, then?"

"Rumors?" I raised a brow.

"You and that girl. The one you were, uh"—he coughed—"fake dating. You're back together, then?"

I couldn't help the warmth that grew in my chest. "We are."

"I'm happy for you. Don't mess it up this time." He winked, and I rolled my eyes.

I didn't plan on it. Losing Juniper once had hurt. Losing her twice would be devastating.

We chatted for a little while longer as we waited for the bull riding to draw nearer. We were both competing in the second section. The first bull riding section was in the beginning of the rodeo, but our section was the very last event of the night.

"Tonight, we have nine more cowboys riding for their chance to advance to the short go."

My bull was already in the chute. I was fourth in the lineup, and Maverick was sixth.

The first rider scored an eighty-four, and the second one bucked off.

I'd visualized a successful ride in my mind, controlling my breathing until it was slow and steady and I was fully grounded.

"That was an eighty-two-point-five ride! Let's get ready for our next rider. You'd have never guessed he was coming off an injury with the week he's had so far. Coming all the way from Silver Creek, Montana, we've got Mikey Tucker on Easy Money!" The announcer rattled off an introduction as I lowered myself down onto the bull.

The scent of burning rosin filled my nostrils as I ran my hand up and down the tail end of my rope. I'd ridden this bull before, so I knew how he bucked straight out of the chute, and I adjusted my seat accordingly.

The guy helping out at the chute pulled my rope tight, and I wrapped the tail around my hand then across my palm.

The world around me started to fade, the cheers from the crowd, chatter from other bull riders, and encouragement for me all becoming static as I locked in.

After taking a deep breath, I slid up to my rope then nodded. Easy Money went exactly where I expected him to, and I adjusted my body accordingly. The arena around me blurred, but I wasn't focused on anything but me and the bull. My partner for eight seconds.

Gritting my teeth, I stuck my chest out and raised my free arm. My legs flexed, and as the bull kicked, I spurred him.

He was mean, but we got the job done, and the eight second buzzer went off.

When I was back to safety, I looked up at the screen just as the announcer called out, "Eighty-nine-point-five for Mikey Tucker!"

It was enough to secure my spot in the Championship short go, and I pumped my fist in the air.

"Ladies and gentlemen, you've traveled from all over the world for one of rodeo's biggest events. We've promised some fantastic competition, and so far these athletes have delivered. But we're not done yet! It's Championship Sunday!"

The uproar from the crowd was deafening, but I smiled thinking about the energy in the arena.

"Quite a comeback, Tucker." One of the other bull riders nodded at me.

"Thanks, man, but it's not over yet." I tried to be humble, but I knew I wasn't going to buck off today. I was determined. My season—despite the injury—had been on a steady climb since Houston, and I wasn't going to let it drop off now.

I'd proven to the press and fans that I was in this. Despite the doubt and the odds, I was climbing back up the world standings.

Now, the only person I had to prove anything to was myself.

Maverick and I had been almost neck and neck, but I'd pulled through to land myself in the number one spot going into the short go. Which meant my ride would be the very last one of the night.

Colter and Reid won the team roping, as expected, and Jake placed sixth in the tie-down roping, so he still cut a check.

Now it was down to bull riding.

"I hope you're not tired yet, folks. Hang in there with us, because it's the event of the night, what you've all been waiting for. The bull riding."

The bullfighters for the night were introduced, and rock music blared through the speakers as the first bull rider climbed into the chute.

I didn't pay much attention to the other rides, only focusing on my surroundings when a score was announced, like keeping a running scoreboard in my mind of what I would have to beat tonight.

The first few riders scored in the lower eighties, and a few in the middle got close to ninety points.

Maverick gave me a fist bump before we parted ways to get by our respective chutes. He'd ride first, then me.

The announcer read off Mav's stats then the stats of the bull he was riding.

"Let's go, Maverick!" the announcer cried out as Maverick nodded, and the bull burst out of the chute in a fury.

He moved gracefully with the bull, matching its kicks and spins with expert finesse.

When the eight second buzzer went off, I was already up on the platform, ready to climb into the chute.

As the announcer called out, "Ninety points!" a wave of anxiety washed over me.

I straddled the top of the chute and took a deep breath as I lowered my knees onto its back.

"Our final performer of the night, *the matchup of the night,* is one you are not going to want to miss! Don't get up from your seats quite yet, ladies and gentlemen. This bull has an eighty-three percent buck-off rate. Many a cowboy has tried to best him, and many have failed. He goes by the name of Play Your Cards Right!" The announcer paused for effect. "Let's see if our cowboy, Mikey Tucker, can ride this old boy to victory!"

Music played in the background, but I only focused on the task at hand as I ran my hand up and down my rope until the rosin was sticky. One of the other bull riders was pulling my rope, and Maverick had run over to offer encouragement.

This time, when I wrapped the tail end of the rope around my hand, I ran it between my pinky and ring finger. This was it. This could very well be one of the most important rides of the year, and there was no way I was going to buck off.

"Let's go, boys," I gritted out as I nodded, and the chute gate flew open.

juniper

The camera zoomed in as Mikey's bull exploded out of the gate, whirling around on the television screen as it attempted to throw him off its back.

My hands had the edge of the couch in a death grip as I watched on the edge of my seat.

"Come on, Mikey," I said under my breath.

Dust flew around the arena as the bull kicked up dirt, and for a moment, the camera only picked up the silhouette of the beast and his rider.

Mikey's arm waved in the air as he kept his balance and flowed with the bull's movements.

"Come on, Mikey! You've gotta ride!" The announcer in the background could be heard as the clock climbed up to eight seconds.

When the buzzer went off, the bull spun a couple more times before Mikey was able to jump and run to safety. The bull, too distracted by the bullfighters, didn't pay him any attention as the camera zoomed in on Mikey, who took off his helmet and held it up in the air in triumph.

"He's back and better than ever, folks! I'd say Mikey

Tucker has played his cards very well and that'll earn him a…ninety-one-point-five for the win! Mikey Tucker is your bull riding champion! What a comeback!"

The television broadcast replayed his ride, displaying his score on the screen before fading out into a post-ride interview.

A reporter shoved a microphone in Mikey's face. "Mikey! How does this victory feel after coming off an injury?"

His lips curved into a smile. "It feels great. It goes to show that a little setback means nothing when it comes to my career. I'm determined to make it all the way this year and prove everyone wrong."

"Any plans to celebrate the win?"

"I have a few ideas." The camera zoomed in on his cocky smirk. "If you'll excuse me, I've got a flight to catch." He spun on his heel to walk away, and cameras flashed in the background as other people raced toward him, firing question after question at his back.

"Do you have a new girlfriend?"

"What happened between you and that other girl?"

"Is this part of your plan to celebrate?"

Mikey turned around to address the reporters. "Not that it's any of your business, but there's somewhere I need to be, and it's very important to me." He fixed his gaze on the camera and winked.

I was just about to head out to grab some food when knuckles rapped against my door. I wasn't expecting any visitors, so I looked through the peephole to see who it was before opening it.

What the—

Standing outside my apartment, still in his dusty jeans, pearl snap shirt, and the baseball cap he always wore backward, was Mikey.

I swung open the front door and threw my arms around him, breathing in his scent—leather, pepper, and sage. Pulling away, I asked, "What are you doing here?"

"Celebrating my win."

I was still struck that he was even here. A hundred questions bounced around my head, but only a couple rattled off my tongue. "But don't you need to be at another rodeo soon? Why didn't you celebrate with the guys?"

"Because I love you, Juniper. I never said it before—that day in the bar—but I knew then. I'd known well before then that I love you. I'm sorry I didn't say it sooner."

I widened my eyes, completely rendered speechless.

The thing about Mikey, though, was that his love didn't need to be the loudest in the room for me to realize it. He may have been the loudest person in the room—boisterous and someone you could always count on for a laugh—but his love was calm, steady, and unwavering.

Even when our relationship was supposed to be pretend, he showed it in the quiet moments. He showed it in his gentle vulnerability and the way he defended me to his friends, his fans, and every person who believed they had the right to his personal life just because he was a professional athlete.

Even though we'd hit some speed bumps along the way, in the end, he still showed up for me and *he chose me*. And

I'd continue to choose him, because the best kinds of love were hard-earned. Fought for.

Love—and life—wasn't easy, but if you could take the bull by the horns and just hang on for eight seconds, the toughest parts didn't feel impossible anymore.

I knew that now.

I took a deep breath before looking him straight in the eyes. "I love you, too. And I'm proud of you. I'm proud of *us*."

Everything that had happened this year—my world being turned upside down, the media questioning his career, his friends—led us to this moment. To now.

For once, I'd never felt so at peace with the unknown.

In this moment, I was choosing to let go of the pain of the past—not feeling chosen, not feeling seen, despite so desperately wanting those things. I chose to let go of the anger and the spite—with the knowledge that I'd be a better person for it.

I was ready to let go of Ava and Brady, too.

My fingers weaved through his hair, and I leaned in as his hands cupped my face and our lips brushed.

I wasn't exactly sure what the future had in store. But if fake dating Mikey Tucker had taught me anything, it was that sometimes the best things in life come unexpectedly.

epilogue

mikey

Ladies and gentlemen, you've been with us for the past nine days, watching the best cowboys and cowgirls in the world compete for the title of World Champion. Tonight is the night where seven new champions will be crowned!"

I surveyed the crowd in the Thomas & Mack arena. Despite it being a sold-out event, I knew exactly where Juniper would be.

All of the trials, sweat, pain, and tears of this year had led to this moment. My ride tonight would determine whether or not I'd go home with a gold buckle. I could practically taste victory on my tongue. I had it within reach, and there was nothing that would tear it from my grasp.

"Best of luck tonight, Mikey." Maverick walked up to shake my hand. He was a shoo-in for the world title—and deserving, at that—but the average title would also be between us tonight.

"Thanks, man." Teasingly nudging him with my elbow, I whispered, "You wouldn't mind bucking off tonight, would you?"

Maverick laughed at the joke, the sound warming my chest. "Man, you know I'd love to do that, but my agent and sponsors would have my head."

"I know, I was just messing. May the best bull rider win."

He tipped his hat as he continued on to chat with some of the other bull riders.

As the rodeo went on, I started to mentally prepare myself and get in the zone, the same routine I'd gone through my entire bull riding career.

Eight seconds. Anything is possible if you can hold on for eight seconds.

I repeated the mantra in my head, letting the world around me fade.

Colter and Reid had roped well, securing a world title for themselves, and Jake ended up placing fourth in the average.

The barrel racing flew by, and when the announcer called out that it was time for the bull riding, I was ready, both mentally and physically, to do whatever it took to win.

Maverick and I were near the end of the section, so I sat down, closing my eyes and letting my breaths slow again.

As each cowboy performed and my ride inched nearer and nearer, the nerves in my stomach swelled more and more. As did the affirmations repeating in my head.

This is it. Whatever it takes to win. You can do it.

Five more riders.

Three more riders.

Maverick's up. Two more.

When the cowboy immediately before me hopped into the chute, I stood, brushing off my jeans and gathering my gear.

"Up next, we've got a bull rider who hails from the great state of Montana. Not only did he have quite the comeback this summer, he's had one hell of a year. He's taking on Whiplash tonight! Mikey Tucker!"

I pulled on my helmet as the announcer read off our stats, climbing up onto the chute to mount the bull. I'd seen videos of this one. He was mean, but that was exactly how I liked them. All I'd have to do tonight was hang on for dear life, throw in a little flair, and hope the judges scored me fairly.

Maverick rode before me, so he was there to help. Even though we were competing against each other for the NFR title, I trusted him. He played fair and wouldn't do anything to endanger me or cause him to catch a fine.

I heated up the rosin on the rope until it was sticky enough on my glove. Maverick pulled my bull rope, and I wrapped it around my hand. Scooting up to my rope, I nodded before tucking my chin and gritting my teeth.

Although the world around me was chaotic—rock music playing over the screaming crowd, bullfighters ready to step in should the ride go awry, dust flying, and fellow bull riders shouting encouragement—I was completely calm. Serene. At peace.

Whatever happened with this ride, I'd be giving it my all, and regardless of what the news and social media said about me, I knew I'd had a damn good career, with plenty more to come.

The bull whipped around, breaking me out of my brief

thoughts. I pushed my chest forward, raising my free hand to match his movements, and when he bucked to the left, I adjusted accordingly.

My muscles burned, but I couldn't give up yet. Every bone in my body was screaming at me, but I could be sore tomorrow. I just had to endure it for eight seconds.

With one final spin in an effort to throw me off, the buzzer sounded, signaling the eight seconds was up.

I did it.

When the bull bucked me off, I ran to safety, letting the bullfighters and barrel man take over. I lifted off my helmet and raised it in the air as the announcer called out, "Ninety-two points for Mikey Tucker!"

After the last few bull riders performed, it was official. I'd won the final round and secured a gold buckle as the NFR Average champion.

I flashed a cocky smile at the crowd, feeling like a million bucks.

But deep down, I was just proud.

After the buckle ceremony and a slew of post-ride interviews, I finally made it to Juniper and the rest of the crew.

She pulled me into a hug, despite how sweaty I was and the fact that I probably smelled worse than a high school boys' locker room. "That was quite a ride, Casanova."

"Would you roll your eyes if I said it was all for you, Peach?" I winked. When she inevitably rolled her eyes, I laughed. "Ah, there it is."

"So, what are we doing to celebrate?" Jake asked. "We've got a couple World Champions and an NFR Champion in our midst. I think that's cause for a big celebration.

I shook my head. "You guys go on ahead. I want to spend some time with my girl."

In the past four months, we'd been long-distance. We visited each other when we could, but for the most part our dates consisted of dinners over FaceTime. I wouldn't have changed it for the world, though. One day we'd talk about living closer—she'd mentioned wanting to go back to school to get a master's and PhD—but for now, she was living out her dreams, and I was living out mine.

Tonight, all I wanted to do was hold her in my arms with no interruptions.

Colter and Reid gave me subtle smirks.

"Hey, we had an agreement," she scolded. "Juniper and Mikey's NFR rule number three: No going back to the room until we've properly celebrated your win!"

"Fuck the rules, Peach. I know exactly how I want to celebrate, and for once, it's not in a bar."

She giggled as I scooped her up in my arms, intending to carry her all the way to our hotel room, hang a *Do Not Disturb* sign on the door, and worship my woman like she deserved.

Because, after all, rules were always meant to be broken.

closed-door modifications

For those who want a reading experience without explicit sexual content (or for those who want to easily find the spice), here are the chapters that include open-door scenes. Please note that each of these chapters include explicit sexual content that is fully consensual.

If you would like to skip the spice, please note the starting points in parentheses that will provide you with the best reading experience. Fully skipping the chapters with spice starting points will cause you to miss out on important scenes and plot points.

- Chapter 4 (page 30 from "Before I could disappear into my head over where I'd heard that name before, I snapped out of it" to end)
- Chapter 16 (page 129 after "No. Fine." to end)
- Chapter 26 (page 198 after "You. I want you." to end)
- Chapter 29 (page 221 after "I'm going to kiss you now" to end)

- Chapter 30 (page 228 after scene break-end)
- Chapter 31 (spice scene ends at the bottom of page 235)
- Chapter 33 (page 251-end)
- Chapter 40 (page 301-305 ending at "What's going to happen now?")

acknowledgments

Four books in and I still never know how long my acknowledgments will be when I type "The End." All I know is that they always end up being more long-winded than anticipated, and I think of it as a blessing to always have so many people in my corner worthy of recognition.

First and foremost to the readers. None of this would be possible without you. Thank you for continuing to read about—and love—these people that I make up in my head. I'm the luckiest girl in the world to be able to do what I do.

Chisum, it takes a whole lot of patience to put up with me and my overactive brain, but you manage to do it every day. I wouldn't pick anyone else to be my teammate—my partner. You're it for me, in this lifetime and every single one that follows.

Casey, for dropping everything to drive an hour and a half to Cody with me and immediately offering to also drive to Deadwood, supporting me through the tough times, and always being down to yap. I can't wait to hear your spicy description for this book.

To my author friends —Alex, Amy, Taryn, Dany, Christina, Ella, Melissa, and so many more—this book wouldn't have seen the light of day without you supporting me along the way. Thank you for listening to my rants, ideas, and everything in between.

To my real life friends for listening to me rant about books all day long. You're so real for that.

To Alissa and the Hot Girls Who Write group, what a badass group of women. Your passion for writing and resilience in the publishing industry inspires me. I'm so glad I decided to join a Zoom write-in on a whim, because if I hadn't, I wouldn't have found this community.

To my in-person writing group, I'm so grateful to have found a group of friends to write with, yap with, and eat really good food with. You motivate and inspire me so much, and I'm so lucky to have met you.

To all of the artists in the book community who I've worked with to create stunning character art, book covers, sprayed edges, stickers, etc., but especially Sam and Mel with Ink & Velvet Designs. You truly outdid yourself with the art of Mikey and Juniper (THE MUSTACHE), and I can't wait to work with you on more art in the future!

I would be nowhere without my incredible team who is truly the cornerstone of every book launch:

PA: Keona @whatskeonareading
Beta Readers: Delaney, Tiffani, Sara, Shaylene, Kait, Keona, Sam, Karlee, Leila, and Savannah
Copy Edit & Proofread: Andrea Halland, Editing By Andrea

Thank you to my ARC team for reading the book early, leaving your reviews, and hyping the book prior to release!

Finally, thank you to my incredible content team. There are trillions of books in the world and millions of authors, yet you choose to read, love, and scream from the rooftops about me and mine.

thanks for reading

If you enjoyed *The Hearts We've Broken*, I would greatly appreciate if you left a review on Amazon, Goodreads, or any other platform!

For more updates on the H.K. Green Universe, subscribe to my newsletter.

H.K. Green is a contemporary romance author based out of Montana, writing raw, emotional stories that will break your heart then put it back together.

Inspired by real-life, relatable challenges, her books feature found families, a healthy dose of sarcastic banter and emotional angst, strong female leads, and the men who'll do anything to give them the world.

When she's not writing, she can be found curling up with all kinds of books, hanging out with her rescue animals, going to rodeos or her family's farm and ranch, and spending time with her real-life book boyfriend.

You can connect with H.K. Green on Instagram and TikTok @authorhkgreen and learn more on her website at www.authorhkgreen.com.